A Shot
of
MURDER

A SHOT
OF
MURDER

A LUCKY WHISKEY MYSTERY

J.A. KAZIMER

MIDNIGHT INK
WOODBURY, MINNESOTA

FIRST EDITION
First Printing, 2019

Book format by Samantha Penn
Cover design by Shira Atakpu
Editing by Nicole Nugent

Midnight Ink, an imprint of Llewellyn Worldwide Ltd.

This is a work of fiction. Names, characters, places, and incidents are either the product of the author's imagination or are used fictitiously, and any resemblance to actual persons, living or dead, business establishments, events, or locales is entirely coincidental.

Library of Congress Cataloging-in-Publication Data
Names: Kazimer, J. A., author.
Title: A shot of murder : a lucky whiskey mystery / J.A. Kazimer.
Description: First Edition. | Woodbury, MN : Midnight Ink, [2019] | Series: A
  lucky whiskey mystery ; #1.
Identifiers: LCCN 2018052802 (print) | LCCN 2018055349 (ebook) | ISBN
  9780738760117 (ebook) | ISBN 9780738760070 (alk. paper)
Subjects: LCSH: Murder—Investigation—Fiction. | GSAFD: Mystery fiction.
Classification: LCC PS3611.A96 (ebook) | LCC PS3611.A96 S56 2019 (print) |
  DDC 813/.6--dc23
LC record available at https://lccn.loc.gov/2018052802

Midnight Ink
Llewellyn Worldwide Ltd.
2143 Wooddale Drive
Woodbury, MN 55125-2989
www.midnightinkbooks.com

Printed in the United States of America

For my sister, Jennie Kazimer,
for your invaluable help in researching this novel,
as well as the numerous brain cells we killed in doing so.

CHAPTER

1

ACCORDING TO LOCAL LEGEND, I was born under a bad sign. A green and white highway sign for those entering or leaving Gett, Florida, to be precise. My parents had been escaping the small town deep in the Everglades of South Florida and their soon-to-be-shotgun-wedded fate when the engine blew on my father's 1977 Trans Am—black like the one Burt Reynolds drove in some movie made thirteen years before I was even born.

The arrival of an eight-pound, three-ounce baby girl had lessened my parents' desire for freedom from small-town life, mostly due to the expense of diapers and formula.

Or so the gossip said.

I tried to ignore the whispers of rumors always circulating through the Gett population of 845. Particularly when it had to do with my family—which it did all too often since I'd returned home from Hollywood to sweltering heat and bugs the size of compact cars. I'd lived in California since graduating college six years ago, working as an

1

actress, and only recently came back to take care of my ailing grand-father and the true love of his life—The Lucky Whiskey Distillery.

"Blue is such a soothing color." Sallie Abbott, the owner of Sallie's Crafts and Such, beamed as she rang up the two cans of light azure paint I'd set on the counter.

Inhaling deeply, a flood of long forgotten memories and paint fumes flickered through my senses, much like an old black-and-white movie. I'd spent countless hours roaming the paint selections as a kin-dergartener, picking out just the right color for my new walls. Like Goldilocks, it had to be just right.

I couldn't afford to make a mistake.

Not when it mattered most.

The memory had me thinking about Jack, as it always did. Which was the reason I found myself at Sallie's today. My granddad's room needed a fresh coat of paint. I glanced at the cobalt label on the paint can, hoping against hope Sallie was right and the color would soothe my granddad, for Jack desperately needed to be soothed … before someone shot him.

An action I considered at least once a day.

Thank God for his nurse, Sweet Jayme Babbitt, a saint in every sense—from the top of her head, often piled high with dark hair, to her elfish feet. Much to her chagrin, Sweet Jayme only stood just over five foot in her sneakers.

Not only did Jayme keep Jack away from the distillery as he recu-perated, which was probably why I hadn't acted on my threat to shoot my beloved cranky grandparent, but also I suspected she spiked his morning decaf coffee with Xanax.

Doctor's orders.

Saying Jack was a good patient was like ordering a bourbon and Diet Coke. It just wasn't done. Not in polite circles.

"The house needs work," I said to Sallie, picturing the Lucky family home. "Especially the living room. I don't think Jack's touched up the paint since the day I was born."

The monstrosity Jack called home was built in the late 1800s by my great-great-grandfather. It had eight bedrooms and five baths, plus a library, living room, and kitchen. Most of which were unchanged in the last seventy-four years, much like Granddad Jack.

"More likely a few decades before that." Sallie's eyes, milky with age but still as intense as ever, stayed on mine. "Be sure that paint ends up on the walls, and not anywhere else in town, girl."

I winced at her harshly spoken warning. Over ten years ago, on a dare after much too much cheap wine, I apparently—not that I had a memory of the event—climbed the Gett water tower with a can of paint. The next morning, far too hungover to think straight, I awoke with emerald paint on my hands and no idea why … until I looked out my bedroom window.

The water tower, which once boasted the town's proud name, now read:

GETTing

Lucky

It was a stupid, childish prank. One the town had never let me forget.

Damn Brodie Gett for his truth-or-dare games that, I was almost positive, had driven me up the ladder. I'd heard Grodie Brodie, as I used to call him, was back in town after a stint in the military. Not that it mattered, for I made a point to avoid all Getts.

Life was easier that way.

Not that one could spit without hitting a Gett in Gett, Florida.

Not only was the town named after the Gett family, but they also made it a point to fill said town with as many of their genetic byproduct as possible. And seeing as each Gett was better-looking than the next, possibilities abound.

"When will you all quit talking about the water tower?" I asked with a sigh.

She chuckled, a sound warmed from years of drinking Lucky Whiskey. "Charlotte, girl, you've been the talk of the town since your dear mommy, God rest her, took a ride in John Lucky's Trans Am."

I'd heard that story so many times growing up. Where it once brought pain, it now gave me comfort. I smiled as I pictured two madly in love teenagers cutting class to go for a joyride in a car that would, nine months later, act as baby's first bassinet.

Sadly, the same car would, only five short years later, take both their lives.

With a sigh of regret for what should've been, I picked up the cans, one in each hand, and headed for the door. "Thanks, Sallie."

"You tell your adorable granddaddy hi for me." She patted her salt-and-pepper hair pulled tightly against her head.

"I surely will."

Who knew Jack was such a catch?

Half grossed out by the possibility, I pushed through the door of her shop and into the humid hell known as Florida. My hair, normally tawny-colored with a fashionable pixie cut, instantly curled, leaving me looking more like the Little Orphan Annie during a walk of shame. I blew out a loud, heated breath. It could've been worse.

Then it got exactly that as I turned a corner and ran smack dab into Grodie Brodie Gett. Literally. My face smashed into his hard chest. The paint cans tipped backward, as did I. Somehow he managed to stop my descent to the ground, gripping me around the waist with his wide hands.

Unfortunately, the same could not be said for the cans of paint. They hit the concrete, hard. One of the lids popped loose, oozing paint onto the pitted sidewalk.

"No, no, no," I whispered, one of my greatest nightmares coming true. I'd never hear the end of this, let alone the incident with the water tower. How could this happen!

At that moment, I glared up at the very bane of my un-Lucky existence.

Grodie Brodie stared at the mess on the concrete and then his gaze traveled to me. As if not quite believing his eyes, he slowly looked me up and down. Not in a creepy way, but more of a general appraisal. However, I could've done without the familiar smirk, the one that likely led to the incident on the tower all those years ago in the first place. "Well, well, if it isn't Charms." His hand lingered on my back for a brief moment before he released me, taking a step back. "You look exactly the same."

Charms, as in Lucky Charms.

I remembered the day in first grade when he announced the nickname to the entire class, which, admittedly, was about thirty kids in all. He stood up in the middle of quiet time, smirking that Gett smirk. His eyes roamed over my red hair and eyes too big for my face. And then he forever sealed my fate with one word: Charms. The other kids laughed. Even Mrs. Crest, our teacher, smiled a bit before shushing Brodie.

Years later, Grodie Brodie added how he'd tasted my charms, and they were indeed magically delicious. A lie, but one that stuck. The first time I'd heard the rumor flickering through our high school of teenagers from both Gett and the larger town of Harker, I'd been studying lines for an audition for the lead role in *The Taming of the Shrew.*

5

The shrew had nothing on me when I ran down the hall to confront Brodie.

I'd screamed in his face until my voice went hoarse. He just stood there, his face devoid of emotion. In that moment, I hated him. Suffice it to say, when I finally auditioned a few hours later, the shrew sounded much more like a squeaky mouse.

I didn't get the part.

I blamed Brodie to this day.

At the memory, my blood pressure rose until my body felt as hot as the scorching sun overhead.

"You don't look at all like you used to," I said as a means of irritating him. Not that it would. The captain of the football team had grown from a boy into a man—a stunning one at that. During his time in the Army, his body had filled out, turning youthful muscles rock hard. His black hair, once shaggy and long, was now buzzed and in order. Everything about him screamed *soldier*.

Nothing like the boy who'd recklessly tried to "borrow" my granddad's pickup, but ended up stalling the stick shift. Rather than blister the twelve-year-old Brodie following his joyride, Jack had shoved him back into the pickup and taught him the basics of stick. The sound of grinding gears filled my head. The ever-confident Gett hadn't been so much so that day. Then again, the first time Jack let me drive his pickup, I'd confused reverse for first, sending the truck into the shallow river bed running along our property.

The memory of Jack's laughter filled my mind.

A sound I hadn't heard since I'd returned home six weeks ago.

"It's been ten years," Brodie said, his thumbs hooked into his belt loops. "I hope I'm not the same stupid kid, doing stupid things to get girls' attention."

I gave him a half smile. "Like you had to try."

"Maybe not all the time. Speaking of trying, how's Jack?" Brodie and my grandfather had an odd relationship. The Gett family with their Gett Whiskey brand had long been the Lucky's rivals for best whiskey in the country, let alone state.

It all started almost two hundred years ago, when my great-great-grandfather, Wilson Lucky, entrusted the recipe for the smoothest whiskey to his best friend and investment partner, Marvin Gett. Less than a year later, Marvin had set up his own distillery only a few miles away, and Wilson had to witness the betrayal every day.

A year after that, Wilson Lucky was dead.

Some say he had died of a broken heart.

However, some believed the legend that declared his death a direct result of a gunshot wound sustained by an irate husband returning home early. A legend Jack denied with a wink whenever asked.

The feud grew under the helm of Rue Gett, Brodie's grandmother and the bane of Jack's existence. She did everything in her power to come out on top, even if that meant sabotaging Lucky. But be that as it may, Jack had always held a special spot in his heart for Brodie, the youngest Gett. I'd often wondered why, but never asked. For as much loss as Jack had suffered, from Grandma Jennie to my own father, he was owed a secret or two.

"He'll be back in the saddle in no time." Not quite true, but why tell Brodie? His feelings for Jack aside, he'd only use it to one-up us. Whiskey and family meant far more than feelings around here. "And your Grandma Rue? My Gosh, she must be in her eighties by now." And as wily as ever, by all accounts. "How's she doing these days?"

"Good. Good."

A loud creak from rusted hinges warned of my impending doom as Sallie charged out of her shop to blister me for the paint spill, and then stopped. She beamed up at Brodie as if he'd recently saved the world. Single-handedly.

Sometimes I hated this town.

"Good to have you home, boy. We sure did miss you," she said.

"Good to be here."

Lovefest over, she turned to scold me, her thin arms motioning with a vigor reserved for a much younger woman. "Look at what you've done. I warned you to be careful, Charlotte."

"I..." I glanced down at the mess, and then back at Brodie. "He did it," I said and walked off, a genuine smile on my face. The first since I'd left the soft, golden promise of the California sun.

CHAPTER

2

"CHAR, DID YOU TEST the cask strength?" Granddad Jack asked a few hours later. "It's gotta be under 125 proof. Any more and we're going to have a batch of furniture polish." He sat in his favorite worn recliner, a glass of water rather than whiskey, much to his dismay, on the armrest.

"I know," I said, placing a tray filled with food in front of him. He looked far too thin, not nearly the big bold presence I remembered. He wasn't eating, and I was getting worried.

Jack had raised me since my parents died in an unfortunate roll-over car accident along Gator Row when I was five. Granddad had taken me in without a second thought. I couldn't imagine life without him. Since my return, every time I looked at him, I saw a seventy-four-year-old man, his hair thinning, skin growing pale. Tired. His gaze not as steady.

He was fading before my eyes, and I had no way of stopping it.

Time, even more than the Getts, was our enemy now.

"I'll check the strength in a moment." I motioned to the food on the plate. Food that looked far too gray in color to taste like anything. "Now will you eat? It's your favorite. Chicken pot pie."

He thumped the tray, sending the plate dancing toward the edge. Thankfully it stayed on the tray, along with seventy-five percent of the pot pie. "What's the point of pot pie if there's no butter in it? I might as well eat chicken soup."

I tried to smile, but it fell flat. He did have a point, but seeing as I'd worked for over an hour trying to make "healthy" chicken pot pie, I wasn't in the mood to argue. Rather than listen to the same complaint I'd heard every night since he'd come home from the hospital, I used a tried-and-true motto. "Doctor's orders."

"Doctor, my ass," he yelled. "Those quacks know nothing—"

Before he went full-court press on the medical profession, Sweet Jayme entered the room, her hair tied back with a bandana and a wide smile on her face. Granddad instantly dropped his rant.

"I'll take it from here," she said, handing him a fork, worn with age and use. "Go check your cask strength, Charlotte. We'll be here when you're done."

I smiled my appreciation and then focused on Granddad. "I'll be back in ten minutes. I expect a cleaned plate and a smile on your grumpy face upon my return." Leaning down, I kissed his forehead to soften my words. As I did, I inhaled his scent. A combination of oak and whiskey.

Taking one last whiff, I left the house, circling the distillery, where grains went from malting to milling to mash, and then on to fermentation in large steel tanks called washbacks, and finally distilling. Separating the alcohol from the water during the distilling process was done in copper stills heated to just under 212 degrees. From there, it would be distilled again before it was ready to sleep for the next four years in a cask created to instill the finest color and flavor.

On my right sat the cooperage cottage, where my cousin Evan crafted the finest whiskey casks in the business, like my father once had. But my mission wasn't in the cottage or the distillery, but the building directly behind the distillery, tucked between it and the swamp.

The structure known as the rackhouse—where two thousand gallons of whiskey sat waiting for the exact right time to be bottled—was like a beacon in the sky. I was, as always, impressed by the sheer height of it. Three stories all packed with aging whiskey and intricate pulley systems to raise and lower casks, to ensure no whiskey was served before its time.

Luckys knew two things. First, good wort wrought grand flavor; and second, whiskey took time to mature. Open a cask too soon and the best of wort couldn't save it.

Each barrel inside our rackhouse spent over four long years inside, sometimes longer. Waiting for that one magical moment where the blurred lines between booze and whiskey sharpened into something wonderful.

What wasn't wonderful was the humidity stalking my every step on the journey to whiskey nirvana. How could it be this sweltering at seven at night? One of the things I missed most about L.A. When the sun set over the ocean waters, the air chilled like whiskey poured over ice.

Not so in sweaty armpit Florida.

Though I had to admit, it felt nice to be outside to hear the buzz of mosquitoes and the cry of wildlife hidden in the shadows beyond the property line.

These days I spent most of my time indoors trying to figure out Jack's filing system so I could pay the stack of bills piling up on his old oak desk. Running Lucky Whiskey wasn't as easy as I'd first thought when I rolled back into town six weeks ago. And I rarely did more than the routine administrative work. The actual distilling and chemistry I left to our head distiller, Roger Kerrick.

Roger and I went back a way. Back to high school and the backseat of his mother's Jeep, to be specific. The memory of the heavy scent of Drakkar Noir and leather seats, of teenage hormones and wet kisses, of Roger's fumbling hands and fogged windows, rose inside me.

Thankfully, I moved on to better after I caught Roger humping the prom queen. At the time, my tears had Jack threatening to stuff the cheating Roger in a cask and toss him in the Glades.

For the distillery's sake, I'm glad he'd refrained.

We needed Roger.

Desperately.

Especially since I was now in charge. I made a mental note to swing by and see Roger in the morning, to find out where we were at with the latest batch. I hadn't seen him in a day or two, and was starting to get concerned. Even an hour too long in the wort room and the grain could shoot, thereby ruining the flavor of the batch.

Or so Jack said.

Sadly, everyone in the county knew I was in over my head, even if I would never admit to such a sin. Whiskey was supposed to be in my blood. Without Roger at my side, I felt like I was swimming in a glass of Old Crow instead of Old Weller Antique.

Using all the strength in my arms, I pulled open the door to the rackhouse, inhaling the scent of wood and whiskey, as I did every time I entered. There was something almost reverent about the rackhouse, with the rows upon rows of casks stacked as high as the eye could see.

With a loud sigh that filled the empty building, I pulled a small copper tube-like instrument from my pocket called a thief. The weight and feel of it brought back a flood of memories. Both good and bad.

Memories of Jack. Of his stern features breaking into a wide grin at the first taste of a new batch. My first kiss had been just beyond the first row of casks. The heady scent of warming whiskey as welcoming as Joey Duggan's moist lips.

The Lucky Distillery was family.

In my years away I'd forgotten the intoxicating smell of fermenting grains. Or how my tongue tingled, much more than other places had during Joey's overly wet smooch, as I anticipated the finest whiskey in the country.

But while Jack had always dreamed of that perfect sip, I'd spent my childhood days daydreaming of life outside Gett, Florida … of walking the red carpet.

I spied the cask the rackhouse manager had left out for me to test. The Lucky emblem embossed on the top. Wiping a bead of sweat from my forehead, I held the thief aloft, the cask—my intended victim.

I stabbed the instrument into the oak like I had done with an ice-pick in my brief appearance on *NCIS*. I used my thumb, holding it over the top to gain enough pressure to suck up a taste of the rich whiskey inside.

I lifted the thief, frowning.

Something wasn't right.

I jabbed it in again. Harder. Still nothing. Was something wrong with the cask? Had the angels taken more than their fair share? More likely the devil was at play. But he wouldn't win. Not this time.

I grabbed a bung puller, which looked a lot like a large, complicated corkscrew, and went to work on prying the barrel open. Whiskey splashed over the edge, falling on my boots with a wet splat. I paused, frowning as the air filled with a pungent odor, like fermenting overly ripe bananas and whiskey.

Was the cask bad? Had air somehow gotten inside, destroying the carefully crafted ingredients? I hoped not. We had orders to fill, and each cask was worth nearly ten thousand dollars.

Using all the strength in what some might call my scrawny arms, I cranked at the bung puller along the edge of the barrel. Ultimately the lid gave way and I fell back a step.

An even fouler odor spewed from the cask, like meat left far too long in the Florida sun. Tears rose in my eyes. Cupping a hand over my mouth, I held my breath. The stench threatened to overwhelm my efforts to keep it at bay. Trying not to gag, I took a step closer to the cask.

Don't look. Don't look, my mind warned, but I had no choice.

Once my brain recognized the horror before me, I let out a sharp cry. "Oh my God." The urge to lose my own chicken pot pie dinner rose up. I had a feeling it wouldn't taste any better coming back up than it had going down. I swallowed gulping breaths until the feeling subsided.

Stumbling back, I accidently bumped the cask with the bung puller. It rocked back and then tipped forward, spilling the very pickled corpse of Roger Kerrick onto the rackhouse floor with a wet plop.

CHAPTER

3

"LET ME GET THIS straight," said Danny Gett, the straight-laced sheriff of Collier County, population just over three hundred thousand.

Even more than being sheriff, Danny loved being a Gett. Loved the long-standing feud between our families. So his interrogating me, in my own far-from-orderly kitchen, after I found Roger pickled in a Lucky Whiskey cask, gave him such glee that he looked like a little kid in need of a bathroom break.

He danced to my right and back to center. His normally handsome, albeit stern, features brightened to Hollywood actor at the Golden Globes giddiness at the prospect of arresting a Lucky for murder. "You just happened upon Roger while sampling the goods," he said, doubt lacing his every word. "Is that what I'm supposed to believe?"

I lifted my shoulders in a shrug, annoyed by the hour-long interview. I'd given him my statement three times. Three times and still he wanted me to repeat every word. Danny hadn't been the brightest kid in school, but this was too much. Why didn't he just listen? Was the inability to pay attention to a single female a Gett trait? "I don't care what you believe, Danny—"

"Sheriff," he interrupted, his tone coolly professional. "Call me Sheriff Gett."

Sure I would. Right after hell froze over and I won an Academy Award. I could hear my acceptance speech now...

"I told you already, I tapped the cask, realized something was wrong when only a few drops emerged, and popped the lid." I thought back, my stomach ache growing when I pictured Roger's pale, whiskey-soaked head floating on top. His light brown hair had danced along the liquid ripples. The moment of death forever locked on his face, mouth wide, as if he hadn't expected his untimely end. Then again, who would?

Blowing out a breath as the memory faded, I added, "When I saw what or rather *who* was inside, I freaked, accidently knocking the barrel over." Roger-infused whiskey had splashed up, soaking my jeans. Jeans currently sticking to my legs as we spoke. "His ... body ... hit the floor, which was when I noticed the bloodstains on the ground, and I ran out to call 911."

All completely the truth.

Except for one tiny detail.

For a brief moment, I'd hesitated. My first thoughts were of the distillery, of what would happen if Roger had accidently fallen inside, smacking his head on the cask and drowning. A ridiculous notion but one that stopped me in my tracks.

Then I remembered the lid and its tight fit.

This wasn't an accident.

Someone had killed Roger, stuffing his corpse in a cask like grave robbers used to do. The tomb raiders would then ship the corpse in the cask to America, where they would sell the body to med students along with the corpse whiskey, aptly renamed rotgut.

Why that bizarre fact popped into my head was beyond me. Shock? Maybe a bit of the macabre? Or perhaps I'd finally lost my mind. It sure felt like it. Nothing appeared quite real, like walking through a nightmare.

Thankfully there wasn't a creepy clown in sight.

After finding the body, I had run to the house on shaking legs and called the police. Since Gett didn't have its own police force, I was forced to wait for the sheriff and his three deputies. Four cops to cover 2,300 square miles of brackish waterways and towns even smaller than our own.

They arrived an hour later, lights and sirens in full use.

Probably the only time they got to use them.

One of the two county ambulances came as well. A ghoulish man, his skin the color of a fading bruise, emerged from the ambulance. I gave him a wave. "Hi, Lester." We'd been in the same science class. I'd let him cheat off my final test on anatomy. Guess it paid off.

He waved back. "Charms."

My fists clenched but before I could correct him, Danny had started in with his questions. "Looks like Kerrick died at least twenty-four hours ago of a gunshot to the chest. So tell me again how he got those post-mortem stab wounds on his head?" Danny stroked his chin and the few hairs growing out of it. As far back as I remember he'd tried to grow a beard to match the one his renowned lady killer of a daddy, Big Paul Gett, had. I swear, in high school, he'd used his mother's eyeliner to fill in the missing patches.

"It was an accident," I said through clenched teeth. "You know as well as I do that I didn't kill Roger."

"Do I?"

17

"That's enough, boy," Grandpa Jack, using a cane, walked into the kitchen. A place I'd rarely, if ever, seen him step foot in. All my life, he'd say cooking was for women then push me toward the mass of canned soup, canned vegetables, and worst of all, canned meats.

To this day, the very sight of SPAM made my stomach roll.

With all that sodium, it was no wonder Jack's skin looked half cured and he had off-the-chart blood pressure. What had he done after I left for college? The sadness on his face that day would haunt me for the rest of my life. But I had to go. Had to find my own joy. After all, Gett was hardly a haven for actors, producers, or even baristas.

The closest Starbucks was fifty miles away in Immokalee.

"But, sir," Danny began, but Jack's cane against his shin shut him up. He winced but didn't cry out. Or, thankfully, arrest Jack for assault.

"It's late and Charlotte needs her beauty sleep," the old man declared for *everyone* to hear.

Damn, did I look that bad? I patted my humidity-curled hair. Sure, I could use a trim, but it wasn't that bad. I hoped.

"You can pester her some more tomorrow," he finished.

"Fine." Danny glared at me. "But don't leave town."

I stifled a giggle when I realized he was serious. Cops didn't talk like that. Not in real life. I guess Danny spent too much time watching old detective shows. Next, would he be booking me, Danny-o? The thought of spending time in the Collier County jail drained my humor much like a drunk did his glass at last call.

Once Lester packed up Roger's body and the cops collected their evidence, whatever that meant, Danny and his deputies left. Silence filled the house. Shock at both Roger's murder and what his death meant to Lucky Whiskey kept Jack and I locked in our own thoughts.

Why would anyone kill Roger?

And why here, at the distillery?

Guilt rose inside me as I thought of Roger. I knew little of his life over the last few years outside the walls of the distillery, too little to even guess at the motive behind the murder.

"Granddad," I said as the night sky grew blacker. "Why don't you go to bed? It's been a long night." I was exhausted and confused. Murder in the heat of passion was one thing, but killing Roger and then stuffing him in a Lucky Whiskey cask was quite another. Not only was the act cold, it was also calculated.

Someone hadn't wanted Roger found. Not for some time. Or had they? Was it my unlucky luck that I picked that cask to test, or had someone wanted me to find Roger's body? Like a grumpy, wrinkled kid, he stomped his foot. "I'll go to bed, but not because you said so." Slowly he rose from his chair and staggered down the hall to the family room we turned into a bedroom after his heart attack. The doctor had, for now, vetoed using the stairs. I wondered if Jack would ever recover enough to live the life he once had. It had been well over a month already. He stopped before he reached his door. "I love you, Char."

Tears rose in my eyes. "I love you too, Granddad." Taking a deep breath, I wiped away the wetness with the back of my hand. Jack hated to see me cry, so I long ago vowed to contain my emotions. It worked about fifty percent of the time.

With a loud sigh into the now quiet house, I sat down at the kitchen table to do some work. I rifled through the stack of bills that only seemed to grow higher each day. Payroll was coming up. A day over twenty families in the town relied on for their next meal.

Life wasn't easy for most folks in Gett. Work was often hard, and even harder to come by. Too often generations of people lived together in the same small house, working until fingers bled and hearts grew weak. From an early age, I'd wanted my freedom. Wanted to become a great actress. Wanted to thank the little people.

I realized now how little I'd known. People in Gett had one thing most in Hollywood lacked—deep, unwavering pride. Not to mention the ability to hold a grudge forever. I thought of the water tower. Of the ugly, hastily splattered paint declaring: *Getting Lucky*. What had I been thinking?

The answer was easy. I hadn't. My first alcohol-infused blackout that fateful night had been my last. I had vowed to never make such a mistake again.

I allowed myself to wallow in self-pity for thirty seconds more, then poured a dram of whiskey into a crystal glass. I took a long sip, willing away the sight of Roger as the whiskey warmed my tongue. Forcing myself to swallow, I opened Granddad's personal checkbook, making note of last month's payments. Property taxes. Groceries (all canned, I'd bet). Insurance. My head tilted to the side to look closer at one particular entry for over five thousand dollars written a few days before Granddad's heart attack.

A check made out to Roger Kerrick.

Why had Granddad written him a personal check, rather than one from the distillery payroll account? And why for so much?

A chill ran up my spine.

If Danny saw the checkbook, he'd suspect the worst.

Taking a long drink, I let the whiskey roll around on my tongue before swallowing past the lump forming there. I glanced at the checkbook and then to my whiskey, making up my mind. Without pause, I tore the carbon copy from the registry and ripped it into hundreds of pieces. Then I swiped the bits from the table, tossing them into the trash.

My second swallow of whiskey burned a path into my stomach, where it sat like a weight. The same sort that had settled into my chest.

CHAPTER

4

THE NEXT MORNING, I woke to the call of Osprey as they circled the surrounding Glades. The distinctive cry warned of danger—the presence of a predator. I took the warning to heart; after all, someone had left Roger dead in a Lucky Whiskey cask.

If that wasn't some kind of omen, I didn't know what was.

Dressing in a plain, light green tank dress and my favorite pair of black boots, I grabbed my purse off the nightstand, the very same nightstand I'd had as a little girl, and headed downstairs.

A sense of déjà vu filled me.

I was maybe fifteen, going out on my first date, dressed much like I was right now except in a cheaper bra and panties set.

Then, like now, Granddad stood at the foot of the steps, a half smile on his face. Ever the pragmatist, he'd grab my chin in his calloused hands when I reached him. His hands had smelled of yeast and sour mash. "Char, girl," he'd say, "don't go *getting* into trouble."

This time his warning wasn't about unintended babies.

"Char, girl," he said when I reached him. His hands still smelled of sour mash, but now they trembled with age and illness. "Don't go *making* trouble."

Now, like I had then, I stared into his pea green eyes and said, "I won't, Granddad."

His snort sounded the same, full of frustration. "What you mean to say is, I won't find out. You pulled that same trick a hundred times while you were growing up. Always too smart for my good." He smiled, seemingly adrift in time, gaze losing its normally sharp focus. His mouth thinned, hand trembling against the banister.

"Granddad," I said as fear filled my belly. "Are you okay?"

He shook off whatever ghosts of the past that haunted him. "I'm fine, Char. You go do your errands." Eyebrow twitching, he added, "I'll be here when you get back."

I patted his hand, leaning in to kiss his cheek. I considered asking him about the check to Roger, but decided against it. I didn't want to upset him. Not now. Not when he looked so frail. Again, sadness threatened. What would I do without Jack?

He'd always been there for me.

Like on the day I'd gotten my first period. I'd been so embarrassed, mortified to ask my grandfather for the necessary feminine products. But Jack had happily driven me to the store, fifteen miles away. We'd rode in silence. My face burning brighter with each mile.

Until Jack said something I took with me to this day. He said, "Never be ashamed to be a woman." And I wasn't. Not now. Or ever.

"Don't forget to eat breakfast," I said as the memory faded. "Sweet Jayme will be here in less than an hour, and if your oatmeal isn't empty..."

"I won't be getting whiskey tonight." He laughed, sounding much more like the man who'd driven his embarrassed granddaughter all that way. "I know the rules, girl. Hell, a year ago I made them."

"And you will again." I waved as I headed out the door. He stood in the doorway staring after me, like he always had. Warmth flooded my chest. I didn't know much, but I knew Granddad would die or kill for me.

Which brought me to this morning's errand.

Who had killed Roger and why?

———

I strode past the Prius I'd driven, packed with almost everything I owned, from Hollywood to Gett six weeks before, deciding on a nice stroll. I needed to stretch my legs and clear my head after last night. It wasn't a long walk to the house Roger shared with his girlfriend, Mary Broome. Just about three miles down the bumpy Route 1. I regretted my decision a quarter of a mile in, my tank dress clinging to my body, drenched in sweat. Three-fourths of the way my boots had filled with perspiration as well. They made squeaking sounds every time I took a step.

Cursing the humidity and once again missing my air-conditioned L.A. studio apartment, I staggered the rest of the way, sucking in the wet air. Mary taught school in the next town over but lived in Gett's Gator Alley. Since the town didn't have much imagination when it came to naming conventions, Gator Alley stood for exactly that— three houses, almost a hundred yards away from each other, backed against the Glades filled with the sharp-toothed beasts.

Therefore, less alley and much more gator.

The last hundred feet or so, I hesitated with every step as the undergrowth surrounding the street thickened. The perfect hiding place for a gator, or any other beastie wishing to do me harm.

With a sigh of relief, I finally stepped on Mary's front porch, which creaked under the assault. The old house looked nice enough. White with yellow trim. Two stories, the first of which was built on stilts. A common occurrence for Gett.

Only a fool built a house on the ground in these parts.

I knocked on Mary's door, not really expecting an answer. After all, she was grieving and must've had plenty of final-resting sorts of errands to do for Roger today. Since Gett didn't have a funeral home—thankfully, for I could only imagine the name—Mary would have to drive forty miles east to the Welcome Home Funeral Home in Bonita Springs.

When the door opened with a groan, I took a surprised step back. Mary stood in the doorway, a brave albeit watery smile on her thin face. She waved me in. "So good to see you, Charlotte," she said in a fragile voice, as if any second she might break. My heart ached for her loss. I'd suffered a few of my own. That pit just below your breastbone never disappeared completely, no matter how much time passed. Though their faces faded, growing blurry with the fog of time, enhancing your grief.

"I'm so sorry ..." I said.

"I know but thank you," she said, sadness flickering in her eyes. "It's so stuffy in here, let's talk on the patio." She led me through her tidy house toward the back porch. A porch sitting six feet off swampland. A bead of sweat, not caused by the high humidity, ran down my face.

When I was a kid, I had a recurring dream about getting lost in the swamp, drowning in the brackish water, never to be seen again. Unlike

25

other kids in town who ran wildly through the swamp, I kept far away from the Glades. When I confessed my fear, Jack said I had nothing to worry about. For the first time in my short life, I hadn't believed him.

"Please, have a seat," Mary said, motioning to a well-used wire patio chair.

The humid climate had rusted the armrest, but otherwise the seat looked sturdy enough. I sat gently, tucking my purse underneath me.

"Can I offer you some sweet tea?" she asked.

"Yes," I said quickly. Too quickly. "Thank you."

She left to pour the delicious, cold drink, leaving me to my own devices. Never a good thing. Specifically with a backyard filled with mangroves trees, mosquitoes as big as birds, and alligators ready and waiting for their next meal.

The snap of teeth, the crackle of birds, and the pop of rednecks firing at anything that moved filled the air. Below me, a wrinkled brown head suddenly popped up. Beady eyes looked me over, as if debating whether eating me was worth the effort. As swiftly as the head of the gator appeared, it disappeared back under the murky water. Even in the heat, chills puckered my skin.

Thankfully Mary returned before I bolted off the porch and ran until I reached L.A.

She set two glasses down. Amber tea, the same color as a fine Irish whiskey, ice, and enough sweetener to rot one's teeth swirled in each glass. She motioned to the sugar bowl she'd also set on the table. I shook my head, unsurprised as she added two teaspoons to her tea. The way of the South. Astounding we hadn't won the Civil War out of sheer sugar rush.

"I know this is a hard time for you," I began. "Again, I am so sorry for your loss."

She wiped a tear away but didn't comment.

"You and Roger lived together?"

At his name, her tears came faster. Still silent. Like in a movie. For me, tears meant a box of snotty Kleenex and noises loud enough to scare my neighbors.

"Yes," she said after a few seconds. "He moved in a year after we started dating. As you know, I'd had some unfortunate ends to a couple of relationships before we met, so I was cautious."

I nodded, remembering Mary's whirlwind courtship and eventual bad breakup with a college boy our senior year of high school. There was rumor of a restraining order, but I couldn't recall the details.

She gave me a watery smile. "Roger kept insisting, and at last I said yes. He moved in a few days later."

"Roger was a good man." I didn't have a clue if that was true or not. Not since we were seventeen, when he cheated on me. We'd only interacted a handful of times since I arrived home. Mostly distillery business. Cask strength and such. Only once did we talk of anything personal, and that consisted of small talk about weekend plans. He'd had some, and I didn't. Shocking, I know.

"Yes, he was," Mary said.

"I hate to bring this up, but can you tell me about a check my grandfather wrote to him a few weeks ago?" I rushed on when she frowned. "I'm trying to get a handle on Jack's finances and any help you can give …"

Her irritation cleared. Southern ladies, which I was—if in location only—never discussed money. It just wasn't done outside the confines of husband and wife.

"I understand. My mamma, God rest her, had troubles remembering too, after her attack. Died soon after."

That was the last thing I needed to hear. Jack wasn't dying. He was too stubborn to let the angels take him and the devil surely didn't want to deal with his crap. "Did you remember Roger talking about the money?" I asked. "Maybe what it was for?"

Redness stained her pale cheeks. "I'm not sure it's my place ..."

"Please."

Her eyes darted left and then to the right, and she lowered her voice as if revealing a grand secret, even though no one but the two of us and a monster gator sat nearby. "The money was for Evan."

"Evan? My Evan?" Cousin Evan Lewis. The bane of Granddad's existence over the last few years. He worked for the distillery on and off as a barrel maker, also known as a cooper. Jack said he was one of the best in the business. He would work for a few months at a time. Then Evan would vanish without so much as a goodbye. Granddad never told me why. I suspected drugs. But again, Southern etiquette deemed such frank talk impossible.

"I'm not sure what it was all about..." She took drink from her sweet tea. "But I do know Evan owed Roger a little money."

My stomach dropped. Was it more than a little?

Perhaps enough to kill over?

CHAPTER

5

"I HATE TO ASK this, but..." I took a deep breath and rushed on before I could think better of it. "Do you know anyone who ... would want ... Roger dead?" Other than Jack or my cousin. Not that Jack would kill unless he had a damn good reason, and a few grand was too little a reason to kill Lucky Whiskey's best distiller.

In the end, it always came down to the distillery for Jack. Bitterness that I hadn't felt in years swelled inside me. While Jack loved me, growing up I often worried he loved the whiskey business more. I swallowed it down, deep inside, where resentments either festered, died, or killed you.

Mary's forehead wrinkled, turning her pale skin even whiter against the darkness of her hair. The poor thing had been through enough and here I was pushing her for reasons someone had killed her beau. Guilt added to the weight of resentment mixed with fear in my belly.

"No one comes to mind. Everyone loved him," she said. "But you should ask around at the Gett. Danny said it was the last place Roger was ... before ... you know."

I did know. Roger's dead-eyed stare swirled through my vision. I took a drink of the sweet tea to wash away the wave of nausea threatening to burst forth. I thanked her, set my drink on the table, and gave one last glance to the gator below. His sharp, jagged teeth shone like ivory in the midmorning sunlight.

Goosebumps rose on my skin, but I shook them off. Gators won't hurt you unless provoked. Or you stumbled onto their nest. Of if you looked good enough to eat. No matter how hard I tried to convince myself, the gator sunning itself a few feet away was much too close for comfort.

"Boots there is a big one. Eight feet by my count," Mary said, following my gaze to the beast. A long stark white scar lined his snout, from below his eye to his razor sharp teeth. "Been here since I can remember."

I nodded, not caring to get to know Boots, or any gator for that matter, any more than absolutely necessary.

"Let me walk you out," she said with a small smile.

I followed her back through the house, catching the distinctive scent of whiskey in the air. But not a bottle in sight. I inhaled deeply. Whoever had recently partaken sure as hell wasn't drinking Lucky Whiskey. I could identify our brand at ten paces—twenty if the person consumed enough. Why was there a competitor's whiskey in Roger's house?

Once at the door I thanked Mary again. I stared into her red-rimmed eyes, hoping to see more than just a grieving girlfriend. Perhaps a murder suspect? But all I saw was my own warped reflection in her pupils.

"If you find anything ... about ... you'll let me know?" she asked, wetness spilling down her cheeks.

"Of course."

"Roger ... he ... ah ... talked about you sometimes," she whispered. "He was proud of what you'd become out there in Hollywood."

A larger lump formed in my stomach. "Thank you," I said.

I gave her a wave before turning toward the one place in town I'd avoided since my return. But I needed information of the desperate variety, and the best place to find it was, and always would be, the Gett Bar & Grill. Not that they served food. The county health inspector saw to that.

———

Ten minutes after leaving Mary, I was seated on a stool a foot longer than my legs. My feet dangled uselessly as I ordered whiskey, neat. Nothing back. Just like my granddaddy had taught me.

The bartender—a young woman I'd gone to school with named Willow Jones—grabbed the cheap watered-down stuff from the shelf. Other than being old enough to wield the bottle in her hands, Willow hadn't changed at all since our school days. In fact, I remembered her wearing the same outfit of jeans and a gray t-shirt on the day I left town.

"Lucky Whiskey," I said. "And it better not be watered down."

She laughed, unsealing a brand-new bottle of my family's pride and joy. A good whiskey, here in the States, was normally aged in oak casks for four years. We tended most of ours for even longer. Therefore, the whiskey Willow poured was likely fermented around the time I lost my virginity, in a car parked around the back of this very bar.

Willow finished the pour, set the bottle down, and shoved the glass my way. I threw a ten on the bar, tapping it to gain her attention. "When did you last see Roger Kerrick?" I did my best impersonation of a cop on a crime show.

She raised an eyebrow. "Who?"

"Really? You're going to claim ignorance?" Everyone in town knew, or knew of, everyone else. Our high school was combined with a few neighboring towns, but it still wasn't so big that you didn't know everyone's name from freshman through senior. She knew Roger as surely as the humidity made for the boldest of whiskey flavor. Add in the fact that she was and always would be Danny Gett's best friend, and her plea of ignorance rang as hollow as the watered-down whiskey on the shelf.

She shrugged.

"Your grandma Martha is going to be disappointed." I let my words settle in. "After all, my granddaddy gave your brother a job when he was down on his luck." My brow inched upward. "Without being asked." Then again, after her brother received his first paycheck he took off for the sands of Miami. Another casualty of topless beaches and the devil's juice. Or, as others called it, rum.

"Damn, Charms, you go for the jugular."

Grodie Brodie Gett appeared next to me, as if conjured up from the same place as mojitos. He laid another ten on top of mine on the bar. "Tell her."

Willow nodded, scooping the two tens into her delicate hands. "Roger was here two nights ago. He was pretty drunk. I booted him after last call, he argued some, but finally left. Must've been around two."

Two nights ago matched the timeline. At least according to Sheriff Danny. When he didn't know I was listening, he had said Roger took his whiskey nap sometime between twenty-four and forty-eight hours before I found him.

"Last I saw of him," Willow said, "he was stumbling through the parking lot." Her eyes slid to Brodie. Just for a second. Enough for the hairs on my neck to stand on end. The two of them had a secret. I could read it all over Willow's poor poker face. Brodie's, on the other hand, looked as innocent as a newborn baby. The lying jerk.

"Did you see anyone with him?" I asked. The last person to see Roger alive might very well be the same one who killed him. My brow furrowed. Was that what the two of them were hiding? Did they know the killer?

She shook her head, sending her long curly copper-colored hair dancing up and down. I envied the color. Had I not known her for most of my life, I would've asked the name of her colorist. Of course, here in Gett, the only place to get your hair cut let alone colored was The Curl & Dye on Main Street.

I turned to Brodie. "Well?"

"Well, what?" he drawled.

"Were you here that night?" I tried to avoid sounding like a scolding schoolteacher for his obviously alcohol-fueled activities since his release, discharge, or whatever from the Army, but I must've failed.

His arms crossed over his chest. "I don't spend all my time here, you know."

"Then you weren't here the night Roger died?"

"Damn it," he said, blowing out a harsh, whiskey-soaked breath. "Why are you flouncing around town asking questions about this? Roger is dead. My brother's smart—"

Willow snorted. "Debatable."

Brodie smirked but continued on as if she hadn't spoken. "He'll arrest the killer."

Unlike Willow, I didn't have a crush on the annoying sheriff. Though, like her, I had my doubts about Danny's IQ. I'd spent many hours tutoring him in high school. Money was money, after all, and jobs weren't plentiful for teenagers around here. I'd gotten a whole years' worth of tutoring payments when I was a junior and he was a senior in danger of not graduating. Yeah, Danny certainly wasn't the smartest Gett in the genetic bunch.

That honor fell to the Machiavellian man next to me. While I'd held a perfect 4.0, Brodie had graduated second in our class, with a 3.9 GPA. Had he studied for the Home Economics final rather than going to football practice, he very well would've passed the class with a perfect grade, thereby tying me for the honor of valedictorian.

"Leave it alone, Charms." He leaned in close enough that I caught his manly scent—the smell of soap and hard work. I guess day drinking took a lot out of you. "For your own good," he added, his tone as cold as the beer in the cooler next to us.

I drew back and then gave a small chuckle. "Flouncing? Really?"

He let out his own laugh. "Too much? You always have had a way of making things more complicated." The humor faded from his stare. "I'm gonna give you some friendly advice." His tone implied anything but camaraderie.

"Gee, thanks."

Lips twisted into a half smile, his features changed from handsome to devastating. He quickly sobered, hot eyes on mine. "Roger isn't worth your life."

CHAPTER

6

FOLLOWING WHAT SOUNDED TOO much like a threat for me to ignore, Brodie snatched my whiskey from the bar, drained it with a grimace, and walked away with a simple, "Later, Charms."

I sat, stunned. My mouth hanging open.

"That'll be seven bucks," Willow said.

"What?"

She motioned to my empty glass. "Seven bucks for the whiskey." A grin washed over her face, taking me back to the girl who had followed Danny Gett around like a lost puppy. "You did want the good stuff."

"But I didn't even drink it. Brodie did."

She shrugged, softening the blow by widening her smile. "Still seven bucks."

"I put ten on the bar!"

Her shoulders shifted again. "That was for answering your questions when Danny expressly said to keep quiet while he investigates, not the booze."

"But … I … ah hell with it." I threw a five and two ones on the bar, unwilling to give her a penny more.

She scooped the cash up, ringing the transaction up in a prehistoric cash register, the kind with typewriter buttons. As I slide from the bar stool, her words stopped me. "You should give Brodie a break."

"What?"

"Brodie." She waved to the door he'd departed moments ago. "He's a good man. Better than most, in truth."

Was Willow giving me advice about men? The world shifted under my feet. "To you, maybe," I said. "To me, he's a pain in the ass."

The corner of her mouth lifted. "I didn't say he wasn't a Gett."

We shared a brief smile. Just two women bemoaning their Gett-related state.

"Can I ask you something?" I said.

Her eyebrow rose. "Depends."

"What are you and Brodie hiding?"

Her features grew hard, shaping her already angular face. "Nothing."

I didn't believe her for a second. Both knew more about Roger's death than they were saying. But how much more?

"Have it your way," I said, holding my head up high as I stormed out of the Gett Bar.

And straight across the street to the Get-it Saloon less than a hundred and fifty feet away.

The Get-it Saloon was once named the Gett Saloon, until a lawsuit filed by the owner of the Gett Bar forced a name change. In a fit of drunken rage after the verdict, the owner of the Gett Saloon, Billy James, climbed a ladder with a can of spray paint, adding a small dotted i between the ts, making it—Getit.

The hyphen came later.

No one knew why. Except Billy James, but he refused to say a word.

Both bars were the same. Too-high barstools. Floor coated in stale beer. And the aroma of desperation with a hint of whiskey. I avoided such places after my fair share of desperate, whiskey-soaked nights, thankfully sans blackout-drunk spray-paint hijinks.

"Well, well," Billy James said, holding his large arms wide as I strolled inside. He looked much the same as he had years ago. Dark hair, tanned skin, and a wide open smile. "If it ain't Gett's most famous resident."

I winced. "When will people forgive me for painting the water tower?"

He frowned at the reminder of my vandalism.

Crap. "Oh, you meant my TV appearances," I said. My acting career might not have set the world on fire, but I had been on TV twice. I always knew which time someone had seen by his or her expression. If they smirked, then I knew they'd seen my stint as murderous Navy lieutenant on *NCIS*. If they avoided my gaze and made an excuse to get as far away from me as possible, they'd seen my role as victim #2 on a national STD prescription medication commercial.

Like STDs were catchy.

"How's Jack?" Billy asked as I crawled on top of the four-foot stool.

"Good." I smiled as he poured me two fingers of Lucky Whiskey. "He's driving poor Jayme crazy."

He waved off the ten-dollar bill I placed on the bar. "I know," he said with a grin. "She tells me all about it every night before we turn in. I'm thinking about buying ear plugs if he don't get better soon."

Billy and Jayme had lived in sin, according to the townsfolk, for the last three years. Billy had asked Jayme to marry him repeatedly, but she always refused, which drove Billy mad. I think she just didn't want to be Jayme James.

"So what brings you by?" he asked. "Besides my company?"

"I wanted to ask about Roger."

His eyebrow rose. "Best distiller around."

"He's dead."

Billy snorted. "I know that, girl. I was taught not to speak ill of the dead. And you shouldn't neither."

If only it was that simple. "Did you see him the night he died?" I asked.

"Why are you interested?" Gazing down, he ran his finger over the top of the beer in his hand. "You don't owe him anything."

"I know ... it's just ..." I began. How could I explain? Roger's dead-eye stare flickered in my head. That vision wasn't something likely to fade anytime soon. "Someone shot him, in my rackhouse. I can't just let that go."

Dipping his head, he took a long pull off the bottle of beer. When he pulled away, a beer-bubble mustache clung to his own whiskery lip. "Yeah, I saw Roger that night." He wiped the bubbles away with his bare arm. "Saw him drunk, in the parking lot, arguing with someone."

"Who?"

He shrugged.

"Come on, Billy." I leaned in. "You know everyone in town. Who was Roger was arguing with?"

He lowered his voice to a scant whisper. "Brodie Gett."

CHAPTER

7

STANDING OUTSIDE THE GET-IT, I tapped my finger to my lips. Armed with evidence that Brodie had likely done poor drunken Roger in, I wasn't sure of my next step. Not only did the town fawn over him, but also his brother was the law. Danny would hardly arrest his kin on my word. So what was I to do?

I needed evidence, or at the very least a motive.

But how would I get it?

Hesitantly, I dialed Mary's number. When she answered, I quickly explained my suspicions. Rather than outright laugh in my ear, she paused long enough for the hairs on my neck to rise. I wasn't crazy. Brodie and Roger had some sort of connection.

"Mary?" I prompted.

She exhaled loudly. "Brodie would never hurt Roger. They were friends."

"Friends can argue," I said. "Any idea what it was about? Was Roger angry with Brodie for some reason?" I could think of ten good ones off the top of my head. Then again, Brodie hadn't tortured Roger throughout his childhood.

"Who knows," she said. "When Roger got drunk …"

Goosebumps rose on my arms even in the sweltering Florida heat. "Did he … hurt you?"

"God, no," she said. "Nothing like that."

"Oh. Good."

"I've dated my fair share of jerks," she said, voice tight. "Roger wasn't one of them. But he knew how I felt about overindulging. So when he had too much to drink, he usually slept it off on the couch in Jack's office."

Which could explain how he came to be on Lucky property the night he was killed and sealed in a cask. "Who knew that he slept there?" I asked, biting my lip.

"Everybody," she said. "Jack. Brodie. Remy. Willow …"

Well that didn't help. In fact, it only added to the list of possible suspects. Who knew if Roger was even the intended victim? Jack had chased off his share of whiskey-poachers over the years. If someone came into the distillery late at night and found someone in the office … Maybe Roger was just in the wrong place at the wrong time.

"Charlotte," Mary said when the silence between us lengthened. "Please let Roger rest in peace. For all of our sakes."

"Of course," I lied. My stomach burned with guilt.

"Thank you," she said. "You'll be at the memorial?"

I agreed after she filled me in on the date and time. Flowers, I added to my mental to-do list. Something bright. A memory from over two decades ago flashed through my head. I stood on the edge of my parents' graves, red roses covering the caskets and tears clogging my throat. Jack took my hand in his large one. He gave it a squeeze, and my fear of the future faded with every shovel of dirt crushing the velvety petals.

For a moment, the vision stole my breath.

"Charlotte?" Mary said. "Are you still there?"

"Yes," I said, returning to the present—to the loss another woman bore. Whereas I'd had Jack, Mary was alone in her grief. The ache for her in my chest intensified. We talked for a few more minutes about the memorial, and then hung up.

Before I could drop the phone back in my purse, it rang again.

"Charlotte," my cousin Evan's voice flickered through the line. I held back a sigh. We'd never been close. Not having much in common. He was three years younger than me, putting him just over twenty-six, and spoiled rotten. He always had been. Evan's mother was the daughter of Jack's only sister. After her husband left, she'd spoiled Evan like crazy up until her death a few years ago. A direct contrast to Granddad Jack. Everything we had in terms of profit went right back into the distillery. There was always something in need of repair.

Not that Jack hadn't done his best by me. He had. I was never in need of anything. I had food in my belly, albeit canned, clothes on my back, though his fashion sense ranked up there with Bjork, and enough spending cash to buy lip gloss, though he wouldn't let me wear it until I turned sixteen. Jack had been both father and awkward mother to me.

To Evan, he was nothing more than a bank with whiskey breath.

Evan had spent the summers working at the distillery under the guise of bonding with Uncle Jack. Much to my disgust, Jack showed him the art of cooperage. An art I'd begged to learn for years. When I asked, Jack would shake his head. "Cooperage is not for girls, Char.

You'll have muscles like a man and then who will want to make an honest woman out of you?"

Growing up I hated being a girl, though thanks to Jack's words of wisdom, I'd never been ashamed of it. Even now I was having a hard time being a woman in the man-dominated profession of whiskey. Thankfully Jack hadn't questioned my rightful place when his heart rebelled against too many cigars and buttered everything.

"Are you there, Charlotte?" Evan asked, his voice shaking slightly.

I closed my eyes. "Yeah, what's up?"

"It's … um … about Roger."

My stomach clenched. "Did you kill him?" I asked, cupping the phone so no one else on the street—not that there was a single soul around—would overhear.

"What?! No. Hell no."

"Oh."

"It's just … I might've owed him a few bucks." He stopped. "Did Uncle Jack mention anything to you?"

I shook my head, realizing a few seconds too late that Evan couldn't see through the phone. The glass of Lucky I'd consumed, along with a lack of sleep, was taking its toll. "No," I said. "He didn't. How much was a few?"

"Doesn't matter."

"Jack should've fed you to the wolves."

"Don't act like you're better than me, Charlotte." He paused. "You left Uncle Jack high and dry. Running off to La-La-Land as fast as your feet would carry you. At least I've been here for him."

I snorted. "For him or for his money?"

"Hey," he began, but I cut him off.

"The gravy train has ended," I said. "Consider Jack paying your debt to Roger the last stop."

Silence. "You know about that?" he finally asked, sounding almost ashamed.

"Yeah, I do." I kicked at a patch of grass growing through the otherwise barren parking lot. I caught sight of my reflection in the paint of the only vehicle nearby and winced. Quickly I ran a hand through my hair. I really needed a cut.

"I didn't ask him to," he whined. "I had everything taken care of."

"Is that so?" Again, I considered Evan as a suspect. Was it possible he'd murdered Roger over a few thousand dollars?

"It doesn't matter anymore," he said darkly. "The distillery is in hock. We can barely afford the next shipment of yeast."

"That's not true." Though it would be now that we lost our distiller. Roger's death would send shock waves throughout our business, everything from the actual chemical process of creating the whiskey to buying the grains and equipment. Jack, and later I, had trusted Roger to do all of it. I couldn't even guess all he did for Lucky Whiskey.

Was Roger's death somehow related to his work for us?

Evan snorted, an ugly sound that drew me back to the conversation at hand, as well as grated on my nerves. "Make Uncle Jack do the smart thing," he said. "Sell to Rue Gett before we lose everything."

"Over my dead body."

His laugh held a cruel edge. "Wonder if Roger said the same thing." He paused long enough to make his point. "You know, before you found him in one of my fine casks?"

CHAPTER

8

HAD I MISSED THE memo for *Let's Threaten Charlotte Day?*

I jabbed my finger on the end button on my phone with force. My nail cracked under the pressure. My last manicured one, painted a vivid green to match my eyes—at least that's what Raoul, my manicurist in L.A., had said in what I suspected to be an affected accent.

Nothing in Hollywood was real, including me.

Not that I'd admit to anyone that I'd never quite felt at home there, not as I did here, in the humidity and swamps. But this wasn't my home. Not anymore.

I didn't belong here.

As soon as Jack recovered enough to run the distillery on his own, if there still was a distillery, I was headed back to Cali and the warm rather than blazing sunshine. I'd finally make it my home. Unpack my life and welcome the smoggy air.

As for now, I had to talk to Jack, to find out if what Evan said was true. Were we closer to losing the distillery than I knew? I flashed to the pile of bills on the table at the house. A pile that grew daily. I hadn't made a dent in them yet. Add in Rue Gett's day-to-day phone calls—calls Jack left unanswered—and I had to wonder if Lucky Whiskey would see its 100th birthday next year.

I also wouldn't mind Jack's opinion of Brodie being my top suspect.

In so many ways, it sounded crazy: Grodie Brodie murdering Roger in our rackhouse.

Not that Brodie looked incapable of killing. In fact, with the five o'clock shadow on his face and his piercing gaze, the possibility sounded more plausible than one would think. Though, I suspected, if Brodie did kill, he'd have a good reason. Or at least, that was true of the boy I used to know. Obnoxious sure, but not a cold-blooded killer. Perhaps Roger wasn't killed in cold blood, but rather in the heat of the moment.

What would Brodie get mad enough to kill for?

Family.

The word popped into my head as I thought back to grade school and the one and only fight Brodie had lost. He'd fought three older boys who'd insulted his daddy. I couldn't quite remember what had been said, only the crazed look in Brodie's eyes seconds before he launched himself at the boys.

And the blood.

Brodie had stumbled away with a busted nose, red wetness staining his shirt, and salty tears he never let fall shimmering in his haunted eyes. As far as I knew, those kids had never again spoken of the Gett family, at least not in earshot of the youngest Gett.

This was something I understood, for I would protect Jack with my last breath.

If that meant skinless, butter-free chicken pot pie for the rest of our days together, so be it.

My boots ate up the distance from the Get-it to the Lucky family home. Cars would drive by, slow down to chat, or give a simple wave. The way of small-town life. I laughed at the idea of the same thing happening in L.A. Drivers there were more likely to run pedestrians over while updating their IMDb page.

When I reached the end of our driveway, I stopped dead, my heart in my throat. Red and blue flashing lights filled the yard. Jack. *Oh, my God. Jack.* Tears spilled down my cheeks as I ran as fast as I could to the house. *Please,* I prayed, sucking in an impossible breath.

I was too late.

In a manner of speaking.

———

As I bulldozed into the house, my foot caught the edge of the carpet, and I tipped forward. Righting myself, I froze. The scene playing out in front of me so ridiculous words failed me.

For ten or so seconds.

Then all hell broke loose. "Get your hands off of him this instant," I yelled in what I hate to say sounded much like a screech. I shoved the lean cop in front of me out of my way. Or at least I tried to thrust past him.

But before I could reach my granddad the cop wrapped his arm around my waist, hoisting me off my feet. "Take it easy," he said in a calm, controlled tone. Which set me off all the more. I kicked at the cop's shin but shouted at the sheriff in front of me, his hand on Jack's arm as he read Granddad the Miranda warning.

"What the hell do you think you're doing, Danny Gett?" I sputtered, unable to fathom what or why he was reading Jack his rights. "Whatever you are accusing Jack of," I yelled, "you're off base."

"Char," Jack said quietly, "take it easy, girl. Danny just wants to ask me some questions. I'll be home in a few hours. No need to make a fuss."

Jack was lying. I could see it in his eyes. The emerald color grew dark when he wasn't being honest. The same color I remembered from the day he told me my parents wouldn't be coming home, but everything would be the same.

Nothing had ever been the same again.

Not bad, just different.

I was different.

Now I couldn't bear the thought of losing what little time we had left. Time still possible to learn and to love a man who'd taken in his orphaned grandchild without pause. "Questions about Roger's murder?" I asked, unsure it was even possible. Jack wasn't a killer. Danny had to know it too.

At long last, Danny faced me, his features hard. "We have enough evidence to hold Jack on suspicion of first degree murder. I suggest you find him a lawyer." His face grew even grimmer. "A damn good one."

———

Standing in our kitchen an hour later, now alone, I stared at the pile of bills I'd rummaged through after Danny left with my grandfather in handcuffs. Completely unnecessary. But Sheriff Danny, the vindictive jerk he was, had insisted. Jack's gaze begged me to keep quiet as Danny led him away.

Wetness rose in my eyes, leaving salty streaks as tears rolled down my face. The truth about the distillery and Jack's arrest had just about settled in. By my calculations, the Lucky family would, if something didn't change and quick, lose the distillery.

We were broke.

And I had no idea why.

The distillery, which was normally in the black, had lost fifty thousand dollars in the last quarter. Was it due to Jack's illness? Or something more? Hemorrhaging money like that would shut us down within the next six months. Sooner, since Jack needed a lawyer, an expensive one to boot.

I wasn't about to risk the rest of his days on a pro bono attorney. Or Danny Gett's investigational skills. After all, Danny had nothing to gain by finding Roger's real killer. With Granddad out of the way, Lucky Whiskey would follow, and Rue Gett, Danny's dear granny, would have what she always wanted.

Lucky Whiskey.

Over my cold corpse.

A knock sounded at the back door, causing me to jump, my hand flying to my throat. The violent reaction felt justified considering there was a killer still on the loose. My bets were still on Grodie Brodie having done the deed.

I opened the door, facing the very man in question. "What are you doing here?" I tried to keep the fear and suspicion from my tone. Why let him know I was on to him?

He raised an eyebrow. "Can I come in?"

"No."

His lips curled into a dark smile, eyes sparkling. "Charms, for once in your life, don't overthink it and let me in so we can talk."

My own eyebrow arched, not nearly as effectively. "How about, hell no?"

"Do you want Jack out of jail or what?"

With a muffled curse, I stepped back and motioned him inside. Jack stashed weapons all over the house, if it turned out that I needed one. Though I had my doubts Brodie would drive over in his noticeably loud Jeep to kill me. Too many people would see him.

Of course, half the town, still annoyed about the water tower, might cheer my demise. "Please, come on in," I said. "But don't try any funny stuff." I'd always wanted to say that. Too much TV as a child, I guessed.

He pushed by me, smelling of whiskey. And not the good stuff. Strolling to the living room, he plopped down in Jack's chair like he owned the place. He even had the audacity to flip the recliner up and lean back. His long legs hung over the end.

My annoyance rose. I was sick of Getts, of the way they lorded over the rest of the town. Everywhere I went, the Gett name stood out. Most notably, as if mocking my return, on the damn water tower. "Why are you here?" I crossed my arms over my chest.

The side of his mouth lifted into that familiar smirk. Oddly, I remembered that smile most from the night I painted the tower. Not that I remembered the actual event, but I sure as hell knew Brodie had egged me on until I climbed up. In school—and now, it seemed—he took pleasure in pushing my buttons. His next words were a perfect example.

"And that concludes the polite portion of the evening. You didn't even offer me a drink," he said, and then went on before I could comment. "I wouldn't say no to a whiskey, even if it's Lucky."

"You're hilarious," I said deadpan. "Now I repeat, what are you doing here?"

He let out a long, weary lament. "I take it your question isn't a philosophical one," he said. When I didn't so much as laugh at his joke, he sighed again. Louder. "Guess you lost your sense of humor in La-La-Land. Happens to the best of them."

"I happen to have a great sense of humor." I added a nod for emphasis, which was sort of like saying I'm a nice person. "When something's funny, of course," I said. "Now tell me why you're here or get out."

"I kindly, out of the goodness of my heart, came to tell you Jack has a lawyer." He smirked.

"What?"

"Yep, the best in the county, which isn't saying much considering..." He paused as if letting the other shoe drop. "But I promise, nickname aside, William 'The Killer' Meir is good at what he does. So you don't have to worry about finding Jack one."

"We don't take charity." Particularly from a Gett. Jack would rather rot in a cell.

I was almost sure of it.

He rolled his eyes. "No charity involved. Jack knows Meir. They've worked together before."

"All right." I lowered my arms, making a sweeping motion with my hands. "If that's all..."

He closed the recliner, rising from the chair. "Not quite. I heard you've been asking around about me. About the night Roger died." His legs swallowed the distance between us in half a step. I had to look up at him, which wouldn't do at all, so I took a large step back, unfortunately hitting the edge of the bookcase on the wall. Picture frames and other assorted knickknacks, untouched for the last forty years in the same exact spot my Grandma Jennie had put them, rattled. Brodie reached out to steady the case, all teasing gone from his face. "Son-of-a-bitch. You really think I had something to do with Roger's death."

The implication that I was an idiot to believe he was guilty raised my ire. "If you didn't kill Roger"—I tilted my head—"why won't you tell me about that night? What were the two of you arguing about?"

"I can't say," he said, voice tight. "Trust me, Charms, I would if I could."

"That's what I thought." I waved to the door. "Thanks for dropping by, but I have things to do ..."

He didn't move. Just stood there like a big dumb rock. "Things like investigating Roger's murder?" he asked, his tone quizzical.

Like it was his business what I did with my time.

I shrugged.

"This is a bad idea, Charms." His face grew hard, intimidating in its coldness. I stifled the urge to shiver in the air-conditioned house. "A man is dead," he said as if talking of the weather. He went on, like he was just an old pal giving friendly advice. "I get wanting to find out who did it, especially with Jack's arrest, but what you're doing is dangerous."

I licked my suddenly dry lips. "Are you threatening me?"

His eyes went wide, practically glowing with pretend innocence. "Hell no. I'm giving you good advice, Charms." His voice lowered to a whisper. "Take it."

Staring into his eyes, I inhaled, and then blew out a breath. "I can't," I said, echoing his earlier answer in the same affected tone. "Trust me, Grodie, I would if I could."

He took another step forward, backing me against the bookcase. "I didn't want to do this ..."

"What?"

"I'm in."

"In *what?*"

"Your investigation." His smirk said he was doing me a favor. "I'm going to help you solve Roger's murder." The smile grew, even as it failed to reach his eyes. "You can thank me later."

CHAPTER

9

MY BROW WRINKLED AS I stared at Brodie Gett's muscular form, wondering what plan he was cooking up now. Did he honestly just offer to help a Lucky? My suspicion grew tenfold. *Never trust a Gett bearing whiskey*, Jack always said.

That lesson I'd learned the hard way. One day Brodie had offered to walk me home from school, through the heart of the Glades. I'd foolishly accepted, trusting him right up until he left me alone except for the monster alligators. We were eight years old.

I could still hear his laughter as he sprinted away. The memory caused my hands to sweat. Was this the same sort of thing? Would I find myself alone, battling my own fears, while Brodie stood to the side and laughed? With a shallow breath, I asked, "Why?"

"What?"

"Why would *you* want to help *me*?"

"For one thing, I'm your prime suspect." He stopped as if waiting for me to deny it. Like I would. If he hadn't outright killed Roger, I bet he knew who had. He shot me a frown when I remained silent. I stifled my smile at his disgruntled look. "Proving it wasn't me sounds like enough of a reason," he said, his tone even.

"And why would I, being a sane person, agree to this?"

A cutting laugh burst from his lips. "Let's forego the obvious debate of your mental status for the moment." His hand went to his chin, rubbing it as if thinking hard. "Instead," he said, "let's focus on the bigger issue. Like it or not, people in this town trust me." That damn time-honored smirk returned. "Hell, I'd go as far as saying they love me." He gestured my way. "Current company apparently excluded."

"Is that so?"

He went on as if I hadn't said a word. "You, on the other hand, painted their beloved water tower, embarrassing the *entire* town." He emphasized the word *entire*. He hadn't needed to. I understood exactly where he was coming from. On my visit to the Gett Bar & Grill, Willow Jones had ignored my questions about Roger right up until Brodie nodded his okay.

I was an outsider, though I'd lived here most of my life.

The town didn't trust outsiders.

Damn, a Gett actually made sense for once.

Better to keep your enemies close, right? Knowing I was about to agree to a deal with the devil, I nodded slowly. "Fine. You can help me. But if you so much as make one funny move ..."

"You'll what, Charms?" He laughed, loud and long, too much so to be genuine. The jerk. "Act me to death?"

My ego rose nicely to his bait. "Hey, I'm a damn good actress."

He snapped his fingers. "Right. I was totally convinced of your herpes outbreak." I opened my mouth to let him have it, but before one f-word slipped out, he waved his hand at me. "Okay, sorry," he said. "You are an amazing actor. Shakespearean in quality if not quantity." He paused, as if awaiting my approval. I nodded, slightly mollified. "Now we can get on with solving Roger's murder," he said. "Where to start…"

I smiled without a bit of humor. "Let's start by you telling me what happened after your argument with Roger."

He sucked in a deep breath, and for a moment, I suspected he wouldn't answer. My eyes widened when he did. "Roger was drunk. We argued, and he stumbled off toward here. I never saw him after that." He stopped, his eyes hard on mine, as if willing me to believe him. To trust him. Like I was eight again.

"I swear to it, Charms," he whispered.

I chose, for the moment, to buy his tale. "So how did he get from the Gett, alive, and end up dead in the Lucky Whiskey rackhouse?"

Brodie shook his head; his razor-sharp hair barely moved. The desire to run my hand over it took me off guard. "We need more information," he said.

My mouth lifted to a one-sided grin as he'd walked neatly into my trap. The one person who would never give me anything, let alone information on an ongoing investigation, just might cough it up for Brodie. "Funny you should say that."

"Why?" he asked quietly.

"I know just who to ask."

His brow rose. "Is that so?"

"Your dear brother," I said with glee, "the sheriff."

His snort grated on my ears, but not nearly as much as his next words. "You want me to ask Danny about an ongoing investigation? One that he arrested a suspect in? Are you crazy?"

Tired of that question, I said, "You did want to help."

He closed his eyes. "You're going to owe me."

55

If it got Jack out of jail, I'd willingly sell my soul. "Name your price."

He shot me that familiar wicked smile. "We'll discuss my terms later."

———

As the sun hung low in the sky, casting a golden glow over the Glades, I followed Brodie's black Jeep CJ-7 in my Prius. We headed across town, the Jeep's small, close together headlights illuminating the way we both knew by heart.

Thankfully Brodie decided on taking the main, paved drag and not the more reckless four-wheel drive path that cut through the swamp, and only, in the end, cut the trip down by thirty or so seconds. The path most in the county knew as Moonshine Run had played a major role in breaking many interstate and federal liquor laws during the long Prohibition period. Lucky Whiskey had contributed to breaking said statutes as well, surreptitiously cooking up batches of whiskey for the outlaws to sell until Prohibition ended. The swamplands kept secrets better than Pastor Reeves, Gett's lone holy man.

As a child, my friends and I would play cops and bootleggers. I, of course, was always a cop. One who more often than not ended up face down in the dirt. Jack would take one look at my muddy face and clothes, and shake his head.

But he never stopped our games.

I smiled at the memory.

Before we left the Lucky family property, Brodie had texted his brother, asking him to meet up at the Gett Diner, but not a mention as to why. Danny had asked, but Brodie didn't respond. We both knew

Danny would not agree if he had an inkling as to what Brodie wanted. What I wanted, really.

We arrived at the diner a few minutes later. I stepped out of my car, surprised by the fresh coat of light blue paint haphazardly splattered on the exterior walls of the single-story building. A neon sign in the window blinked the word OPEN in bright pink, at odd contrast to the newly blue facade.

But it was what was below the sign that shocked me most.

A large piece of cardboard boasted of the *Best meatloaf in the county* in handwritten black lettering. One look at the congealed greasy gravy on a nearby plate as Brodie and I entered, and I decided against risking it.

Cindy Mae, the once perky high school prom queen now pregnant with a fifth child, sat us at a table toward the back. She set down a glass of tap water in front of Brodie. "You're looking good, sugar," she said. Her blank gaze passed over me as if I was nothing more than Brodie's latest conquest rather than a living, breathing, and thirsty woman. "Remember that time we—" she said with a giggle.

"Good to see you, Cindy Mae. How's Colin?" Brodie asked after the father of three out of four of her children. The fifth was to be determined according to local gossip. "And the kids?"

She patted her round belly. "Afraid this one's gonna fall out every time I bend over."

He laughed but the humor didn't reach his eyes. They stayed the same icy color. I wondered if he ever felt real emotion underneath his good ole boy façade. Serial killers didn't. Was that what Grodie Brodie was? Had years of relentless female admiration as well as no teenaged acne warped him so? I smiled at the thought. If only ...

"You want something stronger to drink?" she asked, waving to his water glass. Bits of something floated on the surface of the glass.

Maybe I would forgo a water as well.

She leaned down as far as her large belly would allow. "We got some Gett in the back."

In the back was code around Gett for *We ain't paying the county for our God-given right to sell liquor.*

The side of his mouth lifted, yet he only said, "To keep the peace, I'll have a beer."

Her eyes flickered over my body. "And you, hon?"

"Iced tea, please."

"We only got sweet tea. None of those fancy California teas with fruit," she sneered.

I'd wondered if she'd recognized me. Apparently so. And she didn't look happy about it either. Not that we knew each other well during school. I was a bookish nerd while she dated the captain of the football team—the very man sitting across from me—until they broke up when he left to play for the University of Miami. "Sweet tea is fine." I gave her a warm smile. "Thank you."

She nodded, her gaze a little less hostile, but still wary, like my California ways might include stealing tarnished silverware. "Do you need a minute before you order?"

"Please," Brodie said.

Again, she nodded, this time heading off to fill our drink order. I glanced around the diner. I hadn't been there in years. Not since Jack brought me here for graduation. The very same night Gett became the town of *Getting Lucky*.

"What's good here?" I asked, peeling the sticky, yellowed menu from the table.

"Nothing." He finished his tap water in one drink, setting the glass down. "But the pork chop probably won't kill you."

"Better than the salad?"

"If you like your meal sans bacterial contingent." He grinned. "In Afghanistan, I ate wild goat for three meals a day. Given the choice between yet another steaming goat dish and a Cobb, I'd eat three billys, and their gruff."

I studied his face over the top of my menu. This was the first time he'd mentioned his time away. I wondered how long he'd been deployed, but decided against asking. The more I knew about Brodie personally, the harder it would be to be objective. And I needed to be as objective as possible. One wrong move and Jack would spend the rest of his days in prison garb. For this reason, I settled on a safer topic. "What did you do over there?"

He shrugged. "Advised. Mostly."

"Un huh." I tilted my head. "Are you done with the Army or will you be doing another tour?"

He reached his hand forward, fingers extended like they hoped mine would meet them. They didn't. His tenderness was nothing more than a ploy to distract me. One that might've worked on a good portion of the population. Both male and female.

Nevertheless I'd learned long ago that charm was the actor's best friend. If you charmed the audience, you could forget a line or two with no problem. If you failed to charm them, the reviewers would have your head.

On a pointed pen pike.

I winced, thinking of my first Hollywood review, for a reimagining of Cinderella. It hadn't gone well. I'd played the ugly stepsister for three whole nights until the musical closed. Thanks in part to what Jack declared my rotgut vocals. The reviewer had crueler words. Suffice it to say, the only singing I did nowadays was in the shower.

Humanity deserved as much.

"Why don't we talk about you?" His voice, like a good single malt, swirled around me.

"How about we talk about what you're doing with my prime suspect's granddaughter?" Danny Gett, his cheerless eyes burning, stood over his brother's shoulder, the glower on his face as dark as the food coloring added to the cheapest of bourbon.

Brodie turned. Unlike his brother, his face was devoid of emotion. Had Brodie mastered this skill during his work in Afghanistan? He gestured to his older brother to join us with a simple wave. "Why don't you take a seat?"

With an angry grunt, Danny did, pushing me to the far inside of the booth. He faced Brodie, his eyes vowing revenge. His younger brother didn't seem to care though. That alone apparently made Danny madder. "I told you to stay away from her and out of this," he barked.

Brodie dipped his head. "You did."

"So what the hell, Brodie?"

I chimed in. "*Her* has a name."

Both men turned their glares on me, equal in intensity and looks. Had I not been annoyed by each brother, for a variety of reasons, I might've appreciated the strong, handsome Gett genetics. One thing the Getts didn't lack was attractiveness.

Just morals. And in Danny's case, brains.

"*She* does." A long pause. "*Unlucky*," they growled in unison.

I exaggerated an eye roll. "Funny. But I didn't come here for the comedy or the best meatloaf in the county." I pointed at Danny, stabbing my finger at the innocent air in front of him. "You arrested Jack."

"I did."

"I want to know why. I *deserve* to know why. What evidence do you have against him?"

The elder Gett laughed. Not that his mirth held an ounce of real humor. "You expect me to tell you?" he snorted. "The time in the Holly-weird sun must've rotted your brain."

"I don't *expect* you to tell me anything." I made sure I had his attention before I added, "But I have no doubt that you'll tell your brother."

The laughter fell off his face. "Brodie, do you see what's happening here? It's high school all over again, with Charlotte leading you by your johnson. Wake up before she gets you in real trouble like"—a blush ran up Danny's cheeks—"the last time."

"What?" I asked with a loud, unladylike snort. "You think I led Brodie around? He taunted me, for years. I was the one who got in *real trouble* because of him. He was always daring me to do stupid stunts." I looked at Brodie, at the gleam in his eyes, and the truth hit me like a cut-rate whiskey, leaving a bitter taste in my mouth. "Stunts just like this."

"Take it easy, Charms," Brodie said.

I threw down my napkin. "I'm so dumb to have fallen for it again. You have no desire to help me. You're just playing some game, like always."

"Now hold on—" he said.

I waved him off, rising hastily. In my desire to leave I knocked Danny out of the booth. The good sheriff fell on the floor. The other patrons tried to cover their laughs, but soon the entire diner was filled with humor at the sheriff's expense. Danny's face grew redder and I knew he wouldn't be of help anytime soon.

Not that I needed him or his brother.

But Jack did.

Crap.

I sat back down. Danny was now on his feet, his stance rigid. Anger radiated off him in waves, all directed at little ole me. I shot him my most apologetic smile. The same smile I'd used in the STD commercial on my fake boyfriend, also a herpes sufferer thanks to my character's poor choices.

Unlike in the commercial, Danny didn't give me a forgiving kiss. Instead he continued to glower. One thing Getts hated, besides coming in second best to Lucky whiskey, was looking like a fool. I wouldn't be surprised if he pulled his gun and shot me dead.

"Danny," Brodie whispered, his gaze darting around. "Sit down before you cause more of a scene."

Face still flaming, Danny thankfully listened to his brother, this time opting for Brodie's side of the booth. A good choice, all in all. Cindy Mae reluctantly came back to take our order, for everyone in town knew the famed Gett temper. Their bark was just as bad as their bite. A bite that sometimes destroyed livelihoods if not lives. "What can I get ya?" she asked quietly.

"I'm good," he bit out.

"It's on me," I said as a way of apology.

He turned his heated glare my way. "In that case, hell no."

"Danny ..." Brodie warned.

Danny's face loosened some, and he qualified his statement. "I can't accept Charlotte's"—he paused—"gracious offer if I decide to share information about Roger's case."

I drew back, surprised. But before I could, very likely, stick my foot in my mouth, Brodie spoke up. "What makes you think Jack killed Roger? You know Jack." A smile touched his lips. "He's all bluster, no real bite unless you mess with his kin." Brodie's eyes met mine, and a shiver caused by more than the overly air-conditioned diner ran through me.

"Exactly," Danny said, leaning back in the booth with a smug smile. A smile I wanted to smack off his face. I refrained. But just barely. Had it grown an inch wider, who knows what I might've done.

"Exactly what?" I growled with more than enough bite. "You think Jack killed Roger because Roger was some kind of threat to me?"

Danny's lips curved into a frown, but he shook his head.

"Not to you," Brodie said what his brother obviously wouldn't.

I tilted my head, confused. "Then who?"

"Evan."

CHAPTER

10

CONSIDERING I'D SEEN THE check Jack wrote to Roger to cover Evan's debt, Danny's supposed evidence against Jack didn't surprise me overmuch. "So Jack paid Evan's debt off." I shrugged as if five thousand dollars didn't mean squat to the Luckys. "Why does that make Jack your prime suspect rather than Evan? He was the one who owed the cash." I licked my lips. "If you ask me, he should be in jail for this, not Jack." Way to throw cousin Evan under the proverbial bus. Given the choice between Jack's freedom and Evan's, there wasn't one. I'd save Jack every time.

"Yes, *Jack* paid Roger off." Danny's face grew even smugger. So much so my fist now ached to slap it rather than just fantasizing about such. Luckily for me—and our bank account, for we couldn't afford the bail for assaulting the sheriff—I stopped myself in time. Instead, I stabbed the table with a fork. The bail for vandalism had to be less, right?

"*Jack* also threatened to toss Roger's body into a cask and throw it into the swamp," Danny said, his tone as arrogant as a bad actor during their Oscar acceptance speech. "Guess he never got around to the swamp part." He chewed on his bottom lip. "Makes sense given his condition."

I snorted. "Not likely. Jack would've made good on his threat, no matter his health status. And why would he threaten Roger? He treated the guy like a son."

Danny was far from finished. "Roger wasn't Jack's *only* intended victim."

This time I outright laughed. "You're crazy."

"Come on, Danny," Brodie said in an equally disbelieving voice. "Jack's far from a serial killer."

Danny scowled at me and then turned it on his brother. "You said it yourself. Jack wouldn't kill unless it was to protect those he loves."

I outwardly shrugged, but a chill blanketed me. Danny wasn't wrong. Jack loved harder than most, even if he didn't always show it. Great loss did that to a person. "He's not overly fond of Evan," I lied, "so that's where your theory goes amiss."

Danny grunted. "But Jack *is* very fond of his whiskey."

Brodie took a long pull from the beer Cindy Mae had set in front of him. "Are you implying Jack was drunk and accidently killed Roger?"

"No, no. You misunderstand."

"Then explain what you mean," Brodie snarled at his sibling. "I'm hungry and tired, and the sooner you cut the crap, the sooner I can enjoy my meal." Brodie looked down at the plate Cindy had also placed in his sights. The food swam in grease. Even the still-half-frozen vegetables. "Though *enjoy* might be the wrong word."

Danny stroked the stubble on his chin, a hint of humor in his eyes. "Roger had threatened to break Evan's hands if he didn't pay off the debt."

"So?" Brodie frowned.

"So—"

"Evan is our cooper," I said to cut Danny off. "One of the best in the country. His hands are our livelihood." A surprise to most, but the cask was the most important part of distilling. Use the wrong piece of wood or have the slightest gap in a barrel and the end result tasted of battery acid mixed with cheap kerosene.

Danny wasn't wrong. Besides me, Jack would kill for only one other thing—Lucky Whiskey.

But he hadn't done this.

"Jack took that threat to Evans hands very serious." Danny grabbed the fork I'd jabbed into the table, stabbing one of Brodie's pork chops. He bit into it and chewed. And chewed.

And chewed some more.

That sounded just like something Jack would say. I smiled. Brodie raised an eyebrow. My grin faded. "How do you know what Jack said?"

Danny's smug face loosened—as did his back molars, I'd guess. "That's confidential," he said around the pork chop.

Brodie tilted his head as if sniffing out the scent like a bloodhound. "You don't know, do you? Someone gave an anonymous tip. And you rushed in to arrest Jack."

"Damn it, Brodie." Danny's face grew molten. For a minute I worried the sheriff might stroke out. When he regained his composure, I took a relieved breath. "I took a dangerous killer off the streets," he whispered. "Who cares how we got the tip." He chomped down on the pork chop again, talking with his mouth full. "Besides, Boone confirmed it."

"Boone Daniels?" I shivered at the name and the vile memories it held. "What does that degenerate know?"

"He knows that your granddad threatened him too." Danny wiped his mouth with Brodie's napkin. "At the same time, in fact."

My heart in my throat, I ventured, "Evan owed Boone money too?"

"Owes, sweetheart," Danny said with obvious glee.

Crap. I winced as the implication hit. We couldn't afford another payoff. Damn Evan

Danny wasn't finished delivering the bad news, in a gloating tone. "And Jack's no longer around to bail Evan out. Just who do you think Boone's gonna come looking for if he can't find cousin Evan?"

CHAPTER

11

"DON'T EVEN THINK IT, Charms," Brodie said after Danny left with yet another stern warning to stay out of the investigation, along with a slice of Cindy Mae's cherry pie, charged to our bill. "I mean it," Brodie said to me. "Do not."

"What?" I asked with complete, albeit affected innocence, the sort of innocence that won golden statues of undressed men. Too bad the academy would never know of my brilliant performance.

"Boone is not the kind of guy you mess around with." Brodie hesitated before adding, "You know that as well as I do."

I did. The day of my sixteenth birthday was my first date with an older guy named Boone who hung around our high school, though he'd dropped out the year before. He wore black and sneered at everyone and everything. At the time, I'd equated this with the soul of a poet.

A big mistake, like drinking anything but Lucky.

Our "date" turned out to be an attempted rape in the back of his pickup truck off the side road teenagers probably still used for parking. Had Brodie Gett not stepped in when he did, surely the attempted part of the equation would've changed to outright rape. Brodie had pulled Boone off me, punching him until Boone lost consciousness. He then held me until my tears dried, and rage took over. I added a few bruises to Boone's ribs with the heel of my boot.

After that, we'd left Boone slumped over the back of his truck. Brodie gave me a sweatshirt with University of Miami emblazoned over the chest to cover up my tattered dress so Jack, if he was up, wouldn't see the damage. Nothing could've stopped him from outright murder if he learned of the assault.

His own date long gone, Brodie kindly drove me home, lecturing me on the evils of all guys. Besides himself, of course. For the barest of seconds, I thought for sure he'd try and kiss me. But he didn't, leaving me oddly disappointed.

The next day we never spoke of it again.

We went back to our old ways, him pissing me off to no end with pranks and taunts and me doing my best to ignore his childish antics.

Somewhere I still had that sweatshirt.

According to gossip I'd heard since my return, Boone Daniels hadn't aged gracefully, and was now even more of a scumbag than before. He lived in the trailer park on what, in a town as small and generally poor as ours, was deemed the wrong side of the tracks.

It was swampland for one thing. Gators roamed as if they owned it, much like Gator Alley. I shivered remembering the beady-eyed creature lying in wait below me from Mary's patio.

According to that same gossip, Boone made his living dealing drugs to high schoolers, selling illegal guns to rednecks with poor impulse control (not that Florida law looked down on such actions), and generally making life hell for the good people stuck living check to check in the trailer park.

Danny had reportedly arrested him a time or two, but nothing more than a six-month jail stint stuck.

Boone was bad, bad news.

And I planned on confronting him about a murder.

But Boone *had* made the anonymous call to the sheriff. I was somehow sure of it. The question was, why? Boone wasn't the good neighbor type. The only way he'd have made such a call to law enforcement was if there was something in it for him.

I had to find out what.

With or without Brodie Gett's help.

By the way Brodie watched me, I suspected I just might be going it alone. Fear tingled along my nerves, but my spine and resolved stiffened. Jack's life was at stake. Like grandfather like granddaughter.

I would kill or be killed for one reason and one only—Jack Lucky.

The humor of such a dire sentiment eased some of the tension in my body. Boone wouldn't kill me.

I was eighty-five percent sure of it.

Ninety if one factored in the bottle of Lucky I planned to offer him.

"Damn it, Charms." Brodie crossed his arms over his chest. "If you get me shot I'm going to be real pissed."

I laughed and immediately sobered when Brodie didn't join in. "Oh, don't be such a drama queen." I motioned to the swamp beyond the greasy window of the diner. "You're far more likely to get eaten by a gator."

———

Oddly enough, I wasn't wrong about the gator. The next morning Brodie picked me up in his Jeep and we drove the short distance to the

Wrong Side of the Tracks Trailer & RV Park. Like I said, Gett wasn't all that imaginative when it came to names.

The trailer park hadn't changed much since I'd left. A dilapidated sign in the front as old as Jack announced, *Don't Feed the Gators*.

Or rather it once had.

Someone had changed the feed to another f-word. Seeing as I had my own graffiti past, I forgave the vandal for their lack of creativity.

Rows and rows of run-down trailers sat on three-foot stilts. A few of the renters had tried to liven up their space, planting yellow and pink flowers in foot-long patches of dirt. Rather than pretty up the place, the flowers made it look sadder somehow.

Kids on Salvation Army–purchased bikes, spokes missing from the wheels, rode hell bent around the swampland. A lone dirt pile had turned into a playground for the youths, bikes flying through the air with little regard for their safety.

There was a lesson in there somewhere, but I ignored the knowing glint in Brodie's eyes.

Once we pulled into the parking area—or rather, dirt patch—in front of Boone's trailer, Brodie jumped down from the driver's seat of his Jeep. Boone lived in a derelict trailer that had seen better days, at least a decade ago. The windows, or what used to be windows, were blacked out. And the door hung on one single hinge.

As Brodie landed on the muddy ground next to his Jeep, a brown muscular gator launched itself up on tiny but fast legs, dashing from the nearby mangroves and into the murkier waters a few feet away. The bright morning sunlight sparkled on its wet flesh like diamonds.

Brodie, to his credit, didn't scream like I would have. Instead he leapt up, at least three feet into the air, before diving back into the Jeep. His head landed in my lap in the passenger seat, breath hot on my bare thighs. I was immensely glad I'd opted for shorts rather than a sundress for today's adventure. "Son-of-a—" he yelped.

Seconds later, a round of buckshot peppered the Jeep, hitting the roll bar just above our heads. Flecks of black paint rained down as the air filled with the harsh scent of gun powder. A scent a small-town girl never forgot.

"Get down," Brodie ordered, scrambling to keep low while opening his glovebox. The cold, black steel of a gun glimmered in the light. But Brodie never pulled it free. He never had a chance. The crack of another shell of buckshot loaded into a shotgun stalled his hand.

From my scrunched position in the seat I couldn't see the shotgun or the person holding it. But the sound alone sent a rush of adrenaline spiking through my body. So much so I shivered in the heat of the day.

"Stay here and low," Brodie said as he slid out of the Jeep once again. He kept his hands in the air. The edge of his t-shirt rose, flashing tight abs. "Boone, you and I ain't got beef," he said, his language going good ole boy before my ears. The twang sounded as natural as birth, and yet, it was far from it. "I ain't the law." He motioned to the Jeep where I sat scrunched down. "Charms and I got questions. You don't wanna answer, fine. But we're gonna ask 'em."

"Lucky's here with you?" the ravaged voice of a two-pack-a-day smoker asked.

Brodie lowered his hands. "She is. Why don't you go put on some pants and we'll talk."

"Hell, Gett. You tear into my lot at nine in the morning..." He growled. "You lucky I'm hungover and can't see straight else I would've blow your fool head off."

With those words hanging in the humid air, Boone Daniels, the currently naked scourge of Gett, turned around and marched back into his rusted trailer, pausing momentarily to scratch his hairy butt.

Unlucky for me, I chose that exact moment to pop my head up. The vision will and would always be seared into my brain, blotting out the nice image of Brodie's six-pack.

"Hell, Charms," Brodie said with a genuine laugh seconds later. "That went better than I expected." He patted his body, dressed in a faded gray t-shirt and worn Levis. "Not a bullet hole to speak of."

I laughed, relief making my voice weak. "We never did discuss who'd be doing the shooting. So you'd better keep on my good side, Grodie Brodie."

"Good to know you have one, Charms." His wicked smirk taunted. "I'll be sure and keep a look out for it."

CHAPTER

12

A FULLY CLOTHED BOONE Daniels—meaning dressed in typical redneck fashion of cut-off jean shorts and a t-shirt stained with what I hoped was not last night's debauchery—sat in front of us on a sullied couch. A cigarette hung from his tobacco-stained lips.

Last time I saw him was over ten years ago, but Boone looked as if he'd aged twenty some in that time span. His face appeared shrunken, as if his drug-fueled body was sapping his youth. Brown stringy hair hung out from the back of the baseball cap, so worn, the team logo was unrecognizable.

He rubbed his chin with the loaded .25-caliber gun in his hand. A hand that trembled slightly from the weight. "Now what's all this here about?"

I started to speak, but Brodie silenced me with a quick glance. "We know you called in that tip about Charlotte's granddaddy." Brodie didn't wait for him to deny it. "What we need to know is, why?"

Boone sputtered but it was all bluster, his words at odds with the calculating glint in his hard eyes. "I ain't no snitch."

"Why did you call Danny with that tip?" Brodie leaned in, either unaware or unconcerned about the gun Boone held only inches from Brodie's stomach. His tone suggested Boone tell the truth.

The hard affected gaze in Boone's eyes flickered slightly. He was afraid of Brodie. The tip of his gun lifted, aimed directly at Brodie's heart. My breath hitched for a moment. Did he fear Brodie enough to fire? My lungs withered as the silence grew.

Finally, I couldn't take it anymore. "Boone," I said, forcing his attention to me. My voice was as smooth as the finish of Lucky's best barrel. "Please. Jack didn't do this. You know it as well as I do."

Boone's notice shifted from Brodie to me. The gun swung too. My stomach clenched as I stared down the short barrel. The chrome plating had long ago disappeared, leaving the weapon an off-gray color. A deep chip sat on the front sight.

Brodie shifted in his seat, doing what looked like his best to shield me with his body. Briefly, I wondered if his actions were second nature after serving in the military. "Listen to Charms," Brodie said in a calm, controlled voice. "Jack's been good to Gett. We owe him."

"I don't owe him." Boone's gaze suddenly blazed as he eyed me. "Or any Lucky, for that matter."

"Did you kill Roger?" I asked just as quickly. Stupidly, without a thought for my safety, or Brodie's. "Is that why you turned Jack in, to get the heat off you?"

Boone jumped up, long, thick legs pacing a circle around us. Brodie grabbed my thigh, his fingers digging in. "Let's not annoy the guy with the gun, Charms," he said quietly.

My brain said he was right, while my heart, locked away with Jack in a jail cell, said to push until Boone told us the truth.

Or shot one of us.

Given the circumstances, I hoped for the former but suspected the latter. "What did Roger do that made you kill him?" I asked, my voice calm though my heart slammed wildly in my chest. How much could I push Boone before he pushed back? "Did he cheat you out of some money? Was it a drug deal gone bad?" Not that I'd heard any rumors about Roger and drugs, but why else would he associate with scum like Boone? No rumors at all surrounded Roger's name. Which was weird in a town this small, a place where everyone knew and judged everyone else's business.

Boone froze, the gun in my face. I swallowed hard, but before I could react, Brodie snatched the weapon out of Boone's hands. Without a word or pause, he field-stripped it, removing all the bullets and the magazine in ten seconds. Once empty, he set the pieces on the table.

Boone's glassy, red eyes widened. "How'd you ..." he stuttered.

I snapped my fingers to regain his attention. His unfocused gaze swung my way. "Come on, Boone," I said, my voice growing soft, almost comforting. "Confession is good for the soul."

"Bite me," he snapped. "I didn't kill Roger." He stopped, a smug smile on his dirty face. "Jack did."

I started to rise, but Brodie's hand eased me back. "No, he did not," I said.

Like a child, Boone's face turned red, and he started stomping his foot. "I can prove it."

"What?" I drew back.

"You heard me, you stuck-up bit—"

"Watch your mouth," Brodie cut him off with a warning.

Boone snorted as if he didn't care, but his hand, the one lighting a cigarette, trembled even more. "You've always been her little protector," he said to Brodie. His eyes raked over me, both disgustingly and dismissively. "Is she worth it?"

"Just tell us about this supposed proof and we'll leave you to your day." Brodie waved his hand around at the stacks of illegal weapons and questionable containers of chemicals. "Unless you'd prefer I make my own phone call to my brother, the sheriff …"

"One of these days you Getts are gonna push too much." His fingers twisted into an imitation gun, which he fake-fired. "And then we'll find out who's lucky, and who got get."

His wordplay sounded rehearsed, as if he'd practiced the threat a million times in the cracked mirror above the sink. Be that as it may, as intimidation went, the words left a lot to be desired.

Brodie rolled his eyes but stayed on topic. "The proof?"

Boone looked between us and then lowered his voice to a staged whisper. His cigarette stale breath turned my stomach. "You don't know it, but Jack Lucky had plenty of reasons to want Roger dead."

"We know all about Jack paying off Evan's debt, and his threatening Roger and you if either of you ever loaned Evan another dime, if that's what you mean." I gave him a hard frown to emphasize my words. "So do the cops. Thanks to you."

"That reminds me," he said, brown-stained spittle forming at the corner of his lips. "You tell that cousin of yours he better pay up"—his vindictive gaze fell on me—"or else."

"Are you threatening her?" Brodie's face lost what little humor he had left. His hand clenched into tight fists, ready to beat Boone senseless, that was if he had any sense to begin with. Which I doubted. Not only had he threatened me in front of a witness, but a witness ready and able to tear him apart, piece by filthy piece.

I grabbed Brodie's arm, feeling his hard muscles bunch under my touch. "Unless you want Brodie to smash your face in, again," I said, stifling a smile at the memory of an unconscious Boone lying in a pool of his own urine after Brodie knocked him out twelve years ago, "I suggest you tell us about this supposed reason for Jack wanting Roger dead. Other than the debt, that is."

Ignoring my dig, Boone's features lifted, his lips curving into a wicked smirk. "Roger siphoned fifty grand from Lucky over the last two months." His light-colored eyebrow rose. "Bet you didn't know that."

This time I did jump up. "He stole from Jack?" My anger rose to boiling level. Hell, if Roger wasn't dead, I would've shot him myself. Twice.

"Oh, no." Boone sneered, showing off missing and broken teeth. "He took every dime from the distillery. Lucky Whiskey would go under in another few months if *someone* hadn't offed Roger."

"How do you ...?"

"Hell," he said with a bitter laugh, "with you at the helm, it's bound to go bankrupt anyhow. And then good ole grandma Rue will scavenge through the remains." He turned his spiteful gaze on Brodie. "Isn't that why you're here, Gett? To help your granny steal Lucky?"

CHAPTER

13

"DO YOU BELIEVE BOONE?" Brodie asked as he drove us back to Lucky Whiskey, taking the four-wheeling path that circumvented the main streets. Deep ruts guided drivers along the narrow path. I held the roll bar for dear life as we flew up the steep inclines and back down. Brodie hardly even looked at the dirt path.

"About?" His grandmother's greed? Brodie's deceit? Too many questions whirled in my head to narrow it down to just one. The main one, was I playing right into Brodie and Rue's hands?

He glanced over, his bright green eyes lingering on mine. "About Roger stealing from the distillery."

"Why would he lie? Roger's dead. The only thing he gained was hurting me." I swallowed back the pain, anger, and fear. "I'll have to check the books to make sure. But yes, I think he was telling the truth. If he even knows what the word means." I stopped to hold back a scream as we flew up what looked much like a ninety-degree angle. My hand gripped the roll bar tighter. "What I don't understand is why."

"Why tell you?"

"No. Why would Roger steal from Jack?" Taking my life in my own hands, I released the roll bar for a brief moment in order to shrug. Seconds later, I regretted that decision as we flew up a slope. I dipped backward, nearly falling from the Jeep. Brodie's strong arm caught me in time, pulling me back to my seat.

Once we reached the peak of the incline, I finished my thought. "Jack paid Roger well. Better than most master distillers made. So why did Roger risk his job and his reputation to steal the money from the distillery?"

Brodie failed to answer.

I went on. "You knew him. Was Roger having financial difficulties? Did he need the money for some unexpected expense? Was he sick? Was he planning on proposing to Mary? Or was it something else …?" Like Brodie's interfering grandmother hoping to steal Lucky by bankrupting it like Boone had implied? I didn't voice this, but Brodie responded as if I had.

"No idea." His answer came so quick, so hard and final, it caused me to doubt his sincerity.

Licking my lips, I slowly asked, "Are you sure about that?"

He stepped on the brakes, stopping the Jeep with a jerk. Thankfully I had a firm grip on the roll bar, but just the same, my head whipped back and forth. A headache, which had started about the time Boone had shot at us, grew. I glared at Brodie, but he wasn't paying me any attention. Rather he gazed down at his hands clenched on the steering wheel. Big hands. Rough hands. The feel of his palm against my thigh flickered through my head. It had felt so good, so warm and comforting, yet powerful. Hands that could craft enormous pleasure or tremendous pain.

"Leave it, Charms," he said, snapping me to the present. "It won't solve Roger's murder, or help Jack."

My eyebrow inched up. "And I'm supposed to just believe you?"

To my surprise, he grabbed my chin with his fingers, turning me to face him. His eyes burned into mine. "Yes, you are. I won't lie to you. Not about this."

I jerked away, a piece of me wondering about what he would lie to me about. I pushed the wayward thought to the back of my mind. I had to focus on freeing Jack from jail. That was all that mattered now. "But you won't tell me what I need to know either," I said, frustration clear in my voice.

With an equally exasperated growl, he shoved the Jeep back into gear, and we shot off over hills. Up and down at breakneck speeds. My stomach flipped as we started up yet another death-defying hill, swerving out of the way of a ten-foot gator.

Finally, we arrived behind the rackhouse of Lucky Whiskey. I blew out a relieved breath. Until the snapping of large, predatory jaws sounded from the swamp a few feet away. The sound reminded me of the horror that had occurred in the rackhouse. My eyes narrowed as I scanned the surrounding landscape for both the gator and a clue as to who murdered Roger.

I hadn't thought about this before but somehow, someway, Roger's killer had had to sneak in and out of Lucky property. This path, overgrown with mangroves and weeds, would conceal the murderer just fine. In fact, sneaking was the very reason it existed in the first place.

In the darkness, no headlights on, anyone could have snuck up on a drunk, unsuspecting Roger. Was that how it happened? Had Roger come to sleep it off on the couch in Jack's office, as he'd done countless times before, and instead found himself resting in peace inside a Lucky cask?

I bit my lip, considering. "What do you think about video?"

"In general," Brodie said, his grin going from annoyed to wolfish, "or did you have something more, ah, particular in mind? Not that I have reservations either way."

I rolled my eyes. "I meant, the possibility someone captured Roger's killer on video surveillance. Someone has to have this path under scrutiny."

He tilted his head. "You mean like the cops?"

"No," I said. "Probably not the cops. Not with only three sworn deputies." I had doubts Danny would share the information even if they did. "Someone else. Someone who has property that backs the path. Jack always talked about adding video cameras back here. Just in case." The ending to Jack's just in case always featured Rue Gett and her greedy paws. I decided not to share that bit of wisdom with Rue's grandson. "I imagine other people think the same way ..."

"Worth asking around."

I nodded, happy to have a plan, any sort of plan, in place after meeting with Boone earlier. I'd been so sure he'd killed Roger. Vilifying him was easier than looking closer to home. It seemed every time I found a new suspect, the evidence instead mounted against Jack. Roger's embezzlement was the final straw. If Danny learned of it ...

"Brodie," I began in a sweet tone.

He snorted.

"What?" My arms crossed over my chest.

Another shot of his devastatingly handsome smile. "For most people, the saying you catch more flies with honey is true."

"But not me?"

"Whenever you're nice to me, the hairs on the back of my head raise in warning." He rubbed said hairs, which were, indeed, standing at attention. "Same thing happened right before an IED exploded in Kandahar, nearly killing me."

I gasped, feeling my dander rise. "You're comparing me to a bomb exploding?"

He chuckled. "Something like that. So what is it you're about to sweetly ask for? My spleen?"

I bit my lip, considering the wisdom of asking him to hold back vital evidence in a murder investigation from his own brother. Any ordinary man would tell me to go straight to hell. What would I do if he did? "I know this is asking a lot ..."

He rubbed the back of his neck again, and those damn hairs of warning. "Don't worry about it. I'm not going to tell Danny anything about today."

"Thank you."

He dipped his head. "You're welcome."

I started to climb out of the Jeep.

"Wait." He reached for my arm but dropped his hand before it made contact. "That's it? No offer of undying gratitude?"

I shot him a grin, unwilling to show him any genuine thanks. "Not my style."

"Charms, you're going to be the death of me yet."

His words, spoken in humor, landed on my ears like lead weights. Brodie wasn't wrong. Today, we'd come very close to dying at the hands of a drug dealer. Who knew what tomorrow might bring? If he learned about our investigation, Roger's killer was bound to be unhappy, maybe enough to attempt one or both of our murders. My mind flashed to a vision of Brodie lying in a pool of blood, his eyes wide and unblinking, much like Roger's when he spilled from the cask. I shook the feeling of foreboding away, focusing on the living, breathing version staring at me like I'd lost my mind.

"Maybe you shouldn't help me anymore ..." I began.

"Whoa," He held up a hand, his voice tight. "Where'd that come from?"

"I … this …"

"You're not getting rid of me, so forget whatever is going on in that oversized brain." He gave me a hard frown, as if I'd insulted his manhood. "I can handle myself, and whatever shit you manage to get into."

"Okay," I said, to both appease him and because I needed him. Today showed me just how much. Had he not been there, who knows what could've happened? Boone's animosity for me hadn't mellowed with age. Nor, I found, had mine for him. He was a menace, and always would be.

But with need came fear, but not for Brodie's safety.

What if Boone was right? What if Brodie had lied to me about his involvement in Roger's murder? Or had lied about why he wanted to help me investigate? What if he was guiding me away from the evidence against him? Was I making a huge mistake by partnering with a Gett?

"I'll see you tomorrow, Charms," Brodie said darkly, as if he'd read my mind. He put the Jeep in gear, inching forward. "You can question my integrity some more then."

With that, he roared down the path, his tires leaving deep tread marks in the swampy dirt.

My gaze lingered on the treads. Had I seen those before? Outside the rackhouse where I'd found Roger's body? A few days of swampy weather and Brodie's convenient tear through just now meant there wasn't any evidence to be had on the path. Had I seen anything there before now? I wasn't sure.

About anything.

With measured steps, I headed to the Lucky family home, inhaling Jack's fading scent as I walked through the door.

CHAPTER

14

FOR THE REST OF the evening, I caught up on distillery business, including crafting an ad for a distiller. We wouldn't survive for long under my limited distilling knowledge. I wished I'd paid more attention to Jack's teachings as a kid, but at that time, the distillery felt more like a fairy tale castle than a means of supporting our family of employees.

Exhausted after stirring the mash for an hour, I fell into bed around ten, hardly able to think. The bright morning sunshine, so intense it stung my eyes, brought a far darker realization.

I owed Grodie Brodie Gett an apology.

After he'd done me a favor by going to Boone's, I'd all but accused him of murder. Not that he was incapable of it. The way he'd snatched the gun from Boone's hands proved Brodie's reflexes and speed were well in order.

It was too early to think about murder, and especially too early to think about the smug look on Brodie's face as I did the unforgive-able—apologizing to a Gett.

I buried my head under the covers. I could use a few more hours of sleep. Particularly after Cousin Evan's late-night phone call. Or calls. Since I didn't answer the first couple, he started calling every five minutes. At ten after midnight I gave in, answering with, "What!"

Evan then spent the next five minutes screaming at the top of his lungs. It seemed word had gotten back to him about Brodie's and my little visit to Boone Daniels. A visit Boone still wasn't thrilled about. In spiteful revenge, Boone had called in Evan's marker, to be paid by the end of today.

Evan's hands were at stake.

As was Lucky Whiskey.

And it was all on me.

What would Jack do?

Stupid question. He'd paid Evan's debt once. He'd do so again if it came to it.

But I wasn't Jack. Evan had begged me for the money, but I'd stayed firm. He would never get another dollar to pay off gambling debts as long as I was around. Jack had done enough for him. Time for Evan to sink or swim, minus Jack's water wings.

Suffice it to say, the conversation went from bad to worse after he realized I was serious. He even had the audacity to threaten to make my life hell. I had laughed, but without an ounce of humor. Not only was Jack in jail and my distiller dead, but I was stuck in a town I couldn't wait to leave, filled with people who sat in constant judgment of my every move, largely due to a dumb, childish prank from ten years ago. How much could it get worse?

I regretted my question this morning.

For it was about to get worse, in the form of my needing to apologize to the one man I blamed for so much of the torment I'd faced growing up. The thought turned my stomach. But it had to be done.

Getts might have money, but Luckys had character. We apologized where apologies were due.

Chastising myself for being a big baby, I peeked my head out from under the covers, listening to the house settle around me. When I was a child, right after my parents died, the creaks and groans of this old house would scare me. I'd call out, and every time Jack would come running.

I'd come to rely on his presence for my safety.

I still did.

Jack was my family.

Like it or not, this place was my home.

As were the people of Gett.

Much to my dismay, that included Brodie.

Except … one of those very same people was also a killer.

For in a town this size, a stranger would be noticed, no matter how hard he or she tried to conceal themselves. So that left 842 suspects. I'd left Jack and I out of the pool, as I was sure neither of us had done the deed unless I'd taken up sleep-killing.

Always a distant possibility, though I doubted Roger would've been my first victim.

Swinging the covers back, the cold rush of air sent goosebumps rising on my skin. Rubbing the chill away, I kicked my legs out, rising to my feet. A large purple bruise marred my shin where it had connected with Brodie's dash during yesterday's reckless drive along Moonshine Run. I ran my fingers down the welt, wincing slightly. Considering all we'd done twenty-four hours ago, a single bruise didn't rate a second glance. I was lucky Boone hadn't shot either of us instead of just Brodie's Jeep. Though from the look of sorrow on Brodie's face as he surveyed the damage had said otherwise. He'd run his hand over the marred paint when we left Boone's trailer, muttering about luck and his precious baby. What was it with men and their vehicles? I valued my Prius, but it wasn't an extension of who I was.

I dressed hurriedly, forgoing breakfast and my required intake of caffeine in hopes of catching Brodie before he left his house to do whatever it was a military vet did when he wasn't helping to solve murders. I suspected leaping tall buildings in a single bound.

Or, from what I'd seen, getting day drunk at the Gett Bar & Grill while living off his family coffers. Such a waste.

I grabbed the keys and was out the door by eight. The humidity was low this early, leaving the air crisp and smelling of the approaching change of season and the swampy earth surrounding me. It had rained during the night. My boots sunk into the mud, making sucking sounds with my every step. Not paying all that much attention, which I blamed on my lack of caffeination, I unlocked my small car and slipped inside, seeing nothing amiss.

For ten or so seconds.

With a gasp, my hand ran down the windshield where a crack sat dead center. Had my tires kicked up a rock and I hadn't noticed the chip? I was almost sure the windshield had been fine the last time I drove. The crack hardly seemed worthy of an insurance claim, but I should get it filled before it spread. I added it to my to-do list. Which seemed to grow and grow.

Goosebumps rose along my skin. I started my engine, cracking on the heater to full blast. After ten years in mild California, my body couldn't seem to acclimate to Florida's wild swings between sticky heat and icy air-conditioning. I was constantly too hot or too cold. Eventually the car and my flesh warmed. About the same time as I arrived at the small house on the outskirts of town I'd overheard someone in the gas station say Brodie was now living in.

The white siding of the cottage looked weather-beaten, with peeling paint and pits lining the asymmetrical structure. In an odd contrast, a single bunch of bright yellow flowers sat in a window box below a grime-coated window. I wondered who had planted them, and why? Surely not Brodie. He hardly looked like the daffodil type.

As I was about to exit my car, Brodie's front door opened. A woman appeared. She adjusted her skirt and then leered at a shirtless Brodie, who stood behind her. He grinned back. Next thing I knew, Mary Broome launched herself into his arms.

I looked away, heat burning my cheeks.

My fingers gripped the steering wheel as I debated the wisdom of confronting the couple. He'd lied to me. Clearly. At the very least, he knew more than he was letting on.

At worst, he was a killer who set Jack up.

Anger propelled me out of the driver's seat. Intent on ripping Brodie apart, I stormed up his front walkway. Halfway up, I noticed two things. First, Mary was gone, and second, Brodie stood there waiting for me, that familiar wicked smile on his lips. "Got something on your mind, Charms?"

"I … You …"

He held his front door open, motioning me inside, not an ounce of guilt on his face. "Why don't you come inside where we can talk without the whole town knowing about it?"

Despite my better judgment, I pushed past him and into his small house. People these days paid big bucks for what they called Tiny Houses. The people of Gett mostly just called them home. Generations were raised in the same one- to two-room homes. The same homes that stood the test of hurricanes and time.

Much like the people of Gett.

I glanced around, surprised to see actual furniture rather than milk crate tables and lawn chairs surrounded by beer can pyramids. Okay, no one had actually told me Brodie was a bum now. Maybe I'd filled in those details myself. In fact, the interior of his house was quite beautiful. Oak furnishings with freshly painted tan walls. A bookcase, with more than just comic books, stood against the wall. I cataloged his reading choices. For the sake of the investigation. Not personal interest. I mean, if he had a guide to homicide just laying out…

No such luck. His bookcase was filled with military and whiskey distilling history, and a group of For Dummies books. I had one or two of those myself, not that I'd admit such a thing to the man standing too closely behind me.

"Like what you see?"

I jumped. "Yes. You furnish well."

"Thanks," he said, grabbing a t-shirt off the back of a brown couch. He pulled it over his head and down his muscular chest. "But I'm guessing you didn't come all this way to talk interior decorating."

"You're sleeping with Mary," I blurted, the image of Roger's supposedly grieving girlfriend in Brodie's arms only moments ago burned in my memory. How long had they been sneaking around? And why hadn't I heard anyone gossiping about this fact? "That's what you and Roger fought about." I nodded as a theory formed.

"Not true."

I snorted. "I saw Mary, here, with my own eyes."

"So?"

"Reason number one for murder—a love triangle." I had no clue if that was true, but it sounded good, and I didn't have time to Google it on my iPhone.

He laughed. "Is that so?"

I dipped my head in the affirmative, using an actor's trick as old as time: complete unwavering conviction. Sadly, it also worked for politicians and psychopaths. Not that one could much tell the difference between the two these days.

"Fine." With a sigh he walked into his kitchen. I followed behind, the wonderful aroma of freshly brewed coffee filling my sense. Without asking he shoved a full cup of steaming coffee into my hands. "But you're wrong," he said.

"About?"

"Me and Mary."

My eyebrow rose as I tilted my head. "I'm supposed to believe the two of you never ...?"

He winced. "When you put it like that."

"Roger knew?"

"I think so." He sipped his own cup, looking thoughtful. Surprising since the Brodie I'd known didn't have a thoughtful bone in his body. Calculating, yes. Cynical, for sure. But never thoughtful. "Or maybe not," he said. "It happened long before they got together."

My head tilted farther to the side, and I nearly spilled my coffee on his shiny hardwood floor. I righted the cup before he bemoaned his damaged flooring like he had his Jeep.

"Before I shipped out, Mary and I dated for a few months. Nothing serious." He suddenly scowled, his eyes hard on mine. "Not that any of this is any of *your* business."

I nodded, but asked anyway: "Was Mary the topic of conversation between you and Roger outside the Gett Bar & Grill the night he was killed?"

"No."

"Would you tell me if she was?"

"Probably not," he said with a grin. "Mary dated a real estate developer and a chef after me. Are they suspects now too?"

I pretended to consider this. "Was one of them the last person to see Roger alive?"

"I wasn't the last person to see Roger." He took another sip of coffee. Slowly. Until I wanted to scream. He smirked as if he knew just how I felt. "His killer was. Remember that, Charms."

I threw up my hands. Coffee sloshed over the sides of the cup, splashing my still-cold hand. He reached out to take it. My stomach fluttered in what I told myself was fear.

"Relax," he said, grabbing the towel on the stove handle behind me. "I'm not about to kill you in my own kitchen. Blood stains don't come out of hardwood."

"I'm glad you find this mess so amusing." My hands went to my hips. "A man is dead and another might spend his final days in a cell for something he didn't do."

"Well, at least you got that much right."

Before I murdered Brodie for his smartass remark, I walked to the front door, the very reason for my visit forgotten. "Thank you for the coffee," I snarked.

He followed behind. "Anytime, Charms. Anytime."

Damn him. I clenched my fist, swallowing my pride. After all, he had protected me from Boone, even going as far as to risk his own safety. That had to mean something, right? Maybe he wasn't as bad a guy as I thought. I turned. "About yesterday, I'm sorry ..."

He said nothing.

"Hey, I said I was sorry ..." I glared when he didn't respond again, just stared out the door. Then again, maybe he was the same insensitive jerk I'd known most of my life. "I think I'll strip down to my panties and do a dance ..." I said to gain his attention.

Still nothing.

I stuck out my tongue like a child.

Not a flicker of response.

Eventually, I'd had enough of his ignoring me. "Brodie!" I yelled loud enough that his neighbor's dog, a pit bull named Romeo, started to howl.

Brodie's eyes flew to mine. "What?"

"What is wrong with you?" I gave him a good frown. "I'm trying to apologize, which is a rarity in itself, all but unheard of when it comes to you, and you're ignoring me."

Rather than smile at my half joke, he pointed to my Prius, his features flat. "What happened to your windshield?"

"Nothing." I stopped, confused by the change of subject. "It cracked."

"How?"

"Forget my windshield." I grabbed his arm. His skin felt warm and surprisingly soft. Much too easy to penetrate with a bullet. I couldn't face getting Brodie killed if he wasn't the killer. That was a big if, but even more, I couldn't risk Jack's life by trusting a Gett. "Listen, as much as I appreciate your help in investigating Roger's murder—"

"It's over," he said.

I dropped his arm with relief. That was much easier than I thought it would be. He didn't even bat an eyelash, which annoyed me more than I'd admit. "Yes, I think it's best if I go it alone from here on out."

He grabbed my shoulders, fingers digging in. I tried not to wince. "Are you crazy?" he said. "*You're* done investigating. Do you hear me?" He shook me in case I didn't get his point.

My teeth rattled, igniting my anger. I shoved away from him, my hands pushing at his oversized chest. When he didn't move, even an inch, I gave up. "Who the hell do you think you are?"

"It's time to end this," he said quietly. Too quiet in my opinion.

It sounded like a threat.

I stared into his eyes. The same eyes I'd seen filled with mocking laughter only moments before now filled with violence. This man. This one. He could very well kill.

Had Roger met this Brodie?

I shivered at the thought.

CHAPTER

15

TWO HOURS LATER, WITH enough coffee in me to stock a Starbucks for a week, I sat, hands shaking, at the counter of the Gett Diner. The surface was as chipped and pitted as my emotions. Cindy Mae stood in front of me, the devil's own coffee pot in her hands. "Refill?" she asked in a singsong voice.

"No." I covered my empty cup with my hand. "I've had way too much already."

"Long night with a certain Gett?" Her eyelid lowered with a lascivious wink.

I snorted. "Hardly."

She set the coffee down on the counter, leaning down in the typical juicy gossip stance. She glanced to the right and then the left, as if afraid to be overheard. I suspected Cindy Mae lived and breathed town gossip. "The two of you looked pretty chummy to me."

"Then *you* need glasses. I'm far from Brodie Gett's type." Though Cindy was at one time, and probably still was now, big baby belly and all. Her shiny blond hair and large breasts very much met Brodie's qualifications. I looked down at my barely-C cups and sighed.

Her eyebrow arched.

"I needed his help," I said in my defense, "and he agreed. Nothing lurid going on."

"Needed his *help* doing what?" She leaned closer.

I winced at her implication, as well as the lingering truth. Should I tell Cindy about my investigation? If I did, it would race through Gett like the cheapest of whiskeys. The killer would surely hear of it.

And then what?

Would he be scared out of hiding?

Worth a shot. I launched into my tale, laying out the facts as I knew them. Roger was dead. Murdered. Jack didn't do it. Brodie was the last person to see him alive—other than his killer, if Brodie was to be believed. Not only had Roger dipped into loansharking, he'd also embezzled fifty thousand from Lucky Whiskey.

And there wasn't a good suspect, other than Brodie and my own grandfather, in the group.

"So you see why I needed help," I ended lamely. It sounded sorrier when I said it out loud. Jack would surely rot in prison for the rest of his days.

"I do." She hesitated. "Here's my advice—follow the money, honey."

"What?"

She lowered her voice to a near whisper, even though the diner was empty except for a couple sitting in the back and Billy James, who chatted with the short order cook in the kitchen. "I watch a lot of those true crime shows on the TV." She glanced around again. "You know the ones?"

I nodded. I'd auditioned for roles in graphic reenactments often enough. The dialogue usually went something like, *"Who's there?"* A loud scream. And then a fake death cough. My screeches had never been "real" enough to get me the part, though I'd scared my elderly neighbor a time or two.

Cindy ran her finger across the counter, wiping it on her apron when it came away stained with meatloaf grease. "The one thing all my shows say is, follow the money."

I tilted my head. Could it be that easy? If I found the money—or more to the point, what Roger had done with the money he'd stole from Lucky—would I also find a killer? Damn. I needed to search Jack's records again, see if I could figure out how Roger had gotten his ill-gotten gains. I also needed to talk more with Mary. She knew Roger better than anyone had. And maybe she'd admit to an affair with Brodie, thereby sealing his motive.

On top of all that, I had to get my broken windshield patched, not to mention run a distillery with no distiller. I tapped my lips in wonder. Who distilled for Gett Whiskey?

The two distilleries had a long history of poaching workers. Wouldn't hurt to take a quick jaunt over to Gett's distillery, check out the competition and maybe borrow a distiller or two.

Granddad would be proud.

———

Unfortunately, my trip to Gett Whiskey proved fruitless. Workers in blue coveralls hauled barrels around on carts, but not a one would stop to talk to me. The few I knew by name acknowledged me with small waves but refused to stop and chat. Not that I could blame them. Rue would surely fire anyone who even smiled at a Lucky during business hours.

After about ten minutes of wandering the distillery grounds, a security guard in a gray uniform, gun and taser attached to his utility belt, ushered me through the gate and to my car, windshield still just as cracked as when I left it, parked on the side of the road.

The guard stood there, hand on the gun at his hip, watching as I drove off.

Why Gett needed armed security was beyond me. Sure, the whiskey business had a long history of violence and thuggery. People had killed and died for it. But we'd come a long way since the days of Prohibition, murder, and mobsters.

Or at least I'd thought so until Roger ended up in a cask.

After my futile trip to the Gett compound, I asked around town for the name of Gett's distiller, but everyone claimed not to know. Odd since everyone in Gett knew everyone else's business. Hell, it wasn't long before a rumor about my early-morning visit to a half-naked Brodie had reached my ears.

By the afternoon I'd be bearing his love child.

A few of the old timers, sitting outside the post office playing chess, did say the Getts, like the Luckys, had an open position for a distiller. Not that theirs had left the position feet first. Or maybe he had. Not hard to imagine with Rue at the helm.

Somehow, knowing Rue was in the same boat added a spring to my step. I'd reach out to other distillers around the country for references. See if any names popped up. But first I had to figure out how we would pay a master distiller enough to move to a backwater town in the middle of the Everglades. Any hope I once had of finding a replacement faded as I reviewed invoices and Jack's handwritten ledgers that afternoon. Roger's theft had indeed left us tittering on the edge. One wrong move on my part, and we'd lose everything.

Follow the money echoed through my head. Cindy Mae might be on to something. I pushed back from the desk in Jack's meager office and headed to the rackhouse, where each employee had an assigned locker. Distillery work was often hard, sweaty stuff, especially in the wort room. The locker room was one thing we had to offer that Gett Whiskey didn't; they apparently frowned on employees keeping personal items on company property.

My snooping around inside the men's locker room would draw attention no matter what, so I figured it was better to face it head on. I knocked on the door, announcing myself. When no answer came from inside, I stepped through the doorway. The stench of sweat and body spray hit me full force. I tried not to gag as I headed for Roger's locker at the end of the row. No one had cleaned it out after his death. Did it hold a clue to his killer or, better yet, a clue plus thousands of dollars stolen from Lucky?

Using the bolt cutters I'd found wedged in the coat closet by the front door of our house, I snipped off the thick steel lock, enjoying the final snap. With a hesitant breath, I opened the metal locker. Peering into Roger's life felt odd and intrusive, even after his death. Maybe even more so. I'm sure he would've rather not had me paw through his belongs, especially the tube of questionable medical cream tucked inside a folded shirt. Sadly, I only found a whopping fifty cents. I pocketed it, figuring it was likely stolen from Lucky anyway.

Where I'd hoped to find a clue, I found nothing more than the sad existence of a dead man. The only possible bit of evidence came in the form of a phone number scrawled on a piece of scrap paper. It wasn't a number I recognized. Nor was the large, ornamental handwriting.

I called the number, letting the phone ring and ring, unanswered.

I tapped the number into a database search engine on my phone. No results.

Another dead end.

I winced at the turn of phrase.

If I was going to follow the money, I first needed to untangle Roger's embezzlement scheme. Since I'd barely passed my finance class in college, I opted for a second set of eyes. Eyes that knew where all the proverbial money bags were and are buried. Therefore, I left the distillery and headed into the house. I stuffed all the papers related to the last two year's finances into a plastic bag. Had Jack never heard of a computer? I grumbled as I poured more papers into a second bag.

Once I had everything amassed, I called Crystal Green, Gett's one and only CPA, for an appointment. She agreed to take a look today, if I could swing by her office on Main Street. I had no doubt that she would get the books in order as well as ferret out Roger's embezzlement scheme. Once I knew how Roger had gotten the money, I'd plug the hole to keep any other dirty hands off Lucky Whiskey funds.

And just maybe I'd find a killer.

Before my appointment with Crystal, I drove to the closest mechanic, about ten minutes away. I parked my Prius in the pitted dirt lot, and got out. Jose Garcia, who along with my father had built the very Trans Am I was conceived in, took one look at my windshield and whistled softly. "Unlucky, Charlotte." He laughed, saying something to the two other men in the garage in rapid Spanish. They laughed too. I stifled an eye roll.

"How much will it cost to fill in the crack?" In my head I did a quick calculation of my bank account.

He shrugged. "Fifty or so."

Great.

"How long until it's fixed?"

He shrugged again. This time with more emphasis. "A few hours."

Which in mechanic time equaled next week. I tried not to wince, instead giving him a wide smile. "Thank you," I said, giving him my cell number to call when he finished with the windshield.

"Girl," Jose said, "it's good to have you home."

Tears filled my eyes. I blinked them away. A part of me wished to be anywhere else in the world. The weight of Jack's arrest and Lucky Whiskey's financial straits laid heavy on my shoulders.

But Jose wasn't finished. "Your daddy would've been proud. God rest him."

I had my doubts but thanked Jose for his kindness. I set out to enjoy the walk back to town, which would take about an hour. It would give me a chance to think, I reasoned. And it would have if I hadn't spent all my time worrying about six-foot gators jumping from the marsh on my left. The shopping bags full of receipts gripped in my hands would hardly protect me from steel-locking jaws. Each step brought forth stories whispered around a bonfire. Stories of man-eating gators gobbling up unsuspecting victims.

Only half of which were true.

But half was plenty.

Thankfully I arrived back at what passed for civilization around here without so much as a bug bite. Crystal Green's office on Main Street beckoned, a storefront built, much like the rest of the town, in the late 1800s. A mud-colored stain marked the wall a foot off the ground, a testament to multiple floods over the years.

I opened the door to her office. Bells jangled overhead, sounding homey and inviting. As much as a CPA's office could. Crystal appeared, her brown hair tied back in a bun, glasses hanging off her slim nose. She looked too young to own a business let alone to hold all three degrees from University of Florida hanging on the wall.

"Charlotte." She gave me a quick hug. "It's so good to see you. How's Jack holding up?"

"Good," I said, but I really had no idea. I'd tried to arrange a visit with him yesterday, but he'd refused to see me. His refusal had hurt. But then again, I wouldn't want him to see me behind bars either. Luckys didn't have much in the way of money, but we had plenty of stubborn pride.

That, too often, proved to be our downfall.

"Please, have a seat." She motioned to a single worn chair in front of a nice oak desk, the same type of wood normally charred to make bourbon. A slow smile spread over my lips. One more thing Luckys had in spades—useless whiskey knowledge.

I sat, my legs sticking out as the chair sucked me down into its compressed cushion. Crystal too sat, her body positioned to look down on the client. A power position often used in Hollywood, where z-list actors sat right above screenwriters in the food chain. Odd to see here in Gett. "So what can I do for you?" she asked with a polite, professional smile.

"Jack's books." I passed the plastic bags full of invoices and other financial papers across the desk. She frowned but didn't comment, so I continued, "They're a mess. I need to know exactly where Lucky stands."

"Easy enough."

This is where it got tricky. I didn't want Roger's embezzlement spread all over town. Too many people already knew, though I'd sworn Cindy Mae to secrecy and I doubted Brodie would spread Boone's accusation around.

Could I trust Crystal to keep my secret too? Not that Crystal was in the habit of gossiping, but she could mention it to one person, who would tell another, and eight hundred times later practically everyone in town would know.

Including Danny Gett.

The evidence against Jack didn't need to grow anymore. He was looking at a life sentence at best.

I wrung my hands.

"Charlotte," she said quietly, "I'm not a priest or a lawyer, but whatever you tell me is protected. It stays right here."

I hesitated for a few seconds more. "I recently found out about the embezzlement of fifty thousand dollars from Lucky Whiskey." My voice grew stony. "I need to know how, and if possible, where the money went."

"Oh dear," she said, her eyes widening behind the lenses of her glasses. "Yes, of course. I'll work on it today. Hopefully I'll have an answer in a few hours." A blush rose on her pale cheeks. A blush reserved for southern ladies when broaching a difficult question. "Do you know who stole it?"

"No," I lied with complete conviction. "But I suspect it was someone close to the distillery. An inside job, if you would."

"I'll call you as soon as I know."

"Thank you." I rose, but her next words stopped me.

"It's odd," she said.

"What is?"

"Lucky Whiskey loses fifty thousand dollars, and then Roger Kerrick gets himself murdered."

I said nothing.

She shook her head, her glasses slipping farther down her nose. "It's almost as if the famed Lucky luck Jack often boasted about has petered out."

CHAPTER

16

JACK'S BOASTING ASIDE, THE surname Lucky had always been some sort of cosmic joke to me. Today it seemed more so than ever as I stood in front of the Collier County Jail after picking up my patched-windshielded car. The three-story structure was white, stark white, with few windows. Jack loved the sun. Was he getting enough of it in his 8x10 jail cell?

Anger burned in my chest, and I stomped my foot at the unfairness of it all.

Justice was not being served. Not for Roger or Jack.

With renewed determination to find the real killer, I pushed through the front doors of the jail. A woman in a brightly colored dress held up her hand. "Can I help you?" she asked. Her tone was pleasant but held enough steel underneath that I pulled to a stop.

"Yes," I said. "I'm here to see Jack Lucky."

"And you are?"

"My name is Charlotte Lucky. I'm Jack's granddaughter."

"If you would take a seat ..." She pointed to a row of worn plastic chairs. I moved toward the waiting area. One lone magazine, last year's edition of *Guns & Ammo*, laid on a wobbly table. I sat in one of the plastic chairs next to it, regretting the decision when the handle of the chair oozed some clear substance. I prayed it wasn't biological in origin, but suspected as much.

I leapt up, digging in my purse for the small bottle of hand sanitizer inside. I found it, dumping the entire bottle on my hands. The chemical lemony scent filled the waiting room. Another man entered the jail. He looked vaguely familiar. Where had I seen him before? His cowboy hat and striped shirt made him stand out for sure. As did the very long, pointed cowboy boots on his feet.

"Ms. Lucky," he drawled, tipping his hat. "We haven't been properly introduced. I'm the Killer."

My hand flew to my throat. Was he admitting to murdering Roger? Right here? I tried to speak, but no words would come.

"Mr. Meir," the brightly dressed woman said, "your client is ready to see you as well as his granddaughter. If you'll come with me ...?"

I blinked, realization coming abruptly. This wasn't a killer, but rather *The Killer*. The lawyer Brodie had told me about. The one who would free Jack from jail. I had to believe as much, for the alternative wasn't something I wanted to think about. Not now. Not ever.

"Mr. Meir," I began.

He cut me off, voice kind. "Killer. Please. Everybody calls me that."

Weird, but as long as Jack stayed out of prison, I wasn't going to judge. "Killer," I said, the name awkward on my tongue, "What are Jack's—"

"Everything will be all right, Ms. Lucky."

"Call me Charlotte."

"Charlotte, if you would?" he said, ushering me toward a small room with a table in the center and four folding chairs. The walls were an industrial gray, much like Roger's pallor in death. The thought caught me off guard, as did the memory. Would I ever erase the image from my mind? It was the greatest proof I had of Jack's innocence.

Growing up, my goldfish, George, had lived for fifteen years. It wasn't until I hit high school that I realized the lifespan of a typical goldfish in a bowl was less than five years. When I confronted him, Jack admitted to replacing George six times, all without me ever having noticed.

A man who loved his grandchild enough to do that wasn't about to leave a body in a whiskey cask for said granddaughter to find.

Killer sat down, and I followed suit, lowering my body onto the cold metal chair. Deep gouges ran along the tabletop. As the silence lengthened, I nervously ran my hand across the indentations. I swallowed the urge to whistle.

Admittedly I was as bad at it as I was at singing.

After what felt like a lifetime, Jack staggered into the room. He wore a bright orange jumpsuit and black slippers. Silver handcuffs circled his wrists. The officer who led him in unlocked the cuffs, and Jack rubbed his wrists. Wrists already turning black and blue from a combination of blood thinners and the pressure of the cuffs. My stomach ached. I leapt up, but the officer moved in front of me. "No physical contact."

I sat back down in the chair, facing my grandfather. Once I sat, the guard left to stand outside the door. "It's so good to see you," I said to the man who'd raised me. "How are you feeling?"

"I'm not dead yet, girl," he snorted, "so wipe that look off your face." He softened his rebuke with a smile. Not quite the old Jack, but good enough. "I didn't want you here." His voice trembled with unspoken emotion. Shame maybe? Certainly not guilt. "I still don't, but The Killer insisted."

I tilted my head. "Why?"

William "the Killer" Meir took off his cowboy hat, running a hand through his thinning white hair. "I talked with the DA this morning."

My chest squeezed, barely allowing the word to burst from my mouth. "And?"

"They are proceeding with first degree murder charges." He gazed at my granddad, dipping his head. "I'm sorry, Jack, but they plan to go ahead with charges. You'll likely be arraigned on Friday."

Which was only three days away. Could I find a killer, other than the lawyer next to me, in three days? Failure was not an option. I would do whatever it took.

"I suggest we enter a plea," the Killer said suddenly.

"What?" I screeched, half rising to my feet. "Are you insane?"

"Easy, Char," Jack said, his hands in the air.

I turned to my grandfather. "You didn't do it. Why would you plead guilty?"

"My dear," the Killer said slowly, as if talking to a small, very dumb child, "it's a matter of ten years with good behavior versus a life sentence."

Jack and I looked at each other, and he started to laugh. Humor I did not share in the least. "Ten years or a hundred, I'll still die inside." His eyes met mine. "No plea. That would be lying. Plus, Luckys never settle."

Was Jack referring to me? To my homecoming? Or to my career choice and decision to leave Gett in the first place? He'd never asked me to stay. Never asked me to give up my dreams. I loved him for it, though I now dreaded leaving him to return to my former life. Jack needed me, and at this moment, that was more than enough.

"It's settled then." The Killer seemed oblivious to his word choice. "No plea. We take our chances with a jury." He rose to his feet. The chair he'd vacated groaned as he did so. "I'll leave you and your granddaughter alone."

"Thanks, Killer," Jack said. Meir called for the guard to free him from the conference room. After he left, Jack gave me a crooked smile. "Good man. We're lucky to have him on our side."

I surely hoped so. If I failed to find the real killer, the Killer was Jack's only chance at freedom.

I stared at Jack a long minute. "Mind if I ask you a question?"

"You can ask me anything."

I bit my lip, unsure how to broach Roger's embezzlement. If Jack had indeed known, it would only add to the evidence against him, and if he hadn't, it might be the straw that broke his heart. Did I want to risk it?

"Spit it out, Charlotte," he ordered with a familiar bark.

But the words wouldn't move by my lips. I could only stare into his green eyes, paler than I'd ever seen them. My heart squeezed in my chest. Decision made. Rather than ask about Roger and the stolen money, I tilted my head and gave a grand performance. "What did you want the small batch in again?" I tapped my lips like I'd forgotten. "Was it Spanish Sherry?"

Every year Lucky Whiskey made a small batch—a few gallons of the finest whiskey on Earth. To infuse the special flavors, Jack opted for used casks, ones that had been crafted to ferment the famed manzanilla sherry in Cigarrera, Barbadillo, Spain. After the sherry had reached perfection, Jack purchased the used casks, for a pretty penny, for the small batch.

The flavor complexity alone was worth every cent.

Since I returned the previous month, I'd heard about nothing but the importance of the small batch on the future of Lucky. From day one Jack had drummed the recipe in my head. I knew it inside and out. Therefore, I was hardly surprised, but a tad offended when he saw right through me. Was my acting as bad as Brodie said?

"What's really on your mind, gal?" Jack asked.

I bit my lip, motioning to the gray walls and guard outside the door. "I hate seeing you in here."

"Probably not as much as I hate having to be seen in here."

"Good point." We shared a grin.

"Girl," he said, his voice tight. "This is important."

I leaned in.

"You need to be *very* careful. You're playing with fire." He stopped. "And you're bound to get burned."

I tilted my head, looking as innocent as I could. "What do you mean? I'm not doing anything but running the distillery. Speaking of which, Remy says we can—"

His snort cut me off. "From what I hear, you're running around town with Brodie Gett asking all sorts of questions better left unasked." His eyes grew moist. He dabbed at the wetness with the sleeve of the orange jumpsuit. "This is dangerous business, Char." A single tear, the first one I'd seen Jack cry since he buried his son so many years ago, rolled down his weathered cheek. "I can't lose you."

My throat ached. "Ditto."

"So you'll do as I say, and go back to the distillery and forget the rest of this murder mess."

"Of course," I lied with complete, affected sincerity. "Don't worry about the distillery. I have it under control."

"And Brodie Gett?"

I gave a small laugh. "I have him under control too."

He snorted again. "Watch your back, Char. Getts are no one to mess with. Rue knows where all the bodies are buried."

Jack's words echoed in my ears long after I'd left him.

CHAPTER

17

FOLLOWING MY VISIT TO the jail, I headed back to the distillery. Guilt ate at me for neglecting my whiskey duties. Jack had trusted me to run the distillery during his illness, and now his incarceration. So far I'd failed him and the Lucky family.

Considering not one distiller had magically appeared in my absence, I had to do as much as I could with my limited knowledge to start the process for the next batch. The first step was to soak the barley in water on the floor of the wort room, known as the malting process. There it would sit for days until it began shooting.

Even one day off schedule could and would have long-lasting effects on our distribution, as well as the whiskey itself. And we'd been behind schedule for almost a week.

Much like with acting, timing was everything in the whiskey game.

I parked my car in the empty dirt lot behind the distillery, perhaps two hundred feet from the house. The workers, of which we employed thirty during peak distilling season, had left for the day. The sun was starting to set, leaving a golden glow along the riverbank snaking next to our land. Water was the lifeblood of a distillery. It created unique flavors depending on the season. Deeper in the fall, lighter in the summer months. Winter often gave the whiskey a cinnamon aftertaste like the holiday season.

Any changes to the waterway changed the whiskey.

Jack had pounded this into my head at every opportunity since I was five years old. Hurricanes churned up the sediment. Drought left us wanting. High temperatures, cold ones. Everything had a Butterfly Effect, changing the whiskey. We had to adapt to survive. And Luckys were survivors.

It was what Jack and I did best.

I secured the car and strolled to the distillery door. It was locked. Something we hadn't done until recent events. No one, particularly me, wanted to find another body inside.

It took me a full minute to find the key buried in my purse. I opened the door, inhaling the scent of mash. Mash that would soon be the finest of whiskey. The abrasive scent took some getting used to for the whiskey novice, but for those who'd grown up around the distillery, the odor smelled like home.

Musty, moldy home, but home nonetheless.

My first stop, after I turned on the lights, was the malting room. This was where the magic happened. *Magic* might've been a bit of an exaggeration, considering the malting room consisted of about sixteen inches of warm, wet grains and plenty of waiting.

Lucky Whiskey favored barley as the grain of choice. We bought our malts locally. Used the local waters. Hired locals. We were Gett— as much as one could be without those questionable Gett genes.

For an hour, I stood in the humid room, stirring the grains with a large, wide paddle. As a kid, Jack would let me watch him stir the malt after our canned-whatever dinner. Memories of days gone by tickled my mind. I remembered the heady and bold scent of the grains, so much like the end product. Jack could declare a batch ready by scent alone.

I inhaled deeply, allowing my Lucky sixth sense full release.

Tomorrow the grains would be ready to dry in the kiln. I could smell it.

Four days after that, we'd have a batch ready for the racks.

Excitement built inside me. The same kind of exhilaration I experienced when I took the stage under the bright lights.

My first batch.

One I was in complete control of. I would either prove my Lucky name, or destroy it. As much as I'd fought it, this business flowed through my veins like whiskey through a still. For Luckys, whiskey was life. I'd forgotten that fact while I lived in California, awash in sunlight and minor D-list fame.

Some days I questioned whether I'd return to my former life. To the life I'd left behind when I received a call in the middle of the night. Your grandfather had a heart attack, the caller said. They weren't sure he'd make it at all, let alone the five hours it took me to fly across the country.

My heart in my throat, I'd packed a bag, grabbing the next flight home.

Once it became apparent Jack would live but wouldn't be the same anytime soon, I'd flown back to L.A. to stuff my Prius with a few suitcases of clothes and other essentials for the drive back to Florida. The trip took me four days. Four days of asking myself if I'd lost my mind. Four days of wanting to turn the car around. Even after two months, I still paid rent regularly on my small studio apartment off Sunset Blvd.

Just in case.

Soon I'd have to make up my mind to stay or go.

But not today.

Today I would follow in the footsteps on the Luckys before me.

———

A few hours later, after a dinner of canned vegetable soup and a canned tuna sandwich, I sat in front of my laptop, scrolling through Crystal Green's account reckoning. The distillery was in a little better shape than I'd first thought. Barring any unexpected expenses, we had enough to buy grain for the next batch as well as pay our employees. Employees who were depending on me. At the very leanest of whiskey times, Jack had mortgaged the family home to make sure our employees received their pay. What would I give to honor that practice?

Bile churned in my stomach.

I blew out a heavy breath.

Coincidentally, Crystal had also identified how Roger had embezzled the money. Jack had foolishly trusted Roger by giving him the power to buy grains and equipment with no oversight. Apparently Jack hadn't realized he was paying ten cents more on the dollar for his grain for nearly a year. And why would he? He'd had faith in Roger. If Roger wasn't dead already, he would've been. I would've taken great joy in killing him like my character on *NCIS* had in offing her victims. Though without the ice pick. Too messy for my murderous taste.

Since the malt still had a day left to shoot, I'd take tomorrow off to ask Mary if she knew what Roger had planned with the money he'd swindled. I poured a dram of whiskey into the glass at my elbow, drinking it without tasting the high quality and love that went into making each batch.

CHAPTER

18

THE NEXT MORNING, I woke with renewed purpose, a crick in my neck, and a hangover. At a certain point last night, the whiskey had gone down way too smooth as I worked through Crystal's reports. My eyes blurred, and my head swam. For a few seconds I had closed my eyes.

And fell fast asleep in Jack's chair, his scent surrounding me like a hug.

Now the sun filled the house, as did the noises of the distillery hard at work. Men and women moved barrels back and forth from the rackhouse, filling orders from stores all over the world. We used pulleys and ropes, like our forefathers had before us. Nothing with an engine touched a Lucky cask.

That was a point of pride with Jack. I found it both endearing and ridiculous, but Jack had proven time and again that people and the land made fine whiskey, not technology.

Today the whiskey business would come second. I only had two days before Jack's arraignment, and less time to find a killer. I had to focus. Someone knew Roger's secret. In a town this size, like death and bitching about taxes, that much was a given.

I'd start with Mary, see if she knew what Roger had spent Lucky money on. Had she noticed me a few days ago at Brodie's? She surely hadn't stuck around. Likely embarrassed, if not disappointed, by her one-night stand. I smirked at the thought. As far as I'd heard, no woman ever complained about Brodie Gett's lovemaking skills, but it made me feel better to think, if not say, otherwise.

Taking my time, I dressed in a light blue summer dress with a wide belt. My hair, still wet from the shower, was blown dry. Thankfully the style hadn't grown out too much over the last few months. Though it was no longer sleek. Instead it appeared softer and fuller.

If I intended to stay in town, I'd need a stylist.

And I wasn't sure the Gett Curl & Dye was the best option.

I grabbed a travel mug of coffee, skipped over a canned array of breakfast options, and headed out the door. I wanted to catch Mary before she left for the day.

I wouldn't be that lucky.

I blamed my missing her on the new crack in my very new windshield.

"What the...?" I stood, staring down at the damage. The once clear, shiny window now had thousands of spider cracks running from the large main fracture. I quickly scanned the area for anything that could have caused the damage, like a fallen tree branch or a freaking meteor, but saw nothing. This was no accident. My stomach rebelled at the thought of the rage directed at my poor, innocent Prius. That or the half a bottle of whiskey I'd consumed last night was taking its revenge.

Did someone hate me so much that they smashed my windshield? Was yesterday's small crack just a first attempt? And why?

Was it something to do with my investigation into Roger's murder?

Or something more personal?

Boone Daniels came to mind. He was the sort of coward to damage property in the middle of the night. Then again, my cousin Evan seemed just as logical of a choice. Especially after I sent his calls to voicemail last night. I wasn't up to dealing with his whining. Not when Jack sat in jail with not a single complaint on his lips.

"Damn it." I stomped my foot as my attention focused on the windshield again. I didn't have more money to shell out to fix it, especially if someone was going to continue in this passive-aggressive crusade against my car.

Blowing out an angry breath, I slid into the car, thankful that the fracturing was mainly contained to the passenger side. The vehicle was still drivable, so I did that. I shoved it into gear, and sped down the road, careful to avoid the pothole growing at the end of the driveway.

A few minutes later, after passing a packed Gett Diner, my empty stomach begging to stop in for a quick bite, I'd arrived at Mary's house in Gator Alley. Carefully, I exited the vehicle, watching my every step. I had no desire for a run-in with the gator named Boots.

At least I'd learned that much from Brodie Gett.

I knocked on Mary's door and waited.

No answer.

I knocked again. Harder. The decorative stained glass replica of a blue jay attached to the wood swayed back and forth, as if tempting me to knock again.

"Are you looking for Mary?" A man I didn't recognize, which was odd in itself in a town this size, asked from the dirt road. He was dressed in safari wear, complete with netted hat. I gave him my sweetest smile. "Yes," I said. "Are you a neighbor?"

"Closest one. I live over the hill." He motioned to a speck on the horizon. The dog at his heel barked once, and then quieted.

"Have you by any chance seen Mary today?"

He nodded. The pup yapped again.

"Do you know where she went?"

He nodded again.

"Would you mind telling me?"

He shook his head.

"Pretty please," I added in case that was the magical term to unlocking his jaw.

"It's a school day."

"Excuse me?"

He sighed as if I was too dumb to breath in the same air. "Mary is getting ready for classes to start in a few weeks. She is at the school."

"Oh." I was surprised that she hadn't taken more time off after Roger's murder, especially since she taught second grade. I suspected most of her days were spent cleaning trails of snot off everything in her classroom. Who wouldn't want a head start on that?

"Thank you," I said and started down the steps. I paused at the bottom, wondering how much this neighbor might know about Mary and Roger's relationship. Or more to the point, how much he'd be willing to gossip about it. "Excuse me again," I said. "Sorry to bother you, but do you know Mary well?"

He shrugged.

"How about Roger? Did you know him?"

"A little." He made sucking sounds with his teeth. Barks filled the air as the dog took off for the mangroves. I winced. The poor pup would surely make a nice gator treat. But the man didn't seem phased. He continued to stand there, staring at me.

Wanting to cross my hands over my chest, not that he was paying my girls any attention, I asked, "Were they good neighbors, would you say?" A little friendly chitchat between friends.

He shrugged again.

"Did they have loud parties, or say, arguments?" I asked, when what I really wanted to ask was, *Did Mary sneak out of her house, drive across town, shoot Roger, and leave him in one of my barrels?* I'd probably get another shrug. Which would cause me to run the short distance separating us and beat him with my boot until he cried.

I blew out a long breath, letting go of the fantasy. Where had that come from? Reminder to myself, no more overindulging on Lucky stock.

"Can't say." He sucked harder. I tried not to cringe. How was it I'd found the one person in all of Gett who didn't like to gossip about their friends and neighbors?

"What about seeing any other men hanging around?" Namely Brodie Gett. If he and Mary were having an affair, someone would have seen them together, right?

He shrugged. "One thing I do know …"

"Yes?"

"I liked the water tower when it was yellow." With that, he called to his dog and then started walking to his house without another word.

I stood there, my mouth hanging wide. Brodie was right. The people of Gett still held a grudge for the water tower incident. A vague memory flickered through my head, my seventeen-year-old self, beyond hungover, watching with the rest of the town as a man in a yellow hat climbed the tower to undo my handiwork.

The very same man now walking away from me.

Any and all warm feelings I'd had about Gett evaporated under my hangover and this man's anger.

CHAPTER

19

ABOUT AN HOUR LATER, after fortifying my body with a stale doughnut from the Harker convenience store, I went to school. Specifically, Harker Elementary. The school housed kindergarten through fifth grade. It was technically inside Harker city limits but allowed students from Gett too.

I'd gone to grade school inside the small but brightly painted schoolhouse. I'd loved Mrs. Crest's music class, even though I still couldn't sing a lick. Loved the way the schoolhouse smelled too, like disinfectant and promise. Inside the building seemed much smaller than I remembered. Tiny mutant chairs sat along each wall. Mary stood in the middle, looking a bit frazzled, her hair and clothes in disarray.

"Hi," I ventured with a wave. "Do you have a minute to talk?"

Before she could respond, Mrs. Crest herself walked into the room. She looked exactly as she had almost two decades before, gray hair piled on top of her head frozen in place by a lacquer layer of hairspray. She was the very reason for the hole in the ozone, I was sure of it. "Well, if it isn't the pride and joy of Gett," she said.

Oh, no. Not again. That damn water tower.

She held her arms wide. "You were so good on *NCIS*. We were all so proud. I thought for sure you were a real corpse."

I grinned with relief. I recalled how undead I'd felt during the shoot, after my character was killed off in the second scene. Nothing like laying on a cold, steel table, naked except for a small towel covering one's naughty parts to sear a memory into your mind. I'd fought off a cold for two weeks after. "Mrs. Crest, so good to see you." I hugged her, and then stepped back.

"What brings you by, sweetheart?" she asked, a frown wrinkling her forehead.

I motioned to Mary. "I had a couple of questions … About Roger's memorial and such."

"Such a terrible thing." She dabbed at her dry eyes. "We set up a GoFundMe page to raise money for his final expenses."

I tilted my head, trying not to let anger show on my face. "Is that so? I thought he had some money stocked away." Lucky Whiskey's money, to be precise.

Mary spoke up, her voice cold. "Who told you that?"

"Guess I heard it around town." I hesitated, wondering the appropriateness of asking a grieving girlfriend about her lover's theft. Had our situations been reversed, I wouldn't be nearly as polite. I vowed to tread carefully. "It's not true?"

"I wish," she said. "He barely had enough to cover our rent each month. I told him he needed to start saving for a rainy day." She drew in a shaky breath. "I never … expected … this. Poor Roger." She began to cry.

I grabbed her hand, squeezing tightly. "I am sorry."

She pulled away, as if she couldn't stand my touch. "Why would Jack do such a thing?" Rage laced her words. "Roger thought the world of him."

I caught myself mid-snort. "Jack isn't responsible, no matter what Danny Gett says."

Mrs. Crest's gaze went to the floor.

My heart broke as I realized neither Mary or Mrs. Crest quite believed me.

———

I beat a hasty retreat soon after the awkward silence in Mary's classroom. No closer to the missing money, I considered my next move. In the movies, at the darkest moment, a clue or some sort of sign would literally land at the investigator's feet.

I glanced down.

Nothing. My eyes swept the empty parking lot of the school for inspiration. Any inspiration. Heck, I would've grasped at a straw if one had been within reach.

One thing was in sight. A place I'd vowed never to set foot in again.

Harker High. The bane of my teenaged existence.

Unable to stop myself, I wandered toward the red brick school that housed about four hundred or so hormonal teens. A vibrant green (even in our current drought) football field sat in the back lot. People in Collier County took their high school football seriously. Some even took bets on the games.

Was that how Evan had lost all that money to Roger and Boone?

Before I took another step, the whoop of an ambulance sounded a few blocks away. As far as signs went, it wasn't biblical by any means, but it beat a walk down acne-riddled, Brodie Gett–tortured memory lane.

But I took what I could get.

I jumped into my car, shoved it into drive, and took off.

A few miles up the road the ambulance pulled to a stop in front of the Gett Diner. The meatloaf was enough to send anyone to the hospital. Or the morgue, considering the lights and sirens were now oddly silent.

I pulled next to the vehicle. Lester, the paramedic who'd picked up Roger's corpse, struggled to get his lanky frame out of the driver's seat. "Oh, hey, Charlotte." He gave me a smile and a wave.

"Is everything … okay?" I motioned to the diner. "Somebody sick?"

He laughed. "Naw, I'm just real hungry." I had to smile at his innovation. Though I did worry about his sense of taste. "Care to join me for lunch?" he asked, his large Adam's apple bobbing nervously.

"Sure," I said, happy for a friendly face after my encounter with the grieving girlfriend and my old school teacher.

Together we walked into the grimy-windowed diner, packed with the lunch crowd. Men and women who worked at Gett Whiskey sat opposite their counterparts who I employed. I chatted up a few of them and waved to others as Cindy Mae sat Lester and me at a booth way in the back. She promptly took our order and headed off. The kitchen door smashed into the edge of the seat every time someone opened it.

"Nothing but the best," Lester said with a grin as the door struck the booth again, shaking the glasses of water Cindy Mae had graciously dropped off.

I chuckled. "There are open seats at the counter. Would you like to move?"

A loud crash of dishes obscured my words.

"Can't." His thin blond hair fell over his eyes. "Cindy Mae says I scare the customers, so I have to sit back here."

"What?" I rose, indignant on his behalf. Lester couldn't help his creepy looks.

Before I could make a scene, he held up a hand. "Please sit down. She's not saying it to be mean. It's true."

I shrank back in the seat. "I don't understand. Did you do something to piss the town off?" Like, oh, I didn't know … paint a certain water tower?

"Nothing like that." He gave me a knowing smile. "It's my job. It freaks people out, especially when I get blood on my uniform." He motioned to a stain I had, for my stomach's sake, believed to be ketchup.

"Folks don't like to talk about death." He picked up the grilled cheese sandwich Cindy Mae set in front of him as she slid quickly by. "Let alone like to be reminded of it while eating diner food."

I picked up my own sandwich. Droplets of grease slid down the cheese and onto the plate, where an oily puddle formed. I set it back down. Opting for safer topics, I asked, "Do you … um … like what you do?"

He smirked and I saw the boy I'd once gone to school with. The joker, always looking to make everyone, including the teacher, laugh. "I wouldn't trade it for any other job in the world."

"Good for you."

"Isn't that how you feel about acting?"

I had, at one time. Or maybe I was lying to myself? I wasn't sure anymore. Besides, for the time being, my life was here. Whether I liked it or not. And the jury was still out on that too. Rather than come up with a plausible lie, I said, "Do you work with Danny Gett often?"

125

He wiped his mouth with his sleeve. "Any time there's a suspicious death."

"And?"

He shrugged. "He's okay."

I needed more than a vague *he's okay*. Jack's life might very well be in his hands, for even if I found another suspect (other than his brother, that was), I would have to rely on Danny to believe me enough to arrest the bad guy. Two things I had my doubts he'd willingly do. "I'm worried Roger's killer will get away with murder..."

"Ah."

"What?"

"Explains the rumor I've been hearing."

"Which is?"

He lowered his voice. "That you're investigating Roger's murder with Brodie."

"Who told you that?" While I was, indeed searching for a killer, I wasn't doing so with Brodie. Sure, he'd helped me a little bit. But we weren't chummy. I didn't want anyone getting the wrong idea. Linking any Lucky with a Gett was bad for all involved.

"Does it matter?"

I shook my head.

"So it's not true?"

I winced. "The Brodie part isn't true. The rest..."

He nodded, a wide smile on his face. "Good."

"I thought you and Brodie were friends..."

"We are." He washed down his grilled cheese with a long drink. "It's ... just ..."

"Spill it."

He sighed, loud enough the diner at the next table glanced our way. "The night I took Roger away ..."

126

"Yes?"

He paused, as if weighing his words. Words that might change everything for Jack. "A cell phone fell out of his pocket as I was moving him into the morgue," Lester said.

My brow wrinkled as I pictured the crime scene. "But Danny found his cell phone. It was in the bottom of the cask." Danny had passed the phone to one of his cops before Lester had removed the body. The screen was cracked, as if it had been close to the impact of the gunshot.

Lester appeared thoughtful, chewing his lip along with the remnants of his sandwich. "Burner maybe?"

"Why though?" Twirling the fork on the table, I considered the reasons a man would need a burner phone. None of them were good. "I don't understand it." In my admittedly limited experience, burner cell phones were strictly for those up to no good, like drug dealers. Or cheats.

Had Roger been stepping out on Mary? Or had he only done so after finding out about her and Brodie? I wasn't sure if I believed Brodie when he said he and Mary weren't involved. Though, if either of them had been cheating, keeping it secret in a town this size was near impossible.

Someone would have known.

Was that someone Roger's killer?

"Got me." Lester picked up a pickle from his plate. It drooped sadly. He looked at it but didn't take a bite. Apparently he'd considered the cheater angle as well. "Roger would have had to be a fool to cheat on Mary. She's perfect."

A memory from my high school days flickered in my mind. Lester had talked about Mary nonstop for a full year, until she broke his heart on the night of homecoming when she went to the dance with an older guy from Harker. The memory of Lester's dejected face when he first saw her with her date had stuck with me for some time.

"I have something to admit," he said. "Before I handed it over to Danny, I took a quick peek at the call list."

"You did?" I clapped my hands. My first real clue. "Please tell me Roger put *KILLER* into his contacts." It would make my life so much easier. I smiled at that bit of whimsy.

Not a flicker of humor crossed his face. "No."

"Then what?"

Looking to the left and then the right, he lowered his voice as if sharing a juicy state secret. "The phone had only one number listed in both incoming and outgoing calls."

I leaned in, my spine tight. If he said the number was Jack's, I'd scream. Up to right now, every bit of evidence I found put more dirt on Jack's metaphorical grave. I couldn't overcome much more. "Whose was it?"

Silence grew between us. In the end, his gaze dropped to the tabletop. "Gett."

My stomach dropped. "Which one?"

"You misunderstand." Lester shook his head. "Roger called Gett Whiskey. A lot. I wonder why?"

My hands clenched into tight fists as Brodie's lying face filled my head. The blood pounding in my ears muted whatever Lester said after that. Not that it mattered. I now knew who had killed Roger and why.

CHAPTER

20

DAMN **B**RODIE **G**ETT. **H**E'D led me astray, hoping to divert my attention away from the real criminals—the Gett family.

For reasons that were beyond me, Rue Gett hated Jack. She hated Lucky Whiskey too, which I understood since we beat her brand any day. But her distaste for Granddad was particularly petty.

Jack and Rue played the game of one-upmanship for years, always one doing their best to beat the other. This need to be better than the other trickled down, resulting in a long-standing rivalry between Brodie and myself. As a kid, it made for some awkward moments, like when I got paired with Brodie for a school play. I, of course, was the lead. My poignant Juliet knocked the socks off Brodie's woeful rendition of Romeo. Thank God my high school had deemed the kissing "too explicit" for Gett and cut it from the script.

Jack and Rue sat next to each other in the gymnasium turned theater, watching for the other's kin to mess up in any small way. I never did, not once, which drove Brodie—and by extension, Rue—crazy.

That was, I never messed up until the night of the water tower. That really evened the score over botched Shakespeare lines.

So I guess it made an odd sort of sense for Roger to spy on Lucky Whiskey for Rue Gett. I wouldn't be surprised if Jack didn't have one or two moles at her place of business. But why had Roger done it? And why add in possible criminal theft charges? He'd been loyal, as far as I knew, to Jack for years. Then suddenly he embezzled a bunch of money, causing Lucky's near collapse? Was that Rue's plan? Had she blackmailed Roger into destroying us?

I wouldn't put it past the old bat. She wielded secrets like one did a weapon. The town's politicians, if you could call them that, were deep in her pocket.

Heck, one of her grandson's was the sheriff of the entire county.

And the other ... Brodie ... where did he fit into the puzzle?

Had Roger balked at Rue's plan, causing Brodie to eliminate him as a problem? Or had Rue done the dirty work herself? The picture of an eighty-year-old woman wielding a gun might make some people laugh. But not any of us who knew Rue Gett.

She was a force to be reckoned with.

I doubted she could hoist Roger into the cask on her own. That took the strength of someone much younger. Had Brodie come upon her crime, and now was helping her clean up her mess? Doing anything in his power to keep granny out of jail? Rue held an odd power over her grandsons. They would do anything for her.

And I did mean anything.

Before I could recklessly storm off to confront Rue, my cell phone rang. I checked the caller ID. *Evan*. I winced, debating if I should answer. I opted for no, knowing he'd only whine about Boone's threats to his hands yet again. I swiped to ignore his call, focusing instead on keeping the flies away from my greasy meal.

Minutes later, I thanked Lester for lunch and this eye-opening tidbit about Roger's calls to the Gett distillery. After giving Cindy Mae a casual wave, I headed to the parking lot, and my poor damaged car. Eventually I'd have to give in and get it fixed, but for the moment, I wouldn't give the vandal the satisfaction.

My call phone rang again. I reached for it, sighing as I answered. "What do you want, Evan?"

"The distillery ..." His voice shook so much so it was hard to understand him. "A fire ..."

"What?" I yelled at the word *fire*. Given the explosive contents of a cask, a small fire could soon turn into a blazing inferno, killing all thirty employees within seconds. "I can't understand you. What happened?"

"The distillery ... it's on fire!"

My heart leapt into my throat as the blood left my head. My gaze narrowed to tunnel-vision, and I fought to draw enough air in my lungs. How could this be? I launched myself into my car, tearing out of the parking lot like I was the one on fire, instead of the place my family had lived and died for across the generations.

CHAPTER

21

FLYING ACROSS TOWN, I arrived at the distillery in less than two minutes. Red and white fire trucks blocked the driveway. Smoke, black in color, billowed from the rackhouse. Firemen in protective gear poked holes in the roof to fight the flames. Orange and blue flames were visible against the sunny sky.

Bile burned a path up my throat. I barely managed to open the car door before it ripped from my mouth, landing on the ground with a wet splat. Once my stomach's rebellion subsided, I wiped my mouth with a crumpled napkin I found shoved in my cup holder.

This was bad. Very bad.

The grim, soot-coated faces of a handful of employees scattered around told me how bad.

On shaky legs, I walked as if in a trance, closer and closer to the flames. The heat mixed with the high humidity slammed into me, knocking me back a step. A fireman in full gear minus his helmet grabbed me around the waist, stopping me from getting any closer to the destruction. "Whoa there, girl," he said.

I blinked. *"Whoa there, girl? Did you really just say that?"*

He grinned as he released me. "I did, though I'm now regretting it."

"As you should be." I glanced to the flames and then back to him. "Is everyone ... safe?"

"All accounted for."

"Thank God." I nearly dropped to the water-logged ground in relief. "How ..." I swallowed over the lump in my throat. "How bad is the damage?"

He stared at me for a long moment. "Not as bad as it could've been. The fire was contained to the rear wall." Wiping the sweat from his head, he nodded to the rackhouse. "Maybe ten to fifteen casks lost."

"And the building?"

"It will take a few days to air out." He chewed on his lip, making the thin strip of hair above it wiggle like a worm after a rain. "The smoke is pretty dense, but luckily the oak used in the casks was newer, therefore wet, so the fire didn't spread as quickly as it could've."

Evan had done something right for once. A miracle in itself.

Had we started on the small batch, using the Spanish Sherry casks reserved specifically for it, the whole place might've gone up in flames. For once, luck was on the Lucky side. "Thank you," I said, meaning every word. The firemen had saved Lucky. Without their quick actions, who knows what might've happened.

Laughter filled his face. "You're welcome, Little Missy."

I rolled my eyes but gave a small chuckle. I had to laugh at this misfortune to keep from crying, which is what I felt like doing right now. My eyes scanned the crowd, looking for friendly and not-so-friendly faces. Evan stood with a group of firefighters off to the side. I headed to him, shocked by the anger at the unfairness of it all rising within me.

The Lucky family must truly be cursed. How else could one explain the recent destruction?

Well, there was one other way: Rue Gett.

But I didn't want to even think about her right now. "Evan," I said, looking him over. "Are you all right?"

Soot covered my cousin's face, obscuring his normally handsome features. His hair, once golden, stuck up at all angles, black with debris. Thankfully his hands looked uninjured. "I'm all good. For now," he said, voice hoarse.

"How did it start?" I ignored his veiled reference to Boone's threat, instead asking the group in general about the origin of the blaze. Another firefighter stepped in my way, his salt-and-pepper hair slick with perspiration and fire retardant. He dipped his head. "Ma'am. I'm the county arson investigator."

"Arson?" I choked out the word. Horror rose in me anew. Someone had purposely set fire to the distillery? I couldn't believe it. People could have died. That thought settled in as another rose. There was only one reason for setting this fire—the arsonist wanted to hurt us. Hurt the Lucky family.

Wanted to pound the final nail in our coffins.

The arson investigator rubbed his chin with the back of his flame-retardant glove. "Looks like someone threw an accelerant along the rear wall of the rackhouse."

"Accelerant?" I bit my lip, nearly drawing blood. "What kind?"

He pulled a plastic bag filled with charred pieces of debris, labelled EVIDENCE, out of his pocket. He opened the seal and held it out to me. "Take a sniff. See if you can recognize it?"

I did as he asked, inhaling deeply. The acerbic scent of poorly formulated whiskey assaulted my nostrils. The scent brought a sense memory to mind, but I couldn't place it. "Smells familiar ..."

"A Lucky brand?"

I laughed harder than warranted. "No way. I don't know a lot about running a distillery, but I do know my whiskey. And that is rot-gut, if I've ever smelled it."

"That's what I thought too, but it's good to have a second opinion."

"So what now?" I asked, my gaze on the smoldering, but thankfully no longer in flames, rackhouse roof. The fire had left a good-sized hole in the roof, charring at least half. We'd need to fix it before the moisture compromised the casks. "When can we get back in?"

"County inspector has to come out, check to make sure the building is structurally sound." He shoved the evidence bag back into his pocket. "Which it looks like it is to me. Then he'll give you the all-clear to go back in."

"How long does that usually take?"

"Couple of days." He shrugged. "A week at the most."

My heart sank. In a couple of days, the malt would start to mold and the entire batch would be ruined—if the smoke and water hadn't destroyed it already. We would need to buy another batch of grains, which we couldn't afford. Not to mention the time and manpower it would take to muck out the old, ruined malt. The tiniest bit of left-over mold would ruin the next batch, and the one after that.

"Thank you," I said, voice tight. I refused to cry. Not now. Not in front of my employees. They needed me to stand tall, like Jack, and I would do that. Straightening, I turned to face the men and women who relied on Lucky Whiskey to put food on their tables. "Take the next couple of days off," I said, knowing I was doing the right thing, even if it cost the distillery dearly. "Paid. I'll be in touch once we get the all-clear. Then we'll start rolling on the small batch."

I really hoped we would.

Though, given our luck of late, who knew what might happen.

Lucky's longtime employees hugged me as they passed. Men and women I'd known for all of my life, people who forgave my water tower misdeed or outright laughed at my spark of creativity. I gave each one a weak but grateful smile.

"It will be okay." Remy Ray, the Lucky foreman, patted my shoulder leaving a damp spot on my top, his skin slick from the humidity. "You'll see, Charlotte."

I prayed he was right. The Luckys needed a win.

And we got one.

One that came in the most unexpected way from an unforeseen source.

CHAPTER

22

"Ms. Lucky," a soft voice whispered through the phone, "my name's Emmitt Moore. You might not remember me, seeing as I live over in Harker."

"Sure, Emmitt. I remember you," I lied with only a twinge of guilt. It was hard enough to remember everyone in Gett after being away so long, let alone the names of everyone in the freaking county. "What can I do for you?" I asked, though I really wanted to know how he'd got my number and why he felt the need to call at six in the morning before the sun had even kissed the steamy sky.

I swallowed back my annoyance. One never did get over the ideal of being a good, southern woman. Polite until the end, even if it left shadows under the eyes from lack of sleep.

"Ma'am," he said, "I'm sorry to be calling this early, but my shift just started."

"Okay," I said slowly. As much as I didn't want to be on the phone at six in the morning, Emmitt sounded even less excited about our conversation. His voice shook, breaking occasionally like a high school boy.

He cleared his throat, which only made the cracking worse. "I work at my pa's gas station. The one off Oil Well Road."

"Yes, the Fill 'Er Up." I remembered the worn billboard hanging over the station as I filled my Prius. Gett didn't have its own service station in town, much to the locals' dismay. We had to travel up Route 29 for fifteen miles to the Fill 'Er Up. The lone gas pump was a salvation to Gett. "Nice place," I lied, though I doubted he wanted to discuss the merits of my gasoline choice.

"Thanks," he said, his tone relaxing a bit. "Ma'am, I'm calling cuz I heard about your poor granddaddy's arrest." A short silence ensued. "I'm real sorry 'bout it."

That made two of us. I needed Jack more now than ever if Lucky Whiskey was to survive. "Thank you," I said, my own voice cracking.

"Let me tell you the reason for my call." He stopped, inhaled loudly through his nose if the whistling sound was any indication, and then continued. "We watch the tapes once a week. This morning I watched."

"Tapes?"

"Yes, ma'am."

"Tapes of what?" Had he seen my *NCIS* debut or worse, my STD commercial, and decided to chat about it? I hoped not. It was too early to discuss genital anything, let alone with a complete stranger.

"A few years ago I talked my pa into upgrading his security," he said, voice full of pride. "We retired Rover, our old coon dog, and installed security cameras. The cameras watch anyone who drives up to the pump."

"Smart of you." Was I having a conversation about security cameras before the sun managed to hit the sky? Though it beat herpes

138

outbreaks any day. I tried to keep the snark from my voice. "Bet Rover wasn't as happy with the new system."

"Got that right. Took him awhile to stop chasing cars," he said with complete sincerity. "Now he spends his days searching for vermin under the house."

I tried not to giggle but a few escaped before I could stop them. "Sorry. I was thinking about something else. Go on."

"Ma'am," he said, "I think you need to see the tape for yourself."

"The tape of Rover chasing vermin from under your house?" I blamed my density on the early hour, and the half a bottle of whiskey I'd drank the evening before. Sometimes all one could do was drown their problems in fermented malt. A single one at that. Sadly, it hadn't tasted as good going down as it had days before.

He snickered. And I blushed, realizing my error. "The security tape," I said, my face heating. "You want me to come see your security tape."

"Yes, ma'am."

I grimaced at the phone, hating to drive all the way out to the gas station when I had more pressing matters to attend to, like begging the county inspector to stop over as soon as possible. Oh, and freeing Jack from a lifetime locked away for a murder he didn't commit. With a sigh, I asked, "Can you give me a hint as to what's on the tape?"

"I ..." A pause. "I'd rather you see it for yourself," he finally said.

I glanced at the clock, out of habit. "Okay, I can be there around eight. How does that sound?" That would give me plenty of time to get back in time for the county offices to open at nine a.m.

"Thank you, ma'am," he said, his voice cracking yet again. "I'll be here."

Unfortunately, I would be too, seeing as the distillery was closed until I could get it inspected. Jack was still in jail, and my only other suspects in Roger's murder were a wily eighty-year-old woman and her grandson. I needed real evidence before I could confront Rue Gett or else she'd eat me alive. And even more in the way of evidence before I could approach Danny with proof of his grandmother's misdeeds.

Jack's freedom had never seemed so far away.

CHAPTER

23

AFTER I DOWNED TWO cups of coffee strong enough to set my heart beating double time, I took a quick shower and dressed in a pair of jean shorts and a black t-shirt. I clipped my wet hair back, swiping a sheen of lip gloss on my dry lips.

Once I finished up with whatever oddity Emmitt wished to share, I vowed to contact the inspector. I wiped my finger over the edge of the bathroom mirror. After that, I needed to dust and air out the Lucky family home. While the house had stayed untouched by the evils of the fire, the smoke had left lingering remnants like the scent of charred oak and a fine layer of dust. It was everywhere. No escape from it. Even in the dark of night, smoke and fire had played prominently in my nightmares.

Grabbing yet another cup of coffee, I dug around in my purse for my car keys, finding them, like always, at the bottom of the large bag. A few minutes after that, I pulled out of the driveway and drove the fifteen miles up the two-lane blacktopped road, swerving to miss the occasional gator or other critter trying to cross the road.

Good thing the sun had come up. My windshield was still half wrecked, and Route 29 was dangerous to drive in the dark. Every year at least one person died from an accident on the road, even with the 40 mph posted speed limit. Cars whipped in and out of double yellow lines at breakneck speeds. Where they planned on going in such a rush remained a mystery for the ages.

I spotted the Fill 'Er Up sign two miles before I arrived at the small, independent gas station. Which was a nice way of saying one-room shack with a single gas pump out front. I parked on the side of the building, away from the pump so as not to block it. Then I walked inside, surprised by the blast of cold air that hit me in the face. I wrapped my arms around my body, warding off a shiver. Someone liked their air conditioning.

"Hello?" I called out.

A young man popped out from behind the counter. "Ms. Lucky?"

"Yes." I held out my hand, studying the young man. He wore overalls stained with grease. Acne dotted his face. Oh, the joys of being a teen. "You must be Emmitt," I said with a kind smile. "Thanks for calling me."

A slight blush rose on his cheeks as he took my hand in his sweaty one. "You look different than on TV."

Crap. Had I run into my one and only fan? I hoped he didn't have a ball of my hair bought from eBay. I smiled at the thought. When I lived in Hollywood, a few of my actress friends made money on the side by selling their hair to fans. What those fans did with that hair had kept me awake at night. "They say the TV adds ten pounds, so I'm going to take that as a compliment," I said, smiling brightly as I removed my hand from his. I wiped my now wet palm on the side of my shorts.

His blush grew redder. "Yes, of course."

I motioned around. "You wanted me to watch something, right?"

"Yes, ma'am." He pulled a small TV from behind the counter. The screen had a large crack dead center. "Just let me find the tape." He shot me a small smile and then pushed his way through a storage room door. I peered over the counter and into the back room. Boxes and boxes filled it, in various sizes and shapes. A folding chair sat in the corner, but that appeared to be the only source of comfort.

"Got it," he yelled, and then appeared in front of me, tape in hand. He shoved it in the VCR. I wondered how they even found VCR tapes to use, let alone a working VCR.

The screen flickered and then came to life. The tape showed the single gas pump, one dim light above it. Ghosting images appeared and disappeared, suggesting the tape had been used and reused thousands of time. When the picture cleared, Emmitt pointed with one long, oil-stained finger to the pump. "We're open all night now. We got one of them fancy credit card takers."

"Good to know."

On the screen, a car approached. It was dark in color. But I couldn't tell what color since the tape was shot in black-and-white. Even worse, the angle of the camera failed to capture the license plate. What good was this security camera? I wanted to ask him, but he appeared so proud of the system.

"Look there," Emmitt said excitedly. He again pointed at the screen.

Eyes narrowed, I peered closer. Sure enough, a man emerged from the passenger side of the vehicle. He stumbled around drunkenly, nearly falling. I winced and then straighten, blinking. It couldn't be. "Is that ... Roger?"

I searched for a date, gasping when I saw it in the lower right corner of the screen.

"That's what I wanted you to see." His voice rose so high it squeaked. "Roger Kerrick was *here* the night he died."

"What's the timestamp?"

"3:08 in the morning."

I jumped up and down, giddy with excited relief. My first real clue! I might find the killer yet.

"That's right around the time he died according to the *Collier County Gazette*," Emmitt said, nodding.

Everyone in the county apparently was following the case. I wondered how many had already convicted Jack. Would—or rather, could—he get a fair trial? "If you can believe the paper." The newspaper, once a proud printed edition now a web news daily email, had written a series of reports on Roger's murder. Mostly about Jack's incarceration. One story went as far as connecting my water tower adventure to Roger's murder, claiming criminality was in the Lucky DNA. "I can't make out the driver. Can you?" I asked, squinting like the twenty-eight-year-old woman I was.

Emmitt shook his head.

Together, in horrid fascination, we watched Roger's last minutes on Earth. Sadly, they were mostly as underwhelming as his first twenty-eight years. He staggered to the concrete barrier next to the pump, using the car for leverage as he inched his way back. Once at the pump, much to my disgust, he unzipped his pants. I promptly glanced away. Emmett cleared his throat, his cheeks growing redder as Roger let loose on the pump.

After a few seconds, I turned back to the screen, hoping to learn more than Roger's ability to aim. Thankfully he had finished his drunken urination and now did his best to shove the gas spout into the car.

Except, that wasn't Roger's car.

Or even one I recognized.

From what I recalled, he drove a truck. And Mary had a small white Fiat parked in her driveway when I visited a few days ago. This was some sort of generic four-door. The kind used for company cars. Maybe a Ford Taurus?

Whose car was this? And better yet, who was sitting in the driver's seat?

That person might very well be Roger's killer.

Roger, oblivious to his dim future, was unable to work the pump in his drunken state. He pulled at the line, frowning. When nothing happened, he kicked out at the pump and nearly fell on his butt in the dirt. He caught himself in time, and instead of trying again, he dropped the gas line and staggered back to the passenger side. A second later, he fell inside. The car took off, tires spinning in the gravel, before he could even close the door. Unfortunately for us, dust billowed in a thick cloud, obscuring the back end of the vehicle as it drove off.

Emmitt reached for the off button, but I slowed his hand. "Did you catch the license plate?" I asked, hope fading as he shook his head. I bit my lip. "Can I show this to the sheriff?"

He gazed at the tape, and then to the lone pump.

"Please?"

With a sigh, he pulled the tape from the recorder, handing it to me. "We ain't got a lot of those, so if you don't mind bringing it back?"

"Sure will," I said. Then again, Danny would likely confiscate it as evidence. If that happened, I'd find a way to make it right with Emmitt.

Maybe Danny's team would make out more than I had in the video, use some police techniques to clean up the picture.

I had no doubt the tape held the clue to solving Roger's murder.

For the first time in a very long time, my luck had turned.

CHAPTER

24

"CAN I SPEAK WITH the sheriff?" I asked the uniformed cop sitting behind a large desk an hour later. He grunted, motioning with his head to a frosted glass office with the word SHERIFF etched on the side. I shot the cop a smile of thanks.

I knocked on the door of Danny's office and waited.

"Enter," a voice called from inside. I did as it asked. Danny sat with his broad back to me, his hair mussed. A few lone gray hairs mixed with the dark brown strands. Being sheriff had taken a toll on him. Arresting innocent people did that to a man.

I waited for him to acknowledge me. When he didn't, I cleared my throat, loudly.

"Just set it on my desk and I'll sign it later, Phyllis," he said in response.

"I'm not Phyllis," I growled. "But I do have something for you."

He turned around, slowly. So slowly. As if dreading every second of facing me. I felt the same, but at least I had the decency to try and hide it. Not that I did a great job, but it was resisting the urge to smack him that counted.

"What brings you by, Ms. Lucky?" he asked as if gargling with glass. His fingers clenched around the pen in his hand so tightly I thought it would break. I smiled at the fantasy of the ink-spattered Gett.

Shaking it away, I said, "I think ... I mean, I *know* I have a tape of Roger's last hour of life." I paused for emphasis. An old acting trick used to add drama to a scene. A good pause brought people to tears. "Maybe even his last minutes."

He snorted, apparently not a fan. "You always were a drama queen."

"What?"

"Never mind." He let out a loud, long sigh. "Where's this tape?"

I pulled it carefully from my purse and handed it to him. Danny held it up, his mouth forming a thin line. "What do you expect me to do with this?" he asked with a growl.

"Play it," I said in a near shout.

"On what?" He waved a hand around his office. A fairly nice office at that. On the wall opposite his desk sat a trophy case, filled with shiny relics from his high school days. Danny had wanted to play in the NFL like his younger brother, but he never had Brodie's determination.

If he could, Danny would always take the easy way out. Which explained his hands-off relationship with Willow Jones. She'd obviously loved him, had since our freshman year of high school, and yet, Danny chose to ignore it, for it was easier. *Complicated* wasn't the word anyone with half a mind would use to describe Danny Gett.

I thought back to Brodie's small house. Not a single trophy in sight. Maybe he was more complex than I'd thought. The notion made me a bit nauseated. It was easier to think of Brodie as nothing more than a typical jock jerk.

"Does it look like I own a VCR?" Danny snarled, dragging me back to the matter at hand.

I winced. "I know, but you need to see this. It proves someone else besides Jack was with Roger moments before he died."

His face frozen, and for a second something—maybe fear?—flashed in his eyes. He quickly blinked it away. "Who?" he asked.

Interesting. Did Danny know more than he was letting on? "I don't know," I admitted, and then hastily explained before he threw me out of his office. "They're in shadows."

"You better not be wasting my time, running me around in circles like you do to my brother." After his insult, he rose from his chair and called to a harried woman sitting in the cubicle outside. "Phyllis," he said in his typical curt tone.

She snapped to attention, a guilty look on her face. I knew that look. I'd seen it reflected in the screen of my laptop often enough. Phyllis was an online shoe shopper.

"See if you can dig up a VCR," he said.

"A VCR?" Her eyes widened like she'd never heard the word before.

He snorted. "Yes, a VCR. We're going old-school. Check with Evidence. They might have one."

"Yes, sir," she said, picking up the phone on her desk.

Danny thanked her and then shut the door. He stared at me for a long moment, his face as hard as stone. Typical Gett. "You need to stop butting into my investigation."

I raised an eyebrow. Like that was going to happen. "And you need to find out who really killed Roger."

Danny ignored my interruption, seemingly warming to the topic. "Under any other circumstance, I'd haul your ass to jail for obstruction, but seeing as your granddad is a friend, I'm going to let it slide."

I held back a snort. Jack was hardly a friend of Danny's.

149

He added, "This time."

"I—"

He drew back, frowning. "Let me be clear. Next time, you aren't gonna be so lucky." He smiled at his own unfunny pun. Like I hadn't heard it a million times before, from his younger brother.

Anger burned in my chest, not quite escaping my throat. Before I could let him have it, Phyllis came into the office, a dusty VCR in her hands. I was impressed with her speed. She set it on the desk and then began connecting the frayed wires to Danny's computer. It took five minutes to figure out the right adaptors and a few more to finally get the tape loaded.

The screen flickered to life as she pressed various keys.

Roger's form appeared.

A chill ran up my spine as if a ghost had run his ethereal fingers up it.

Danny leaned in, his eyes squinting as if he needed reading glasses but was too vain to wear them. His hand stroked his chin. "Play it back from the beginning," he said to Phyllis.

She did as he asked. The machine squeaked as the tape rewound to the start. Slowly, frame by frame, we watched as the car pulled up to the gas pump and Roger stumbled out. I again suffered through his public urination, and then the car and Roger were gone.

"Play it one more time," Danny said, leaning in until his eyes were less than an inch from the screen. "Stop it," he ordered when it reached 37 seconds.

Phyllis did.

The tape froze on Roger, his hand on the top of the car, and the outline of the driver.

Danny straightened. "Stay here," he said to me in a tone suggesting he could care less if I listened to him or not. "I have to make a call."

"Now?"

"Yes." Without another word, he yanked out his cell phone and left the office. I watched him through the doorway as he paced back and forth in the hallway, his phone glued to his ear. He wasn't happy, if the coldness on his face was any indication.

Danny's eyes locked on mine. He stepped forward, slamming his office door to prevent me from eavesdropping. As if I could read lips. I stifled an eye roll, focusing on the computer screen. I sat with my hands in my lap, the face of a dead man a foot away. "Can you make out the driver?" I asked Phyllis a few seconds later. She shook her head. I let out a sigh. The only clue I had wasn't enough to free Jack. Not until we identified that silhouette.

My eyes remained locked on the screen, taking in every detail until I thought I might go blind. My eyes blurred as I memorized the way Roger's hand rested on the hood. Memorized the outline of the driver. I even memorized the shape of the decal on the windshield. I now knew every inch of the vehicle. And yet, not a clue as to the color of the paint. Frustrating to say the least, like auditioning for a coveted part only to learn the director's girlfriend also wanted it.

After what felt like hours, Danny returned, his face pinched. He appeared older than he had a few minutes before, as if whoever he'd talked with had sucked the life out of him. "I'll call you after I've taken care of it," he said to the person on the other end of the line, and then hung up before facing me. "Thank you for your input."

"*What*?" I frowned. "What does that mean?"

"It *means*, I'll take the tape under advisement."

"That's it?" I rose, my limbs shaking with fury. "Are you kidding me? You'll take the tape under advisement?" I stomped my foot like a child. I would've screamed like one too, if it would get Danny's attention. Which I knew it wouldn't. He liked his women endlessly meek, like Willow Jones. "That tape proves Jack wasn't with Roger," I declared. "That someone else killed him!"

He held up a hand. "Calm down."

"I will not." Now I did yell. When it didn't help, I took a deep breath, doing my best to get my rage under control. It wouldn't do Jack any good if both of us wound up in jail. "*Please*," I said, "you have to—"

"I don't *have* to do anything," he said, his body as rigid as his voice. "Listen to me, and listen good because I won't say it again." He waited for my full attention. I gave it grudgingly. "Stay out of this or you're going to get hurt."

"Is that a—"

He cut me off. "Go back to your distillery where there's real work to be done."

I flinched, knowing he was half right. I had neglected the distillery since Jack's arrest, and now we'd almost lost the entire thing. I needed to call the county inspector to find out when he could come out. "Can I have the tape, please?" I said to Phyllis.

Danny snatched it out of her hands before she could pass it my way. "This is evidence," he barked.

"But you said—"

"I didn't say it wasn't." He tapped his fingertips with the tape. Tap. Tap. Tap. The sound frayed my last nerve. He tilted his head, eyes on mine. "Could be Jack in the driver's seat. We don't know. Therefore, this is evidence until we sort it out. *We* as in the *cops*"—his gaze flickered over me—"not some half-assed actress with delusions."

My body vibrated with rage at his hastily hurled accusation. I might be delusional, but I was a hell of an actress. To prove it, I smiled my best smile at him, nodded, and left the office without giving in to my baser impulse to knock Danny upside the head until he gained some sense.

Mostly because I didn't have the hours it would take to spare.

Once outside, I released a muffled scream. A cop walking on the other side of the parking lot stopped cold, his hand going to the gun on his hip. He looked my way, measuring the threat. I gave him an apologetic wave and then slid into my car. I pounded on the steering wheel until my anger subsided. The palms of my hands gave out before my rage did. I rubbed away the stinging in my hands, working the tingling away, and finally my anger.

Danny might've dismissed me and confiscated my only hard evidence, but I wasn't going to let that or his warnings to stay out of the investigation stop me.

Not until Roger's killer was securely locked up behind bars and Jack was free.

CHAPTER

25

SINCE I WAS AT the police station, I decided to drive across the parking lot to the jail for a visit with my granddad. I knew he'd balk, but I needed to see him, needed to know he was all right. More so, I needed to bask in his strength.

Once I was allowed to finally see him an hour later, I knew I'd made the right decision. Jack gave me his grumpy smile and the anger at Danny and my fear for the future faded. That being said, I didn't let Jack see the fear of what might happen to him on my face if the tape proved useless like Danny thought. I focused our talk on the distillery, and Jack seemed happy to oblige.

Of course I never once mentioned Roger's embezzlement. He'd find out about that soon enough. I just hoped it wouldn't be the final straw that broke his already damaged heart.

We did talk about the fire and how to proceed with the repairs. Unfortunately, our deductible was more than the repair would cost. I'd have to find the cash somewhere. The idea chilled me to the core.

After our visit, I sat in my car in the parking lot and dialed the county inspector's office. A snotty receptionist informed me that the inspector would be over to check the structural integrity in two weeks. Not a minute sooner, no matter how much I pleaded. A few seconds later, she hung up on me. I stared at the phone for a long minute, taking steadying breaths.

From there, I headed to the diner for an early dinner, my stomach rumbling. My only caloric intake since this morning had been a Jolly Rancher I'd found tucked in my driver's seat. Mind you, a lint-coated Jolly Rancher. My mind and body needed to refuel.

I also needed to regroup. Sort through my list of suspects. Rue Gett remained at the top of the list. Especially after the way Danny had acted. Had he seen something on the tape that suggested the driver to be Rue or maybe even Brodie? Was that why he snatched the tape?

Alone at the counter of the Gett Diner, I mapped out my suspects on a napkin. At the top, I placed Rue, then Brodie, followed by Boone, Danny, Evan, Mary, and Unknown. The unknown category bothered me most. The possibility that Roger had been killed simply for being in the wrong place at the wrong time always loomed. Then again, only someone familiar with Gett, Florida, would know about the Lucky distillery along with Moonshine Run. Blowing out a harsh breath, I eliminated Danny and Mary from the list. Both had alibis, as far as I knew. Danny was at the station at the time, and Mary was in bed, her car parked in the driveway all night. Which left Rue, Brodie, Boone, and my own cousin.

Crap. I needed to find the driver of that car in the video. Only then would I have enough proof to convince Danny or, if need be, go over his head to the Attorney General.

Until then, I needed to eat.

After Cindy Mae, who looked even bigger in the belly than she had yesterday, took my order of a chicken fried steak (a risky choice, I was sure), I mentally reviewed the footage. Nothing jumped out at me to indicate Rue or Brodie was the driver. But something on the tape had grabbed Danny's attention. I was sure of it.

I had to find a way to approach Rue Gett. She was my best chance at solving Roger's murder. Even if she hadn't killed him herself, I was positive she had her hand in it somehow. Why else would someone frame Jack, let alone leave Roger's body in a Lucky cask?

For as long as I could remember, Jack and Rue had been at each other's throats—except for the day of my parents' funeral. While Jack and I stood at the graveside, Rue and all of her offspring and their offspring arrived at the cemetery, all dressed in black even in the hot, sticky weather. Rue had separated from her family to give her condolences to Jack.

The memory had stuck in my five-year-old brain for one reason. I'd been terrified that if I let Jack out of my sight for even a moment, he'd disappear too. Like my parents, who'd kissed me on the cheek a few minutes before an unknown car had struck their Trans Am, sending it flipping end over end, into the brackish marsh along the roadway.

That day, Rue had wrapped her thin arms around Jack, holding tightly. Together, the two competitors mourned a great loss, as if it was a loss to the Gett clan as much as to the Luckys. Cousin Evan had broken them apart a few minutes later when he grabbed Jack's leg. In his defense, he was only two years old at the time.

As if conjuring him up from humid air, Evan appeared at my side in the diner. He looked better than he had yesterday, having washed away the soot from the fire. "Hey Charlotte," he said loudly. Too much so for just a casual meeting. "Mind if I sit?"

Jack would've had my head if I said no, though I wanted to. Very much. I didn't need Evan's whining right now, let alone his badgering me to sell out the Lucky name.

Ever the polite southern hostess, I motioned to the stool next to me. "What can I do for you?" I asked, taking a drink of the sweetest tea I'd ever tasted. I tried not to gag as sugar coated my tongue and teeth. Surely I'd need to go to the dentist for a mouthful of cavities if I stayed in town much longer.

Cindy Mae must've seen my disgust, for she came over with an extra glass of water when she took Evan's order. She set the glass of water down without comment. "What'll it be, hon?" she asked Evan in a friendly tone.

Once he'd requested a grilled cheese with extra mayo and bacon and Cindy Mae left, he gave me a timid smile. "I know we had a bit of a blow up a few days ago ..."

"That's true."

His grin grew even more sheepish. "I'm sorry about that." Twirling the fork on the counter, he seemed to wait for my apology. Which wouldn't be coming anytime soon. Evan had milked Jack, embroiling him in this mess of Roger's murder. I wouldn't let him use Jack or the distillery again.

When he moved his fork to his other hand, I noticed a white wrap of gauze and two metal supports around his middle finger. "What happened? Did you burn your hand in the fire?" I asked, but I suspected a different answer—Boone. He'd made good on his threat to injure Evan's hands.

"Do you really care?" Evan asked in a familiar whine.

I shrugged.

Cindy brought us two plates packed with food. The aroma crossed my nostrils and my mouth began to water. I picked up my own fork, unafraid of the pan-fried piece of cube steak in front of me. Though I should've been, given the charred edges. When she left, we dug in. For a few minutes silence reigned as I chewed through the overcooked meat.

"I care about Jack too," he said, his mouth full of food. Peas and carrots swirled around his plate. "You might not believe this, but I wasn't the one who asked Jack for the money."

I set my fork down, my jaw thanking me for the break between bites. "Then how did Jack know you were into Roger for five thousand dollars?"

"He must've seen us arguing." Evan swallowed then took another bite. Again, chewing with his mouth wide. "Jack hates when anything disrupts the whiskey," he said, "and nothing's worse than having your distiller and your cooper arguing. Anger makes for sour whiskey, Jack says."

"But you knew Jack planned on paying Roger off." I tilted my head. "And you could've stopped him. If you wanted to."

He nodded.

My eyebrow rose. "Did you also know about Jack's threat to toss Roger in a cask?"

He nodded, slower this time.

Oh, no. Had Evan killed Roger and then framed Jack for the deed? It was possible ...

"I didn't kill Roger!" he yelped when I remained silent. "Yeah, I knew Jack had threatened him," he said. "But why would I kill Roger when Jack had already paid him? I'm not stupid, Charlotte, no matter what you might think."

Was I that obvious? Did I care? Not really. Evan had burned his bridges with me. No one used Jack. How would Evan react if Jack had cut him off as well? I wiped my lips with the napkin folded neatly next to my plate. "Maybe you got mad when Roger wouldn't loan you any more money because of Jack's threat." I warmed to my theory. "You found him drunk and vulnerable at the distillery. One thing led to another..."

"You're crazy," he said.

I continued as if he hadn't spoken, "And then you got your revenge on Jack by framing him for murder."

He slammed his injured hand on the counter and then cried out at the pain. Dishes rattled. Cindy Mae started over, but I held up a hand to stop her.

"I have an alibi for that night," he hissed.

"Oh, yeah?" My other eyebrow rose to meet the first. "Tell me all about it."

"I don't need this," he said, throwing his stained napkin down. "I came here to talk about the distillery, and you're starting in on this crap. I'm done."

"What about the distillery?" Had something else gone wrong? My stomach rolled at the thought. We couldn't stand much more.

His face hardened, but his tone stayed pleasant enough. "Charlotte, let's be reasonable. We need to sell the distillery to the Getts before it's worthless." He smiled sadly, which I didn't buy for a moment. "Right now we have some inventory not destroyed in the fire. Sell it to them, and the equipment." His eyes shined brightly. I could practically see the wheels spinning in his head, and not the kind normally associated with deep thought, but rather a roulette wheel, red and black swirling around. "We can walk away with a few hundred grand."

I laughed without a bit of humor. "And I'm the crazy one? You're certifiable. Jack would never go for it."

"But Jack's not here." He shot me a knowing look, one I dreamed of punching off his face. "He's looking at spending the rest of his days in prison. It's up to you and I, his heirs, to take care of business." Rubbing his hands together, he added, "Think about it. You could go back to L.A. with enough cash to live the good life."

Good life? What a joke. Cousin Evan, in that moment, moved even farther up the suspect list. He now sat just below Rue Gett. Both had means and motive. And he never did get around to offering an alibi. Had he killed Roger by accident? Then, in the heat of the moment decided to frame Jack, thinking he could then sell Lucky Whiskey after Jack was locked up?

I knew he had it in him.

As a kid, he'd acted like a spoiled brat, wanting his way no matter what. He hadn't changed much over the years. I could see the anger burning in his gaze. If he'd had a weapon handy, he very well might have used it when I next spoke, "That's never going to happen, Evan. Jack entrusted Lucky to me. I'm his one and only heir."

"What?" he choked out.

"You heard me," I said, leaning in. "And the only way Lucky Whiskey will go to the Getts is over my dead body." Given the situation, I should've chosen my words with better care. Something I'd surely regret later, but in the moment it was all I had.

A smile spread slowly over his face. "You should look at getting the windshield of your car fixed. I wouldn't want anything bad to happen to you, dear cousin."

With that less-than-veiled threat, he slammed his fork into the counter with his injured hand, inches from my own uninjured one, and then left.

Without paying for his meal.

Figured.

CHAPTER

26

FUMING, I PAID FOR our meals and left Cindy Mae a nice tip before leaving the diner. I paced in front of my car, muttering like a madwoman, until the haze of anger left my vision. I'd had about enough of men talking down to me today. Let alone admitting to breaking my windshield like the petulant brat. I'd take the money for my replacement windshield out of his paycheck.

Let's see how he liked that.

Sadly, my bad luck with men wasn't over yet.

After leaving the diner, I stopped at the local convenience store; a place you could buy milk at ten at night. No later though. After ten p.m., all the business on Main Street closed. As I set my purchases of Red Vines and Diet Coke on the counter, Boone Daniels slithered up to my side. His breath smelled of a familiar cheap whiskey. An affront to my Lucky senses, but I couldn't place where I'd smelled it before. He moved closer, until my shoulder touched his chest. My stomach rolled as goosebumps rose on my skin. I wouldn't let him intimidate me.

"Hey, there," he slurred. "Where's your boyfriend?"

I ignored him.

"That will be five twenty-five," the cashier, Margaret Johnson, said, distaste clear on her face.

I didn't know which of us she found so offensive. Regrettably, I put the odds on me. In Gett, one could be a drug-dealing dirtbag, but don't you dare paint the town's water tower and run off thinkin' you're better than everyone else or there would be hell to pay.

Boone gave a lurid chuckle. "No man around to save you this time." He moved even closer. I squeezed my arms next to my body to avoid touching him. "I want what I'm owed. But I'm willing to take it out in trade," he whispered, his breath hot on my neck. The whiskey scent coming off of him in waves lingered in my nostrils.

Was it the same brand used as an accelerate at the rackhouse?

I frowned, trying to remember the strong, acidic scent.

Could be.

Which made me angry enough to lose my good sense and enrage a man I knew capable of evil by giving a short laugh. "I don't need anyone to save me, as you so eloquently put it." I stopped, turning to face him. My eyes ran up and down his scrawny frame much like his gaze had done over my body seconds before. "Especially from the likes of you."

His eyes grew small and mean, meaner than normal, as he hitched up his jeans. "I'm gonna show you just what the likes of me can do to sluts like you."

I ignored his comment and handed Margaret a five-dollar bill and a quarter. I scooped up my items and headed for the door. He reached out to grab my arm, but I maneuvered away in time. He laughed. Hollow and cruel. The same laugh I remembered from that night in his truck, his hands pulling on my clothes. I'd begged for him to let me go. He'd merely laughed harder.

I'd never felt so helpless. So vulnerable.

And then Brodie had appeared.

A good reminder that I at least owed Brodie the benefit of the doubt about Roger's murder.

I hurried to my car, hoping Boone wouldn't follow. He didn't. Though he had parked his truck right next to my Prius. It stood at least two feet higher, with chrome rims and small headlights. The truck was so close I could barely squeeze in without smacking my head into his side mirror. He'd done it on purpose, I'd bet on it. I considered breaking off the mirror, but I denied the childish urge. I was an adult. A responsible one.

How was it I still felt like an awkward teen trapped in a town that never understood me?

Once I was inside, I popped the automatic locks on my doors and started the engine. A blast of hot air, much like Boone's breath sans the rotgut whiskey, spilled from the vents. I twisted the knob to cool and shoved into gear.

The sky started to darken, leaving the street a golden color. This was my favorite time of the day, when the sky joined the rest of us in a nice whiskey-colored hue. All I craved was to go home, slip into a pair of sweatpants and a grungy t-shirt, and sip some of Jack's premium stash.

I had a lot to do tomorrow, starting with the county inspector. I had to find a way to get him to survey Lucky as soon as possible. Had to.

In two weeks, Lucky Whiskey would be in bankruptcy rather than on the verge of it.

Lucky us.

Tears welled in my eyes. I brushed them away with an angry swipe. My cell phone rang, ruining my pity party before it could go full-fledged. I looked at the caller ID. The number was blocked but had a local area code. I debated answering it, but it might be Jack or his lawyer, so I did with a tentative, "Hello?"

"Ms. Lucky?" Emmitt of the *Fill 'Er Up* station asked, again his voice cracking like the teenager he was. I imagined him, acne-riddled face and all, his sweaty palms holding the phone. I remembered my own slick palms the first time Joey Duggan's lips touched mine in the rackhouse.

"Hi Emmitt," I said, shaking off the vivid memory. A memory I'd long associated with the first sip of a single malt. "What can I do for you?"

"I'm sorry to be calling so late, ma'am."

"No problem," I said automatically. Seven was late to most folks around here. Particularly the ones who fished the Glades. Days started much like mine had, before the sun broke the sky. "Did you remember something new?"

"No, ma'am." He hesitated. I could virtually see his *aw shucks* face through the phone. "My pa ... he wants our tape back." A nervous giggle crackled over the phone. "Says it's our only one left, and we can't find no more to buy."

Guilt filled me. "Oh, Emmitt. I'm so sorry. Sheriff Gett took it as evidence." I bit my lip. This was my fault. Maybe I could buy a tape from Amazon.

Wait a minute ...

"Emmitt, I think we have some back at the house." I smiled as the recollection hit me. Jack, in the spur of the moment when I was around thirteen, had bought a monstrous video camera. The kind that used VCR tapes.

A week later, he'd shoved the camera and the tapes in a box at the back of his closet. Like most things that weren't whiskey-related. I'd bet my life the tapes were still there, packed away in their cellophane, untouched.

"Oh, ma'am, that's wonderful. My pa … well, I appreciate it."

"No problem." I rubbed my chin, the fantasy of an evening in sweatpants and grubby t-shirt vanishing with my words. "Give me an hour or so to find the tapes and I'll drive them over." I hung up with a smile. Good deed of the day virtually accomplished.

CHAPTER

27

ON MY WAY TO find the VCR tapes in Jack's closet, I passed the Gett Bar & Grill. A lone vehicle grabbed my attention. Brodie's Jeep sat parked next to the front door. Like it had so many times before.

I considered stopping to ask him about Roger's burner cell phone and its calls to Gett Whiskey.

But the thought of dealing with yet another man who believed he could boss me around or use his size to intimidate me kept my car on its current path. I could always catch him at Roger's memorial in a few days.

It was better this way. Less chance of me taking my frustration with his brother out on an intoxicated Brodie. Who knew how'd he react? The Gett name, at best, was on the line. And I knew how protective they were of it.

Even as I thought it, I knew it was nothing more than an excuse. I wasn't ready to deal with Brodie just yet. We hadn't spoken since the day I caught him with Mary. I wouldn't say I missed him, but it was nice to have a sounding board for my crazier theories. One of which featured most of his family.

I reached the Lucky family home a few minutes later. I parked the Prius close to the house in case someone, namely my cousin, decided to break one of my other windows in the few moments I was inside.

As I unlocked the front door, I inhaled the scent of whiskey and wood with a hint of yesterday's fire. Thankfully, leaving the windows open today had helped clear the stench.

Taking a minute, I considered all the hiding spaces a box of VCR tapes could be. I searched each closet on the main level, not finding a single tape.

Chewing on my bottom lip, I debated heading upstairs to Jack's room. I hadn't stepped foot inside since I'd returned home, but there wasn't really anywhere else to look.

As I opened the door uneasiness flickered through my body. This was Jack's sanctuary. His inner domain. Always had been. Forever would be.

As a child I'd avoided Jack's personal space, knowing it was the only place where he could be alone. Truly alone. He hadn't asked to become a parent again in his fifties, a time when other men bought fancy cars and went on fabulous vacations. Instead, Jack had stayed here, at Lucky Whiskey, raising a girl he most often didn't know what to do with.

His room smelled of him. Of good whiskey and Granddad.

Taking a deep breath, I headed inside. The room looked like most bedrooms—a bed, a nightstand, and a dresser that occupied the right side. On the left sat a half-empty bookcase and the closet. A single picture of my grandmother on their wedding day sat on the table by the bed. I wondered if Jack still missed her. Or had her memory faded like my parents' had slowly vanished from my mind?

Shaking off the melancholy, I opened the closet door. Luck was on my side—a dusty box sat on the top shelf, neatly labeled in Jack's scrawl with the word KEEP.

I wasn't sure what that meant. Did he plan on keeping the box or the contents? Did this box contain his most prized possessions? An odd thought considering Jack wasn't the sentimental type.

Or was he?

When I'd returned home, I was surprised to see Jack using a clay mug I'd decorated in third grade for his nightly dram of whiskey. It was lopsided and florescent pink with *World's Best Granddad* etched into the side. The mug was beyond ugly.

From the wear and tear, Jack apparently drank from it every night.

I pulled the box down, astonished to see a carefully wrapped stack of yellowing letters inside. Definitely keepsakes. There were also two VHS tapes. I bit my lip, debating whether to read the letters. Maybe they were from my parents? Or my Grandma Jennie, who died before I was born? My fingers itched to pull at the edge of the frayed ribbon holding the cluster together.

I set the box down, grabbed the tapes, and walked away.

I didn't even make it to the door.

Spinning around, I ran back to the box and yanked off the ribbon. I opened the first letter addressed in a woman's flowing handwriting to *My beloved*. My eyes scanned the content, stopping before things got hot.

In my hands I held the original booty call.

My face burned at the realization.

I tied the letters back in place, shoving them deep inside the box. As I did so, my hand brushed a stack of newspapers at the bottom. I pulled the first one up. It was dated the day after my parents died on a lone highway. According to the newspaper, their car had flipped three times, eventually landing in a ditch. Both were pronounced dead at the scene. Alcohol was not a factor. An eyewitness claimed to see a dark vehicle leaving the scene of the accident. Police weren't able to identify the vehicle.

For a long time after the loss, Jack obsessed about finding the car. The sheriff at the time, Glenn Hay, offered little in the way of comfort or evidence. If he hadn't needed to take care of me, I suspected Jack would've spent the rest of his life searching for the person responsible for his son's death.

Tears spilled down my cheeks at the unfairness of it all. I angrily swiped them away.

My mom had been a year younger than I was right now.

I carefully placed the newspapers back inside.

One last item caught my eye. It was a Valentine's Day card with a big red heart on the cover. My fingers caressed the edges as the years faded away. Kindergarten. My first valentine. A young boy with bright eyes and a wicked smile—before I knew just what a wicked smile could do to a woman's knees.

Grodie Brodie Gett.

He'd handed me this card in the small coat room at the back of our classroom. He'd also tried to kiss me. I'd punched him square in the nose. Blood spurted from his nostrils and tears formed in his eyes. It was at that moment that I'd gained my first nemesis as well.

Why had Jack saved this card?

With a frown, I traced the frayed, yellowing edges before placing the valentine back in the box. I picked up the VCR tapes and slowly made my way out of the room.

I glanced back once and then firmly shut the door.

———

Ten minutes later, fortified by Red Vines and Diet Coke but no whiskey as of yet, I put my Prius into gear and headed for the Fill 'Er Up. My mind wandered to the tape Danny had confiscated. Something bothered me, but I couldn't place it. I frowned as detail after detail flickered through my head. Still not a one gave me a clue as to who was driving the car.

I passed by the Gett Bar & Grill again, not surprised at all by the sight of the black Jeep front and center of the parking lot. However, it was a shock to see Boone Daniels's truck in the parking lot next to Brodie's Jeep. As far as I knew, Boone was 86ed from both bars in town.

He was a true troublemaker. I gave a thankful shiver to be in the relative safety of my car and at least a hundred yards away as I drove past.

I kept both my hands at ten and two on the steering wheel as I pulled out onto the pitch-black county road. I hated driving at night. Mostly because I hated driving with my overly large eyeglasses. Thankfully my eyesight hadn't reached the point where I needed to wear glasses all the time, but the plastic frames felt heavy on my face.

Add in the splintered view out the windshield, the creepy atmosphere of fog in my headlights, and the assorted night sounds of life in the Glades, and by the time I reached the halfway point, my grip was so tight on the wheel my fingers ached. Consciously, I relaxed each finger, one at a time as I blew out a breath, laughing at my own ridiculousness. I'd learned to drive on darker, more twisted roads than this. Roads even the most daring of drivers refused to travel.

Living in L.A. had softened me, just like Brodie had accused.

I thought of Brodie, of how he'd tried his best to distract me. Was it because of his or his grandmother's guilt? Or was there something else? Something I was missing?

From what seemed like out of the very Glades themselves, bright headlights appeared in my rearview mirror. Blinding headlights, so intense I had to avert my gaze. Perspiration dampened my palms as my fingers once again tightened against the padded wheel. The headlights grew more concentrated as they drew closer to my back bumper.

"Go around me, jerk." I held the wheel steady, slowing.

The lights were less than a car length from me now. I flipped my rearview mirror up to keep the high beams out of my eyes. At the same time, I tried to make out the outline of the vehicle. It wasn't simply a car. That much was for sure. The beams hit too high. They were close together too.

Like a Jeep.

Was that Brodie behind me? My heartbeat decreased to near-normal. What did he want? Was he trying to annoy me? Torture me like he had when we were younger? A cruel joke played by an equally mean spirit? I slowed down even more. If it was Brodie, he'd either flip around me or flick his headlight for me to stop.

Unless he was drunk.

A real possibility, considering his Jeep sat in the parking lot of the bar all day long. Would Willow be reckless enough to allow him to drive? Considering my parents' deaths on a road very much like this, due to some likely drunk driver, the very idea sent my blood boiling.

My anger lasted for a few seconds more, replaced once again by fear.

The vehicle behind me sped up, whipping over the double yellow line and into the lane next to me. My heart leapt into my throat. This was bad. Really bad. What if Boone was the driver and he was looking for revenge? His truck stood about the same height as Brodie's Jeep. The headlight even looked similar in shape.

I stepped on the brake, holding my breath as I slowed to thirty miles an hour. Rather than pass me, the dark vehicle slowed as well, staying in my blind spot. My back grew slick with sweat and I clung to the wheel.

Metal crashed against metal. The screech drew a scream from my own throat. I held onto the wheel as it wobbled in my hands. The Prius jerked to the right as the other vehicle slammed into my side for a second time. My smaller car was no match for the bigger vehicle, crumpling under the impact. Another cry tore from my lungs as the Prius hit the shoulder. Gravel flew up and weeds battered the side of the car.

My poor little car couldn't take the onslaught any longer. One more hit sent it flying off the edge and into the darkness. The already cracked windshield shattered as the vehicle flipped. I wasn't sure how many times I rolled. It felt like forever, and yet, it happened in an instant.

My life wasn't what flashed in front of my eyes though. Just the headlights of the other vehicle.

The Prius eventually landed upside down in the ditch. My seatbelt had locked during the crash, leaving me flailing in the air. Blood briefly obscured my vision as it welled from a cut on my upper lip. I couldn't tell if it was from the glass or from biting myself. I wiped my hand over my eyes, hoping to sweep away the shards. In a panic, I pulled at the belt, grabbing for the button that no longer seemed in place. Finally, my shaking fingers found the latch. My body immediately fell and my head hit the wheel as I crashed into the steering column.

Hard.

The oxygen whooshed from my lungs. I must've blacked out, for when I woke, I lay in a foot of icy ditch water filling the car. The stench brought tears to my eyes, much more than my injuries did. All and all, I'd survived the crash with only minor damage. No broken bones or extreme internal injuries as far as I could tell. Everything worked as it should.

And then I moved. Each action produced a fresh wave of pain shrieking through my brain. Icy wetness seeped into my bones and I started to shiver. Violently. Mostly from shock, I guessed. Not that my brain could make such a connection. Pain and terror had taken control.

Especially when the crunch of boots against broken glass sounded from the darkness. Someone was outside. The bright, close pair of headlights of the other vehicle backlit a pair of the black work boots worn by a third of the men and a few women in the county. The boots stepped closer.

I held my breath, willing the shivering to stop. It didn't, but at least it gave me focus.

Had my would-be killer come back to finish the job?

Glass crunched under his or her feet.

Was I going to die? Right here, on the highway like my parents had?

Poor Jack. Not only would he lose his only grandchild, but he'd spend the rest of his days in prison for a crime he didn't commit. Anger alone gave me strength. I wouldn't let Jack down. Not this time. I struggled to see up and through the missing windshield for the person's face. "Who's there?" I croaked.

The crunch of glass under boot stopped.

Suddenly the ditch water surged up.

In front of my eyes, a beast at least eight feet in length darted from the trench toward the land. The boot steps began again, but this time faster, and in the other direction. The vehicle started and then drove off, headlights swinging around, then red taillights disappearing into the mist.

Tears ran unabated down my face, mixing with blood. I let out a hysterical laugh, filled with relief.

Until two beady eyes appeared in front of me.

In my imagination they glowed angry red in color.

I blinked a few times to clear the vision. The alligator drew closer. But I failed to see just how close, for, thankfully, unconsciousness took me away.

CHAPTER

28

I WOKE TO A not-so-gentle tug on my eyelids, followed by a bright white light. Not the kind you ran into. This one scorched my irises, sending a wave of pain shooting through my head. I tried to pull away, to stop the burning intensity. But something or someone held me fast. I struggled, lashing out.

"Take it easy, Charlotte." The firm but calming voice eased some of my panic. The light faded, and slowly my gaze focused on Lester's thin face, his lips pinched with concern. "Do you know where you are?" he asked. "What day it is?"

Did he think I was stupid? I knew exactly what day it was …

Except when I went to tell him, I couldn't, for the life of me, remember. What day *was* it? Tuesday, maybe? I rubbed my head, concerned when it came away flaked with dried blood. Numbly I stared at the blood staining my fingers. "Was I in an accident?"

His head nodded in the affirmative. "Good girl. Do you know who I am?"

"My brain's a bit scrambled, but not that badly." I licked my dry lips, wincing when I tasted coppery blood. "How did you find me?" I asked, the hazy memory of flipping over and over, glass breaking and the sound of crushing metal. Then, for some reason, I remembered a glowing set of red eyes.

Panic threatened again.

I took a deep breath. My heartbeat failed to slow.

Lester must've disliked the look on my face. "Don't you dare pass out again."

"I won't," I lied, feeling as if I would do just that. "I'm all right. Just a little bruised."

He snorted, an unpleasant sound against the pounding in my brain. "You're still going to the hospital."

I now had the where question answered. I was in Lester's ambulance, wrapped in a cocoon of blankets, Lester in front of me as his co-paramedic drove with lights and sirens to the county hospital. The vehicle smelled of disinfectant and the grease of grilled cheese—much like Lester himself. "I don't ..." I frowned. "Did the other vehicle call for help?"

His face darkened. "What other vehicle? Was someone there with you? Did they see you wreck?"

Was there another car? I couldn't quite remember. I thought so. I remembered seeing headlights looming larger. Bright ones. Then the sound of metal against metal ...

"I ... yes." I snapped my fingers, causing the bones to ache. Who knew a thumb held so many bones? "There was. It ran me off the road." My gaze flew to Lester's as realization dawned. "Someone tried to kill me!"

This time it was Lester's face that looked not so good. "Get the sheriff on the radio," he said to his partner. "Have him meet us at the ER."

"Can't say I'm real surprised by this." Danny Gett stood over my hospital bed in his off-duty uniform of Levi's, a t-shirt, and a backwards ball cap. For the life of me I couldn't figure out the need for men to wear backwards ball caps all the time. Even those who were actual ballplayers.

I glowered up at him. Hard to do while wearing a hospital gown, my bare butt exposed, but I managed. "What's that supposed to mean?" Had Danny had a hand in my current condition? Even as I thought it, I dismissed the possibility. For one thing, I was pretty sure he would've used his gun rather than chancing an accident if he wanted me out of the way.

But what about his brother? The bright glow of a Jeep's headlights flickered through my mind.

"Not what you think it does." His face pinched and then flattened. "The legend is true."

"What legend?" I asked, though I knew exactly what he would say. I'd heard it all my less-than-charmed life.

He confirmed it. "That you, Charlotte Lucky, like the rest of your clan, were born under a bad sign."

I rolled my eyes. "I'm alive, aren't I? That proves I'm lucky."

The grim look on his face suggested otherwise. "You're lucky to be alive, I'll give you that." He paused, chewing on his bottom lip. "I took a look at the scene," he said.

"And?"

"Seems you went off the road and flipped three times before landing in the ditch." His shoulder lifted and then fell. "That damn road needs better lighting. I've told the county a million times. Someone's gonna die." He glared down at me. "Once a week I get a call about another *tourist* driving too fast …"

"Excuse me?" I pushed my body up, regretting it instantly. Every muscle ached. I ignored the tourist dig to focus on his real insult. "Did you just imply the accident was my fault?"

His dark eyebrow rose. "Are you saying it wasn't?"

"Yes! Many times now." I threw my legs over the edge of the bed, swallowing back a wave of bile tempting to erupt from the back of my throat. Parts of my body I never knew existed suddenly declared their presence, and not at all politely. "Someone smashed into me. On purpose."

He held out a hand to stop me from rising. "Take it easy."

"I will not." My voice escalated into a shout. "Someone tried to kill me, and you sit there, holier than all Getts, saying it was my fault."

"I was at the scene," he said, like a genuine know-it-all. "The damage is consistent with the driver overcorrecting, resulting in the vehicle flipping." He hesitated, as though weighing my mental state. His voice softened, and for a brief second he sounded like a human rather than a mouthpiece for the Gett family. "Trust me, Charlotte, I've seen it a hundred times."

My head began to pound. Rings of silver light flickered in my vision. I took a gulping breath. When the wave of dizziness passed, I said, "I don't understand … Someone hit me. I swear it."

He drew in a long breath, letting it out deliberately. "Listen, I know it's hard to remember in cases like this …"

"It was a Jeep." I rubbed my hands together. I couldn't get the image of Brodie's Jeep out of my mind. The small, round, close-to-getherness of the headlights. It had to be a Jeep. Had to be.

All warmth vanished from Danny's face. "What are you implying?" His eyes smoldered much like the gator's in the ditch had. "Are you saying my brother had something to do with this?"

I wasn't sure what I was saying. One thing was sure: I hadn't accidently flipped my car three times. Someone had hit me. If it wasn't Brodie's Jeep, then whose was it? And why had they tried to kill me? Was it due to my investigation into Roger's murder? Or something more personal, like the damage to my windshield?

I started to stand again, unhooking the machine tethering me to the bed.

I had to see Brodie's Jeep.

See if it had any damage from crashing into my Prius. I had to know the truth. Know if he'd tried to kill me. The very idea was crazy. And yet, someone had run me off the road.

"You aren't leaving this hospital," a man in a white lab coat said without looking up from the clipboard in his hand. A man I'd failed to notice before. "Get back in bed or I'll have the nurses restrain you."

When I opened my mouth to argue, he added, "You're also not wearing any pants."

With great reluctance, plenty of annoyed grumbling, and red cheeks (upper, not lower), I laid back in bed under the covers. Once I was settled back in, he grabbed my wrist, checking my pulse.

He released my arm, then nodded to Danny. "As shocking as it is, her tests have come back negative," he said. "No internal injuries or broken bones. Not even a concussion. We'd like to keep her overnight for observation—"

"No," I said though the tremble in my voice suggested otherwise. "I want to go home. Now."

He ignored me as if I hadn't spoken. "Her core temperature is a bit low. She must've laid in that ditch for at least an hour before someone came across the accident to call 9-1-1. She's damn lucky to be alive."

An hour? Really?

"Have you checked her blood...?" Danny asked sheepishly.

I leaned forward again. "Are you kidding me? You think I'm drunk?"

"Relax," the doctor said, "please. The test came back clean. No alcohol or other substances in her bloodstream."

Danny nodded, tilting his head, eyes watchful. "Do you still believe that someone ran you off the road?"

"On purpose." Tears gathered in my eyes, but I refused to let them fall. I would hardly give Danny Gett the satisfaction. "*Someone* tried to kill me. And why do you think that is, Sheriff?"

He shrugged, but I didn't buy it for a minute. Danny knew as well as I did why.

"Because I am making them nervous. Whoever killed Roger knows I'm on to them." I wanted to say Brodie's name, but something held me back. I was far from certain it was Brodie's Jeep that forced me off the road. Now that I took a moment, I was sure I'd seen other Jeeps around town. Furthermore, it could've easily been a case of road rage. Some drunk targeting a small Prius.

If so, why hadn't they called the police right after the accident?

What kind of person just walks away from a scene like that? A killer. Of that I was sure.

CHAPTER

29

UNDER THE COVER OF night, I snuck away from the hospital like a drunk stealing sips of whiskey from a hidden flask. I wanted nothing more than to fall into a deep sleep in my own bed. Since I didn't have a car anymore, I had to rely on the Collier County Taxi. And I do mean, one lone taxi and driver, in all of the county. Thankfully the driver didn't comment on my sad attire of two hospital gowns tied together to conceal my butt, since the doctors had cut away my clothes to assess my injuries. I staggered into the taxi, wincing with each step.

Thirty minutes later, I flopped facedown into my bed, dropping into its soft, fluffy comforter. No sooner had my head hit the pillow than I was snoring loud enough to wake myself.

Too little of a time later, a buzz saw reverberated through my brain.

Literally.

Just outside my window some jerk was happily pounding, hammering, and sawing away. Whistling too. I wished him a plague of warts.

My eyes flew open, realizing what I was hearing. Someone, or what sounded like a lot of someones, were working on the rackhouse.

I jumped from bed. A bad, bad idea. My muscles, the very ones that had hurt last night, had atrophied and now refused to move without intense pain. I staggered to the bathroom, choking when I saw my bruised face in the mirror. A long, jagged cut followed my eyebrow and reached into my hairline. The blood from the gash had congealed in my hair. I ran a hand through it. My hand came away black, though how much was from blood and how much was from soaking in swamp water was unknown. In addition, my upper lip puffed out, giving me a bee-stung look. The kind women usually paid dearly for. And all it had cost me was a Prius and a quick trip to the ER.

Next time I'd kiss a wasp.

Against my better judgement, I disrobed and took a quick, scalding-hot shower. My muscles eased as the water massaged them. Within a minute I could stand upright once again. The cut on my head, which the doctor had declared needed a bandage and no stitches, burned as the water pounded against it. But that didn't stop me from scrubbing every inch of my body. Twice. At long last I felt almost human and stumbled out of the shower.

Foregoing my normal two cups of coffee, I headed downstairs and outside. Since the county inspector wouldn't be here for several more days, I had to stop whatever work had been done to the rackhouse. Last thing we needed was a hefty county fine.

"Hello?" I called to the broad-shouldered back of the man with the saw in his hands. Muscles bunched and released with each movement. For a moment, I stood mesmerized by the sight. Then the man turned, ruining my pleasure. He slowly removed his safety glasses, studying me head to toe. He winced when his gaze landed of my face.

Not the sort of thing that helped a woman's self-esteem.

"Damn," Brodie said, reaching out to touch my damaged skin. I pulled back before he made contact. Not that I feared his caress, but I didn't want what looked like half the town crowded around to witness his concern. More rumors flying around about Grodie Brodie and me would only add to my current host of problems.

Brodie dropped his hand. "Looks painful."

"I'll live." My head started to pound, at odds with my declaration. "Longer than you, if you don't stop sawing."

"Now, was that nice?" He raised the saw. The blade gleamed menacingly in the sunlight. "I'm here, doing you a favor, and this is what I get?"

I ignored his complaining, not in the mood for it after last night. "Favor? Is that what this is? Because it feels more like the Getts trying to stir up trouble, seeing as the county inspector hasn't given his approval to do any work."

His free hand flew to his chest. "I'm hurt. You need to have more faith in your fellow man."

"I do." I flinched when my battered lips cracked as I tried to smile. "Just not those with the last name Gett."

His eyebrow rose, but he didn't respond, instead he restarted the buzz saw and turned away. The noise drowned the string of words falling from my mouth. Most of them starting with the letter F.

Every time I took a breath, the saw idled, but as soon as I spoke again, he revved the engine.

"Bro—"

More revving.

"You—"

Louder still.

"Man-baby!" I yelled.

Sadly just as he cut the engine. Workers nearby spun around, eyes wide.

"Damn y—"

The chainsaw sputtered to life again.

I'd had enough of this game. I smacked his arm. "Stop. Please," I added when it seemed like he planned on continuing to torment me.

He shut the saw off, turning to face me. "What?"

I took a calming breath. Brodie was, even if his ultimate plan was to ruin us, standing there, along with half of Gett Whiskey's employees, trying to help us rebuild after the questionable fire.

"We aren't supposed to go inside the rackhouse until the inspector gives the okay." I paused, fear for his and my own employees filling me. "It's dangerous."

He waved to a man I'd never seen before. The man looked both terrified and in awe of Brodie. His eyes were wide, face pale. "George," Brodie said, motioning from George to me, "I'd like you to meet Charlotte Lucky, the owner of Lucky Whiskey here."

George tipped his baseball cap. "Ma'am."

I gave him a warm smile. "Do you work at Gett? I'm so thankful for all of your help."

"No, miss." He looked from me to Brodie. "I work for the county."

Oh no. My stomach dropped. "Are you going to fine us? Please, you have to understand, I didn't know Brodie had this grand idea to fix us up today. I would've stopped him had I known."

Brodie snorted.

184

"With violence if necessary," I added, meaning every word.

"No fine, ma'am." His gaze returned to me. "Mr. Gett *asked* me to come out to inspect the rackhouse early this morning."

"Oh."

"Lucky Whiskey is welcome to do whatever you need to do to get back in distribution, at least in an official capacity." He chewed his lip, the hair above his upper lip dancing. "We all heard about your recent misfortunes. I hope this lessens some of the burden."

Wetness threatened to leak from the corner of my eyes, but I managed to blink it away before Brodie or anyone else noticed. "Thank you."

He nodded, clearly uncomfortable.

"Thanks again, George," Brodie said, patting the man on his shoulder. "Rue sends her regards." At the mention of Brodie's grandmother's name, George's face grew gray in color. I winced, feeling sorry for him while wondering just what dark secret Rue held over the man.

Blackmail was her specialty after all.

George did the smart thing: He said nothing and slowly crept away.

"You forced him to come here." I tilted my head. "Why?"

"Why what?" Brodie looked honestly confused, as if his reasons were as clear as the water we used for Lucky's Finest. "It's Gett. You need help. We're here to help." He looked down at me with a grin so patronizing I nearly smacked it off his handsome face. "Guess it doesn't work that way in L.A."

Not even close. Often when the fancy mansions slide off the cliffs after a rain, the people on the other side of the 101 cheer, happy their view has opened up. "Whatever your motives," my voice rose, to include the men and women of Gett willing to spend their day helping

185

out their fellow man—or in this case, pathetic-looking woman—
"Thank you all. You have no idea how much we appreciate your help."

"Beers are in the cooler. Cleaning supplies in the back of my Jeep.
And you"—Brodie pointed at me—"back to bed. You look like hell."
With that pronouncement, he revved up the saw once more and went
to work.

CHAPTER

30

I DIDN'T QUITE FOLLOW Brodie's command. Instead, I took a moment to personally thank every one of the people from both distilleries. Some of the workers from Gett I recognized, as they'd worked for Lucky at a time or two. I shook hands with each and asked if I could aid them in any way. Most looked at me with sympathy, and sometimes downright horror.

I must look worse than I thought.

The bruises all over my body had started to ache again. After I thanked everyone, I headed for the house to down half a bottle of Advil. The doctor had prescribed painkillers, but I needed to stay alert so I opted for the Advil and a thermos of coffee. It almost did the trick.

Once fortified with enough caffeine to fuel an army, I headed back outside to help however I could. Which turned out to be very little. Every time I tried to do something, one of the workers jumped in and took over.

Like I was cursed or something.

The *or something* turned out to be Brodie Gett.

It soon became apparent Brodie had ordered the workers to keep me as far away from the heavy lifting as possible. They wouldn't even let me wipe down the copper stills used in the final distilling process, a job a tall two-year-old could do. Feeling much like a petulant one, I stuck my tongue out at his broad back.

As much as his high-handedness bothered me, I did appreciate the gesture, especially when the Advil wore off a few hours later.

My goodwill toward Brodie Gett vanished much sooner.

Since no one would let me do anything, I journeyed toward the house. Might as well get some paperwork done if nothing else. My stroll brought me in the path of Brodie's Jeep.

Headlights, and then my car flipping end over end flashed through my mind.

As I passed his Jeep, I quickly surveyed it. I stumbled, nearly falling. I grabbed onto the Jeep, my heart slamming in my chest. Brodie's right fender was dented and a streak of white paint, the very same color as my Prius, stood out on his dark undercoat.

Running a hand over the whiteness, I frowned as it flecked away. Had Brodie truly tried to kill me? Until this moment, I'd only toyed with the idea he was capable of murder. But now …

"What's that look?" Brodie suddenly appeared at my side, shooting me a grin. "You look like a drunk at last call."

I tried to smile, but it came off more as a grimace. "I was just thinking about Jack, and how much it means for the town to come together to help us," I lied.

"Right."

Unable to control myself, I recklessly waved to his Jeep. "Looks like I wasn't the only one who had an accident last night."

His eyes narrowed and his lips thinned. "Are you accusing me of something?"

"Not at all." I touched my nose to make sure it hadn't grown after that lie. It hadn't. But it did hurt to touch.

The frown didn't leave his face, but rather intensified until the heat of it threatened to start another fire. "Do you think I'm a coward? That I'd stoop so low as to run you off the road because you … annoy me?"

His statement hurt more than I cared to admit. I wasn't the annoying one in our relationship. He was, dang it. "Did you?" I asked in a clear voice, at odds with the queasy feeling bubbling in my stomach.

"I take it I need yet another alibi. Fine." He threw up his hands. "First of all, the damage to my Jeep happened six hours before you landed upside-down in the ditch. Second, though it's not any of your business, I was with … someone last night, when your accident happened." He hesitated. "If it comes down to it, they can vouch for me."

I'd have bet the distillery that someone was of the female persuasion. "Does *someone* have a name?"

"Why? Are you jealous?"

"No," I snapped. Maybe too fast. Was I jealous? I didn't think so. Brodie, while extremely good-looking, wasn't my type and I sure as heck wasn't his. So who was? Who would alibi him?

I had my money on Mary. Since Roger's death, the two of them had gotten chummy, apparently resuming their former relationship. Was that more motive for Roger's demise? Had Mary killed him to get with Brodie? I smiled at the thought.

But no. That didn't fit. Why commit murder when you could just break up? This brought up another question. What about Brodie? Had he wanted what Roger had? Was his desire for Mary enough to kill for?

"It doesn't matter," Brodie was saying. "I didn't run you off the road. But someone did, or so Danny said you believed."

"I was there when it happened. So I think I'd know." I gave a pointed look to his Jeep. "Someone in a dark-colored Jeep hit the back of my

189

driver's side, causing my car to spin out. They did it on purpose."
I frowned when he failed to look convinced. "You don't believe me."

He shrugged. "People drive like idiots. I'm sure the driver was nothing more than some drunk who misjudged the amount of room he had to pass you."

I considered this. At the time the other car had seemed so deliberate. Could Brodie be right? Could the accident have been nothing more than that? The fear that had filled me since the night before lifted a bit. My muscles, once bunched tight, relaxed. I took a long, deep breath. Maybe Brodie was right. It was an accident. No one wanted me dead. Especially not one of the Getts.

Then I saw it. As clear as day.

An inch-long sticker on Brodie's windshield.

The very same sticker as the one on the car in the video of Roger's last moments.

CHAPTER

31

I STARTED TO ASK Brodie about the decal, what it meant, but stopped myself in time. Somehow he was connected with the murder, whether he pulled the trigger or not. The sticker proved it. I had to find out what it stood for, and then I'd have the killer or killers. Adrenaline shot through my body. So much so that my hands shook.

"Charms?" Brodie said, concern apparent in every muscle in his handsome face. "You okay?"

Thinking fast, I said, "I could use a glass of water."

"Of course." Moving around the Jeep, he reached into the cooler, pulling out an icy bottle. Beads of sweat dripped from it. Damn. I needed him away from the Jeep so I could get a better look at the sticker without tipping him off. Channeling my inner brat, I frowned at his outstretched hand. "Ice?" I asked with an internal wince.

His eyes narrowed, and for a moment it looked like he would protest, but he just nodded. "Your wish is my command." He tossed me the water bottle, which I caught with only a mild cry, and then headed for my house.

He'd agreed much too rapidly for my peace of mind.

Maybe I'd always expect an argument from him. A snide comment here, an unkind word there.

Too much residual high school insecurity.

I was a big girl now. I shouldn't let Brodie push my buttons again.

Once he entered the house, I ran as fast as my sore muscles would carry me to the front of his Jeep. I ran my eyes over the decal, the scowl on my face growing. Where I'd expected to see a name embossed in the plastic, I saw nothing but white. My finger brushed the sticker, feeling around. The label wasn't flat, but instead raised at certain points, as if it held a secret larger than the name of Roger's killer.

Was it one of those thingies that protected expensive clothing? Not that I shopped in stores like that. What was it doing on Brodie's Jeep and the killer's car? I used my fingernail to dig around the adhesive, but the decal wouldn't come loose.

Damn.

Brodie appeared in the doorframe of the house. I jumped away from his Jeep as if scalded. He walked over to me, his face fixed in a cold stare. He pushed the glass of ice in his hand at me. "Still don't trust me, huh?"

"What?" I stammered. "I … ah …"

"Forget it, Charms," he said with a frown. "I'm not a fool. I can see you were checking the Jeep's damage."

"I …"

He snorted. "Can't think of a plausible lie?" He glanced at the Jeep, and then at me. "I don't know why I even bother. I get it. I'm a Gett. Untrustworthy." The starkness in his face almost had me blurting out the truth, but I stopped myself in time. "Have it your way," he said. "Once I'm done here, you go your way, and I'll do my thing. Never should the two cross." With those parting words, he headed back to the rackhouse.

I didn't see him for the rest of the day.

Not that I wanted to.

Yet, guilt weighed on me, mainly when I noticed his Jeep, in the same place it had been parked this morning, as I prepared for bed. I turned the lights out, my last thoughts of Brodie and that damning decal on his windshield.

———

The next morning, the decal hadn't left my mind. Though I was thankful the memory of the betrayal on Brodie's face had. I knew, deep in my heart, the sticker was the clue I needed to find the killer. Lucky for me, Gett wasn't big on the future of electronics. Smart phones aside.

Which meant the one and only electronic shop in the county, about an hour north, would know what a decal like the one on Brodie's Jeep was for, and likely who it was purchased by. If I could track down the reason for the decal, I would eventually find the killer. Sure, it would be easier to straight out ask Brodie, but would I be able to trust his answer?

I doubted it. Particularly if it involved Rue Gett.

Dressing swiftly, or as fast as one could when bruises covered 50 percent of your body, I tossed on a pair of jeans and a plain white t-shirt. I opted for my boots rather than sandals, even in the ninety-degree heat. In a town built on swampland, the odds of encountering slithering wildlife were fifty/fifty on a good day. For a minute, I longed for the non-snake-riddled sidewalks of L.A. Then I remembered L.A. had its very own variety of snake. I'd fought off my share of casting couch producers during my brief acting career. It was one of the things I didn't miss.

Today's adventure would take me fifty miles north to Immokalee, a town of about three hundred thousand, with its own Starbucks. My taste buds flickered to life at the thought of a venti vanilla latte. It had been far too long since I'd drank the caffeinated goodness.

But my dream cup of coffee would have to wait.

I parked Jack's pickup truck—a beat-up 1970s Ford Jack vowed to drive until either it or he took the long, lone highway—in the lot behind a strip of shops. My odds were on the truck going first. The poor thing, gas pedal to the floor, barely hit sixty on the interstate. Cars had whipped around us at incredible speeds. My heart leapt in my throat every time I caught sight of another car on the pickup's bumper.

By the time I'd arrived at the electronics store, my hands ached from my hard, tight grip on the wheel.

My accident had affected me more than I'd first thought.

I took a deep breath, rubbing the imprint of the steering wheel cover from my palms. Once I'd collected myself enough not to sound like a blabbering idiot, I stepped from the pickup, smiling as the bright Florida sun warmed my chilled skin.

I'd always liked Immokalee. It was ten times larger than Gett, but held on to the small-town appeal. Small row houses with perfectly manicured lawns, even under the damaging rays of the sun, stood proudly like soldiers ready for battle. The storefronts were clean and neat too. People walked around in shorts and t-shirts, smiles and welcoming hellos on their faces. Very different than L.A., where the only welcoming smiles were from mid-western tourists. Smiles they often lost, along with wallets and watches, before their trips were over.

I strolled into Collier Electronics with a mission in mind. The store looked like a smaller version of Best Buy. Fancy electronics lined the rows, as did teens with backpacks. One couldn't even pass the video game aisle without a contact high from the amount of acne medicine and cheap weed.

"Can I help you?" asked a friendly woman wearing a red vest, her hair streaked in typical Florida style. Lots of blond, black roots.

"I hope so," I said "Can you tell me a little about those electronic stickers? You know, the ones they use on clothes to stop thefts or have on cars ...?"

"Oh, RFID stickers. Let me call Brent. He's our RFID expert," she said as she used the intercom.

Brent arrived a few minutes later, a red tie and vest covering his chest. He pushed up his black-rimmed glasses as his eyes slid over my body in a less-than-professional way. Considering the bruises on my face, his appraisal was only mildly annoying.

"Hello there," he said with a confident grin. A very confident smile for a guy with thick glasses and a pocket protector. Then again, nerds were in. I thought of all my Hollywood friends, with once perfect eyesight, who'd suddenly developed astigmatisms after a popular magazine coined the term Geek Chic. "How can I help you, Mrs. ...?" he prompted.

This was where I was to say, "Oh, I'm not married," which would provoke an invitation to dinner at the very least. Given Brent's confident manner, perhaps his invite would hold a little something extra, like a chance to see the backroom where "the magic" happened. Why not forgo the inevitable? "Jones," I responded. "*Mrs.* Jones."

His brow wrinkled, sending his glasses farther down his nose. He pushed them back in place with a single finger. "Do I know you?" he asked, tilting his head like an owl. "You look very familiar. Are you from around here?"

Crap. I knew what was coming, but still his next words made me flinch. "Oh, that's it!" he said. "I saw you on TV. A commercial." His grin turned into a leer, the kind normally associated with my STD fame. His eyes fell on my breasts. "You do good work."

"Thanks," I mumbled. "Brent, listen, I need your help with a little problem."

"Anything for a star," he said, and sadly meant it. I imagined much of his life was spent in front of the TV, fantasizing about scantily clad women and dreaming of being a hero. The angel on my shoulder told me to leave it alone, but the devil won out in the end.

I blinked my eyes up at him. "Thank you. You're my hero."

And just like that Brent turned into one.

He walked me through what RFID was, explained how it worked and the different types. Basically it boiled down to this: the decal on the vehicles held a tiny electronic chip that used radio frequencies to do various things, like indicate when someone walked out of a store without paying for an item.

"What would it be used for on a car windshield?" I asked, though I had a fairly good idea. Transponders. The kind used on HOV lanes of the highway in the richer counties like Miami-Dade. A plain ridiculous notion in Gett. So why did Brodie and the killer's vehicle have them?

"They could have plenty of uses." He pulled out a small RFID tag from a stack on the shelf next to us. "For example, a business could use them to track an employee coming and going." He picked up another sticker, larger than the first. "Or even use the chip to unlock a gate or open a garage door."

I frowned, remembering my brief trip to Gett Whiskey a week ago. A week that seemed much like a lifetime ago. At the time I'd wondered about the lack of a guard at the gate, and yet, an armed one roaming the grounds. But what if Gett used an RFID system to unlock the gate?

Hope faded as my list of suspects went from a few to anyone who worked at Gett or had worked there in the recent past. The pool of suspects was now as wide as the mouth of Lake Immokalee.

Disappointment stiffened my tone. "Is there any way to know what or who a sticker belongs to?"

"By sight?" He shook his head. "No. Unless it's labeled of course."

"Of course."

His fingers rubbed his chin, much like an evil genius. "Thatv is, unless you have an RFID reader."

"Show me," I said, following him to a rack of what looked much like all the other computer equipment. Plastic boxes in different colors filled with circuits and wires. Not one piece of equipment looked familiar. I felt oddly out of my element. Thankfully Brent knew everything about each piece.

"Voila," he said, pointing. "You said it's on a car, right?" he asked. "Must have a high frequency."

I shrugged.

He smiled, knowingly. "What you need is an ultra-high frequency RFID reader."

If he said so. "How much do they run?"

"Six hundred," he said. "But you're in luck. I have a refurbished Juno handheld for three forty-six."

I grimaced, remembering my near-empty bank account and a distillery barely producing small batch whiskies. "Can I rent it? I only need it for a couple of days."

"I wish I could…"

"Please," I added a husky plea to my tone. The very one that won me the STD commercial in the first place. "I really do need it."

"How about you buy it and then bring it back for a full refund in a few days?" he whispered. "Maybe then, we can grab a drink?" When I didn't respond, he said, "A coffee?" His voice hopeful.

I hated to break his nerdy heart, and he had helped me. "Sure," I said. Then I noticed he was staring at my breasts again. I crossed my arms over my chest. "Coffee only."

"You got it, babe." He handed me a device that looked like a fat TV remote with a red laser on the front. "Looking forward to our date," he said louder than needed.

"Right," I said. "Can you show me how to use this?"

"My pleasure." He took a step forward, too close for comfort. His breath smelled of coffee and that chemical fragrance of spray mint breath freshener. Not the most pleasant of scents. Ever so slowly, he offered instructions for the reader. All of which amounted to: point the red laser at the decal and press the green button. Supposedly the owner or other info would show on the small screen.

Not rocket science but from the look in his eyes, much too much for a woman with my small brain to handle. I wanted to stomp on his foot, but refrained. After all, he was much less likely to let me borrow the reader if I did so. Then again, he might like it. That thought kept me far from his foot, let alone his thin body.

What felt like an eternity later, I left the store with the reader tucked firmly in my purse.

Soon I would have the answers I needed. A shiver ran through me despite the warmth of the Florida sunshine.

CHAPTER

32

ARMED WITH AN **RFID** reader and a rusted-out pickup, I made my way back to town with only a brief stop at Starbucks. The vanilla iced latte went down much too smoothly. Before I even hit the highway, I was sucking on the ice cubes with regret. I'd never been one to savor anything but a fine whiskey. Savoring took time. And time, it felt like, was the one thing none of us genuinely had.

Now that I found myself in possession of an RFID reader, I needed an RFID sticker to test. The one vehicle, besides the killer's, that had just what I needed was Brodie's Jeep.

Considering I saw the Jeep parked at the Gett Bar & Grill more often than not, I detoured toward the watering hole.

Surprisingly Brodie's Jeep was not in the parking lot.

And just as unfortunate for me, Willow Jones was.

She leaned against the brick, one jean-clad foot kicked over the other. She held up her hand in a small wave as I drove by. In order not to raise suspicion, or rumors I was stalking Brodie, I parked the truck and got out.

"Hot out," I said, inanely.

She nodded, a small smile flickering over her face.

"Slow day?" I motioned to the empty parking lot.

A single shoulder lifted.

I frowned as a single tear ran down her pale cheek. "Are you all right?"

She swiped at the wetness. "Why wouldn't I be?" She snorted. "I've done nothing with the last ten years of my life. Spent it waiting around here, while I should've been exploring the world. Today was the last straw. I'm done with Gett. For good."

I knew how she felt. As a teen, I'd longed to be free of Gett, and the Getts. But I learned an important lesson upon my return. The things that had drove me away, the broken pieces inside me, hadn't magically glued themselves back together once I stepped beyond the town limits. I wanted to tell Willow as much, but she'd disappeared back inside the bar.

I stood staring at the door of the bar.

Then I turned back to the pickup to find the one Gett who might free Jack from prison.

Or rather, his Jeep. I'd gladly avoid the man.

Frustration filled me when I pulled up to my house. Brodie's Jeep wasn't in the drive. Yet noises from the distillery drew me. Maybe Brodie had parked around the back? I headed inside Lucky Whiskey, inhaling deeply as I did every time. My blood warmed and my body relaxed just being there. Workers smiled and nodded as they passed. It was good to be up and running. They knew it as much as I did, probably more.

Longtime foreman Remy Ray gave me a wave, his hand shaking slightly from Parkinson's disease. Remy had been the foreman for as long as I could remember. Jack's right hand, many times. "How's it going, girl?" he asked with a wide smile, showing off two missing front teeth.

I swallowed back a retort at the blatant sexism. The whiskey business was not what anyone with the ability to see or hear would call progressive. Plenty of men were shocked to see a woman drink whiskey, let alone know enough about it to run a distillery. Not that I did. Yet.

Nonetheless, Remy didn't mean any harm by his words. The old-timers all called me girl. Why wouldn't they when my very own grandfather did the same? "What's going on, Remy?" I asked, waving around the rackhouse. "Things getting back to normal?"

His grin grew. "The wort's cooling as we speak."

"That's great news," I said with excitement. The wort process was the most delicate step in making a smooth whiskey. The mash was stirred for hours, sucking down the sugars that were eventually fermented in large steel tanks called washbacks. Sixty-seven hours later, the vapors collected in the fermentation process were placed in the copper stills. The process was repeated twice more until the finest whiskey was born. "Anything I can do to help?" I asked.

He looked me up and down slowly, his grin quickly changing to a familiar frown. "You should rest."

His words sounded much like Brodie's, which reminded me of the question I wanted to ask. "I'm fine. But thank you for your concern." I bit my lip. If I posed the question wrong, I'd tip the killer off for sure as well as piss off a large contingent of the town. "You used to work at Gett, right?"

He shrugged. "I sometimes moonlight when Rue asks. Jack doesn't mind," he added, as if I might. "He says it's good to know the competition."

"It is. For sure." I patted his arm. Tremors rippled just underneath his skin. "What I wanted to ask about is Rue."

His stern features grew more so, bushy gray eyebrows near swallowing his face. "What about her?"

"How's she getting along these days?"

Remy's shoulders lifted into another shrug. "She's getting up there. Celebrated her eightieth a few months ago." His smile was back. "Hell of a party."

Rue Gett, though she might not be an outright killer, knew how to throw a killer party. Everyone in town was invited to her yearly birthday bash, and they came, stomachs and livers ready to enjoy the finest spread in five counties. The whiskey served wasn't bad either. Not Lucky, though; Rue made a point of that. Though, surprisingly, she did invite the Luckys every year. Jack's name was always written in her scrawl on invitations.

I thought back to the letter's I'd found in the box in the back of Jack's closet and frowned. Was it the same scrawled writing? Take away the ravages of age, and just maybe ...

Ridiculous. Rue and Jack? That was crazy. They hated each other. Competed at everything. They were far from star-crossed lovers. The very idea sent a laugh bubbling from my throat. "Did Roger go to Rue's birthday party?" I asked once I regained my sanity.

"Sure. Everyone in town went." His smile dimmed somewhat. "Even her youngest grandson. I remember because he and Roger had a bit of a dust-up."

"Brodie?"

"That's the one. Fighting over a girl or something." He shook his head, as if a woman didn't rank high enough to merit fighting over. "Rue put a stop to it. Smacked that boy right upside the head. The two men shook hands and parted ways."

"And that was that?"

He snorted. "You know better than that, girl. Roger wasn't one to let anything go that easy. Remember how he pestered you after you caught him with that other girl?"

I nodded. For a few weeks, he refused to let me alone. Then suddenly, he stopped bugging me. Simply gave up. Or had he? Had Jack had a hand in it? I'd always wondered, but never asked.

Remy rubbed his whiskery chin. "Given the chance, Kerrick would've caused that Gett boy some pain." He stared at me for a long pause. "You watch out, girl."

I blinked at the quick turn in conversation. "For what?"

"You don't want to be on the Getts' bad side either."

"I'm not..."

He placed his weathered hand over mine. "Keep it that way."

CHAPTER

33

A FEW HOURS LATER, after dealing with a long list of distillery business, I found my way once again to the Gett Bar & Grill. More precisely, to the dirt parking lot just off to the side, to repeat my earlier attempt at reading Brodie's RFID sticker. If the decal came back registered to Gett Whiskey, I'd bring my evidence to the state's attorney with the help of Jack's lawyer. Let's see Danny Gett try and bury it then.

Unless Danny had already destroyed the tape.

Damn. No way around it. I had to find the killer's car. The same one on the tape. Emmett could swear, under oath, he'd seen it on the tape.

Luck was on my side at this moment. Brodie's Jeep was parked in the spot closest to the bar. I snorted. Not hard to find good parking when it was barely eleven in the morning. Maybe Brodie was having a harder time adjusting to life outside the military than some? Or maybe I was just projecting my own career crossroads. One day soon I'd have to decide if I wanted back in the limelight. But not today. Today I was playing the role of homicide detective. A role I was far from born to play.

I parked Jack's pickup, jumped out, and readied the RFID reader in my hand. Moment of truth. If this decal was from Gett Whiskey, I had proof that someone closer to Gett Whiskey had killed Roger, and not my grandfather. I took a deep breath.

And my phone in my pocket buzzed to life.

I practically jumped out of my skin as I dropped the reader in the dirt. I scrambled to pick it up while quieting my phone. Was the ringer always this loud? My heart slammed in my chest as the bar door opened. I ran back to the pickup as fast as my battered muscles could carry me. My cell gave another shrill screech. I glanced down to see who had ruined my plans. The caller ID shocked me to my core.

Rue Gett.

Was she some kind of witch who could see the future? Or perhaps she had someone following me? My eyes danced around the landscape, spotting no one out of the ordinary. I answered slowly, unsure. "Hello?"

"Charlotte," her voice warmed the airwaves, "how are you, dear?"

She hadn't even bothered to introduce herself. I looked even harder for a tail. Seeing none, I focused on the phone. "Rue. Good to hear from you," I lied. Considering she'd never contacted me personally before, the hairs on my neck rose in warning.

"Dear," she said, voice shaking, "I hope you'll do me the honor of joining me for dinner tomorrow night after Roger is laid to rest."

What the hell? My frown deepened. Dinner with Rue? I'd expect Grodie Brodie to ask me on a dinner date far sooner than his eighty-year-old grandmother. I wasn't sure I'd have a better answer for him than the one I gave Rue. "Ummm," I mumbled.

"Please." She sounded strangely weak, as if age had caught up with her.

I didn't buy it for a moment.

Rue used her advanced age as leverage. She always had, though she hadn't always been in her eighties. Then again, maybe she was sick and Brodie hadn't told me. At least that would explain why he was home in Gett with seemingly nothing really to do.

"Sure," I said, unable to think of a genuine reason to decline. Other than her being an outright murderer intent on doing me in too. I grinned at the thought. I was far more likely to die outside the Gett estate than in it.

Unless Rue planned on cooking dinner.

Her kitchen exploits were the stuff of legends around Gett. Some claim her husband died so he didn't have to endure another Rue-cooked meal. As soon as Gett Whiskey turned a profit, Rue had hired a cook, a no-no in the decade before bra-burning.

"What time would you like me there?" I asked softly.

"Oh, dear, I'll have a car pick you up."

I shook my head, realizing too late she couldn't see me. Heat stained my cheeks. "No, that's all right." I didn't want to be trapped at the Gett estate. Plus, I'd have a better opportunity to look around for clues if I walked there. Not sure what I expected to find, but I knew there was something there. Had to be. Every cell in my body screamed the Getts were somehow involved.

"If that's what you want ..." She trailed off. "Shall we say eight o'clock?"

"Sounds good," I said, though I would've preferred a thief to the eye. Unwillingly, the image of Roger's head, stabbed multiple times by my own thief, came to mind. Okay, so maybe not. "See you soon." I hung up, unable to believe my continued bad luck.

When would I catch a break?

"Hey Charms," Brodie said. "You're looking a little better than the last time I saw you."

My head whipped up, surprised to see him standing in front of me, a hesitant smile on his face. "Um, hi," I said. What did he mean a little better? Was that an insult? I patted my shaggy hairdo. I really needed a haircut.

His eyebrow rose. "What are you doing here?"

My back straightened. Like it was any of his business where I went. "I wanted a drink."

"Go home," he said in no uncertain terms.

"What?!"

He leaned in, all six-foot of him. "I said, *go home*. This is no place for you."

Rather than intimidate me, his gravely tone pissed me off. I laughed without humor. "Who made you boss?"

Rather than answer my question, he asked one of his own. "Boone's inside." He smiled cruelly. "Want to come say hi?"

"You can be a real jerk, Brodie Gett." With that, I climbed into Jack's pickup, RFID scanner on the seat next to me where I'd thrown it when Rue called. Starting the pickup, my gaze lingered on Brodie's Jeep, and then back to the man himself.

A man who stood with his hands behind him, watching me.

Like predator to prey.

"Another time," I whispered to the RFID reader.

CHAPTER

34

Since Brodie had ruined my chance at reading the decal on his windshield, I drove down Main Street, dreading my next stop even more than I did dinner at Rue's. I'd tried hard to avoid it, to continue to live in denial as I had for the last few weeks, but Brodie's words had burst my bubble.

It was true.

I needed a haircut. Badly.

Specifically, before my dreaded dinner date with Rue Gett, who, on top of her perfect manners, always appeared immaculately dressed, not a hair out of place, placing judgment on those of us without innate style and grace. Next to Rue, I felt like a clumsy, oversized oaf. An oaf with Little Orphan Annie hair and too many cuts and bruises to count. Though I knew Jack didn't care, I didn't want my appearance to embarrass the Lucky name. My water tower adventure had done enough.

I had one option to fix myself up—The Gett Curl & Dye.

Might as well make the best of it.

I entered the hair salon, if one could call it that, and was greeted with eleven eyes flying my way. Yes, I said eleven. Mrs. Branson lost her eye years ago after a hunting "accident" that also ended up killing her abusive husband. Speculation was, her gun had misfired right around the time Boris took the same caliber bullet to the noggin. Not that a single person in Gett had cared—well, other than the sheriff at the time. Boris was an outsider after all, born two towns away. Everyone had warned Mrs. Branson not to marry a man from Kent, but she'd gone and done it anyway.

I raised a tentative hand. "Hi."

"Well, well, if it ain't Charlotte Lucky," Nanette Rogers said, snapping the gum in her mouth. We'd gone to school together until she'd dropped out her sophomore year. The official story was, she left to spend time with her great aunt. The unofficial version added in a pregnancy, and later a closed adoption of said baby. Either way, when she returned to Gett, Nanette was no longer the same girl. She got herself a job sweeping hair at The Gett Curl & Dye and never looked back.

"Haven't seen you around much," she said. "Not since you climbed the water tower to paint it. What did you write again?" She snapped her fingers before I could respond. "That's right. Getting Lucky." The other ladies glared at me. "A little on the nose for my taste," she said, popping her gum again.

When would people forget? I wished my drunken amnesia regarding that night could spread to the whole town. But it wasn't to be. So I affected a warm smile for the speaker with teased hair tall enough to make a Texan jealous. "It's good to be home. But, as you can see"—I patted my own hair, thankfully not quite as big—"I'm in need of a trim."

She snapped her gum yet again. An annoying habit, but one I'd put up with as long as she didn't snap it out of her mouth and into my hair. She gave me a wide smile, as if she knew exactly what I'd been thinking. "I ain't one of them fancy Hollywood stylists."

I wasn't quite sure how to take that so I opted for a change in subject. "Where's Mrs. Bennet?" I asked after the woman who'd cut my hair every month like clockwork up until my seventeenth birthday.

The same haircut, mind you.

One similar to every other girl in school who also had the pleasure of a cut at the Curl & Dye. After years of repression, I admit to some experimentation when I arrived at my college dorm. Bangs and bleach, as well as a rainbow of colors, all self-administered, sometimes with disastrous results. In fact, I'd spent most of my senior year at college in a hat.

"Smoke break," Nannette said, motioning to the back. "Damn county won't let her smoke inside, even though it's her shop. What's next?"

I didn't comment, but I did breathe a little easier. The back of my neck still bore a scar from when I was twelve and Mrs. Bennett's cigarette ash had fallen just so. "Maybe you could give me a cut then?" I asked.

She looked me over for a long minute, then swung her empty barber chair around. "Sit," she ordered like one would an animal.

I sat.

Her hands yanked on my locks. "You could use a touch up on your color too."

"Sure," I said, my voice shaking only a little.

She nodded in the mirror, then left for coloring supplies. I counted to ten, willing away my panic. It was only hair. I could always get it fixed when I returned to L.A. I thought of the horrified look on Jaz, my

Hollywood stylist's face, and winced. He'd have my head for this. My stomach rolled, but I managed a small smile when Nanette returned.

She lined up bottle after bottle. "So what brings you in? Hot date with Brodie Gett?"

"What?" I choked. "Where did you get that idea? Brodie and I are not an item." What was it with this town? Just because a man and a woman shared the same space for a few minutes didn't mean they were involved in a hot affair.

Nannette grunted. "Sure, honey."

"No, really," I said, voice rising. "We are not involved. I swear it."

She tsked. "What's wrong with you? That Gett boy is fine." She shook her head. "Of course, he, like all the Getts, knows it. Gett's gift to women. Even my mom declared she wouldn't kick him out for eating crackers in her bed."

"So?"

She laughed. "Mom's in her fifties, with a bad hip and half blind to boot."

I'd walked into that one.

"Last I heard he was dating that Winter girl," a lady with her hair piled high on her head declared in an enhanced southern drawl. The drawl reserved for the juiciest of gossip.

"No, no," said Mrs. Drift, the one and only Sunday school teacher in the county. "They stopped hooking up, as the kids say, last month. He just up and dumped her." She shook her head as if unable to understand. "The girl was devastated. Foolish thing expected a ring."

"From what I hear, he started seeing the Lewis chit a few days after that." Mrs. Branson rubbed her good eyelid. "A week later she called my granddaughter, crying about how distant the Gett boy was. He ended things a few days later."

Another woman, younger than the rest, caught my eye. She looked vaguely familiar but I couldn't place where I'd seen her before. Her eyes were red rimmed, and it looked as if she'd spent most of her days crying. A shame, for without the aura of sadness around her, she practically glowed in that perky blond college kid way. Her blond coloring had started to fade though, leaving her skin tone even more washed out. She gave me a small smile that didn't reach her eyes.

"He's a womanizer for sure," Mrs. Drift said. "Just like his brother, his daddy, and his granddaddy before him." Her eyes met mine in the reflective glass. "You keep that in mind, girl."

"We are not—"

"I'm surprised nobody's shot one of those Gett boys for their womanizing ways yet," Nanette said, her gaze also on mine in the surface of the mirror. "No, it's always the good ones who are killed far too young."

I frowned, pulling from her grip on my hair. "Are you talking about Roger?"

"Say what you will about him, Roger loved his Mary." She gave a loud sigh. "June Wicket said he bought flowers every week." She sighed again. "Now that's love. The Gett boys, especially Danny—who I hear is dating three women, not one of them the right woman—could learn something from that."

The young woman, the one I couldn't place, leapt from the hair drying chair, hand over her mouth as she ran for the door. She pushed through it like barreling through a line of linebackers. I watched her run down the street and out of view as the door swung closed.

"What's with Nancy Jeanne?" Nanette asked, staring after the young woman.

Mrs. Drift looked up from an out-of-date magazine featuring a wedding picture of Brad and Jen. "You don't know?"

"What?"

"The girl's pregnant," she said, as if that explained everything. When the rest of us apparently didn't share her understanding, she added, "Guess who the father is?"

"Who?" Nanette leaned in.

I sat, trapped, between the gossiping women, wanting nothing more than to shove my hands over my ears and follow poor, pregnant Nancy Jeanne out the door. This was what I'd both hoped to avoid and prayed would happen, just not about an illegitimate pregnancy but rather the first lady of Gett herself, Rue Gett. Careful what you ask for.

"None other than Danny Gett," she whispered to the shocked gasps of those around her. She beamed, as if relishing her new role as lead gossip. "My boy, Benji, saw her get into his squad car a few days ago."

Mrs. Branson, seemingly more put off by her losing the gossip limelight than the gossip itself, sucked on her teeth. "So what? That doesn't prove anything. The Meade boy spends plenty of time in the backseat of Danny's squad car. Such a delinquent that one is ..."

Mrs. Drift smiled as if savoring her next statement. "Danny picked her up at Doc Wilson's place."

"Ah," the group collectively said.

"Who's Doctor Wilson?" I had been away too long if the town had managed to acquire their own doctor. Why hadn't anyone told me? And why did it automatically mean Danny was sleeping with the much younger woman? Let alone fathering her child?

"He's not really a doctor, at least not one with a fancy degree," Nanette said.

"He's a vet," Mrs. Drift said. "Works on the livestock."

She said the words so matter-of-factly that I frowned. It was as if nothing was wrong with a vet acting as an OB/GYN. Typical Gett.

"Oh." My sadness for poor Nancy Jeanne grew. Danny Gett could certainly afford a real baby doctor. What was wrong with him?

I bet Rue would have a fit, if she knew. Firsthand, I knew how she felt about illegitimate children. She'd never let Jack hear the end of it regarding my parents' marital status at the time of my birth. Then again, it was hardly a secret from the rest of the town either. In kindergarten I was introduced as *that bastard Lucky girl*.

If Rue learned the truth, she would have Danny and Nancy Jeanne married within a week.

For one brief moment, I considered blackmailing Danny to get Jack out of jail. I dismissed the notion out of hand. I wasn't stooping to acting like a Gett. Danny and his younger (much too young, in my opinion) baby momma could live in peace. Though I did feel sorry for Willow Jones. Danny's soon-to-be-daddy status had to be killing her, which explained her outburst outside the bar. I wondered if she would make good on her threat to leave Gett. And just how would Danny feel? If he ever *felt* anything.

"Are you going to Roger's memorial tomorrow?" Nanette asked, pulling me from my thoughts as she yanked me back in the chair by the hair. "We're booked all day today because of it." She sneered. "Guess everyone wants to look their best to pay their respects."

I squirmed at her tone.

"Such a shame." Again, her gaze met mine in the mirror.

I winced, for all eyes were on me, and looking none too happy. Did they believe the lies about Jack? "My granddad had nothing to do with Roger's death." I nodded for emphasis when no one looked convinced by my passionate denial.

After an awkward few seconds, Mrs. Drift spoke up. "We know that, sweetheart. Jack's a good man." Even as she said the words, I could see not one of the women agreed with them.

For Jack's sake, for the sake of future Luckys, I needed to find Roger's killer and fast before malicious gossip tainted the Lucky name forever.

"Now, what do you think about going a little bigger?" Nanette said, teasing my hair to unprecedented heights.

CHAPTER

35

THE NEXT MORNING I woke to the worst bed head in history and the best surprise of my life. My grandfather stood at the edge of my bed, his arms crossed and a frown on his bearded face. Not a shackle in sight.

"Girl," he said, "is this how you run my business? Sleeping all day?"

"How ...?" I rubbed my eyes, sure I was dreaming and Jack would disappear at any moment. When he didn't, I jumped out of bed, throwing my arms around him. I held him tight, afraid he'd vanish into the ether if I let go. He'd lost weight, and dark circles rimmed his eyes. Not as bad as the pair I was sporting, but blackened nonetheless. "How did you get out?" I pulled back to smile at him. "Did you break out? Are you a fugitive on the run?"

He laughed, big and bold, like I remembered. "Not quite, Char girl."

I stared at him for a long moment before saying, "I couldn't make the bail, even if I put up the distillery as collateral. So who sprung you?"

"No clue," he said, but his eyes wouldn't meet mine. Jack was lying. But why?

"Are you sure?"

"Leave it alone, Char. The cops put this dang ankle monitor on," he pointed to the object around his leg, "Then they opened the gate, and I left before someone changed their mind."

"Really?"

"I'm a semi-free man." He shot me a quick grin. "As long as I don't go more than three hundred feet from the house, with the exception of any and all doctors' appointments. Guess they don't want me to die until I get Old Sparky."

"That won't happen." My tone conveyed complete conviction. When he raised an eyebrow, I added, "They haven't used Old Sparky since 2000."

"Lucky me," he said with a greater laugh. "I'll get lethal injection then."

"I won't let that happen either." I ran my finger up and over my heart, making a sign of the cross. "I promise. I'm close to figuring this mess out."

His bushy eyebrow, badly in need of a trim, rose. "I can see that." He motioned to the multiple bruises covering my arms and face. "Real close. I don't want you involved in this anymore. Do you hear me, girl?"

I agreed with a nod, having absolutely no intention of listening to him. I patted his arm. The skin felt papery thin under my touch. "I'm going to let the professionals handle it from here on out."

The suspicion fell away from his face, and he patted my shoulder lightly in return, as if afraid to add to my current collection of welts. "That's a good girl. Now what do you say to a nice homemade breakfast?"

"Sure." I smiled up at him brightly. "What will you be cooking us?"

We gorged on a breakfast of eggs and bacon—turkey bacon, much to Jack's disgust, but seeing as I was the chef, he had little choice in the menu. We talked of inconsequential things. Never once did I mention the murder, his arrest, or the trouble at the distillery. Which left us with weather highlights and local gossip.

Oddly enough, Jack refused to believe the worst of Danny Gett, even though I'd witnessed Nancy Jeanne's meltdown with my own eyes.

"Danny's a lot of things, girl," Jack said, slurping at a glass of orange juice I'd squeezed moments ago. "But that boy is nothing like his daddy."

Danny and Brodie's father, Big Paul Gett, had quite the love 'em and leave 'em reputation. All my life I'd heard whispered stories about his long line of mistresses and even a bastard or two. I'd even met one of his longtime mistresses once.

Danny and Brodie's mother ignored the rumors, acting like a picture-perfect first family of Gett. I'd felt sorry for Danny and Brodie even as I did my best to steer clear of them. It had to be hard living in Paul's reckless, womanizing shadow.

"I know," I said to Jack. "But I saw her face. Nancy Jeanne was devastated by the gossip about Danny and three other women."

A puzzle to be sure. But one I didn't care about. Not unless it helped me find a killer.

After we finished eating and I cleared the dirty dishes, I grabbed the keys of his old pickup and drove to the Wicket Bouquet flower shop in Harker.

The Wickets were known to most people in Gett. June Wicket's mother had been born and raised in our town limits. The only reason June had left Gett was to open the flower shop in a town large enough to support one. Not that Harker was all that big, population around 3,000.

The Wicket Bouquet was the only flower shop for fifty miles, therefore, the only one men used when in the doghouse with their wives. It was also the only shop in a fifty-mile radius to buy flowers for Roger's memorial. I only hoped June would have something left in stock.

I opened the door of the shop, inhaling the warm and welcoming scents of jasmine, lilacs, and roses. My breathing instantly slowed, as did my pulse. Nothing like a flower shop to ease one's stress. Vibrant colors, reds, yellows, and greens filled my eyes, almost too many for my brain to comprehend.

"How can I help ..." June appeared from behind a large fern. "*You.*" She sneered the last word when she saw it was me, telling me that June still held a grudge. At the time of my unfortunate prank, June Wicket had been in charge of the town's conservation committee. Which normally was a place for the town gossips to share notes. Until that fateful night.

I'd made June look bad and she wasn't going to let me forget it.

"Hi June." I gave her a friendly wave. "Lovely shop."

"Thanks," she muttered. "What is it *you* want?"

"I'm back in Gett," I said, in case she didn't know. A fact I doubted. "Helping Jack while he recuperates from his heart troubles. By the way, thank you for the beautiful get well displays sent to the house by Jack's friends." I pictured Jack among the bouquets. He'd hated them. Made me toss each one out as soon as they arrived. To Jack, flowers were for two things—courting and funerals. He'd declared he was too young to die and he wasn't up to any courting just yet.

Or ever.

As far as I could remember, Jack had never brought a woman home. He'd loved and lost once. Never wishing to repeat it. My mind flashed on the stack of letters I'd found in Jack's bedroom, but I shook

219

it away. Whoever those letters were from was Jack's business. I wouldn't intrude. At least no more than I already had.

"Your grandfather is well liked," June said, dragging me to the present. "Or he *was* until he, true to the Lucky nature, acted on his baser impulses."

CHAPTER

36

I TRIED TO KEEP the artificial smile plastered on my face, but it slipped a few notches under June's cruelty. Breathe, I ordered my lungs. After they complied I motioned to a small *Gone but not forgotten* wreath on my right. As much as I wanted to tell June to choke on it, I said, "Can I buy this, please?"

"Why?" She sneered again. "You Luckys planning on killing someone else?"

As much as I wished June dead at the moment, I opted for a less violent approach. "Not today." I laughed like she'd made a hilarious joke. "But I would like to buy Mary some of your fragrant flowers. Hopefully it makes her feel a fraction better." That much was true. I couldn't imagine how difficult tomorrow's service would be for Mary. Losing someone you loved was bad enough, but losing them to a senseless crime … My heart ached for her.

"Oh." June's attitude lost some of its edge. Her face, however, remained cold. "We have two sizes, and can deliver"—she stopped, raising her thick eyebrow—"if you don't plan to attend the service."

"Oh, I'll be there." My smile hardened. "You can count on it."

Her face pinched, as if my sheer presence in a house of God would rain fire on the faithful. Her reaction instantly brightened my day. I bit my lip to keep from laughing while I acted like I was deciding between the different, albeit by a slim variance, of sizes.

She stood there, fuming.

Finally, I pointed to the larger of the two. "I'll take that one. And yes, please deliver it."

Nodding, she headed behind the counter to ring up my purchase on an antiquated cash register. I suspected she hadn't heard of Quick-Books, let alone the computer age. I glowered as she added the total up by hand on the paper next to her.

What seemed like an hour later, she said, "That will be eighty-seven dollars. We only take cash." *From the likes of you*, was implied in her tone.

"But it says you take Visa." I waved to the register, with the VISA sticker on the side under a *We accept* sticky note.

"Misprint," she said with a shrug.

"But it's in your handwriting."

"What can I say?" she scoffed.

"You can say you'll take my Visa." My voice rose.

"Sorry, no."

I pulled out my wallet, counting out enough money to cover the cost. Thankfully I had two dollars to spare. Now to get down to the real purpose for my visit. "Can I ask you a question?"

She nodded, though her heart wasn't in it.

"Nanette at the Curl & Dye said Roger bought Mary a bouquet each week." If I could trace Roger's Visa card purchases, maybe I could find the Lucky Whiskey's embezzled funds. Or better yet, another motive for his murder. I didn't like my weak one at the moment.

Yes, Rue wanted Lucky Whiskey, but that was nothing new. She'd never killed for it before. Something had to have threatened her way of life to act in such a manner.

June snorted. "Not from me."

"What?"

"That man didn't buy *Mary* a single rose from my store."

Something in her tone had my ears perking up. Had she emphasized the word *Mary*? I crooked my head. "But he did buy flowers here."

Looking around as if to make sure no one else was in the obviously empty shop, she began, "That—"

Bells jangled from over the front door of the shop. Our eyes swung to the interloper. June froze, her mouth hanging open as Grodie Brodie Gett strolled inside. At once, she shoved a receipt in my hand and pushed me toward the door with a hiss. "You better mind your own business, missy, before someone minds it for you." She tossed in a nasty smirk. "If he isn't already."

CHAPTER

37

I STOOD OUTSIDE THE flower shop, anger burning inside me. Damn Brodie. He'd ruined yet another chance at gathering evidence in Jack's favor. What was it June had planned on saying? Had Roger bought flowers from June, but not for Mary? Did he have a secret lover somewhere?

I shook my head at the thought. If he did, surely everyone in town would know about it. Just like they knew about Danny and Nancy Jeanne. Just like they insinuated about Brodie and myself.

Leaping into Jack's pickup, I noticed the RFID reader on the floor under the passenger seat. Why not? I picked up the reader and went in search of Brodie's Jeep. I located it around back, gleaming malevolently in the sunlight. I turned on the reader, practically dropping it when it let out a loud screech. A warning light flashed.

Low battery.

Unbelievable.

I set the reader on the ground, searching my purse for backup AAA batteries. I knew I'd put some in there a few days ago …

"What's that?" Brodie asked from his position above me.

I leapt up, nearly colliding with his broad frame. "What's what?" I barked to hide my guilt. Offense beat defense any day. "Are you stalking me now? No means no, Brodie."

"Funny," he said, his tone implying the opposite. He motioned to the chip reader with his boot-clad foot. "What is that?"

I licked my lips, thinking. "Breathalyzer."

"Is that so?" He laughed. "Looks more like a RFID chip reader."

"Oops, guess I should return it to Radio Shack then." I picked the reader up off the ground, dropping it my purse. "So what brings you by? Picking up flowers for your alibi?"

He grunted. "Not quite. Grandma sent me over to buy a fresh bouquet as, apparently, she will be having company for dinner after Roger's service." He let out a long sigh. "Though she refuses to tell me who. I hope to hell that she's not trying to set me up again." He stopped, looking me up and down. "I swear to Christ, the women in this town are mental."

I smiled with saccharine sweetness. "Present company excluded, right?" How I wanted to tell him who Rue's dinner guest was, but I kept my mouth shut. Brodie was way too smart to leave me alone with his grandmother when she very well might be to blame for Jack's incarceration and Roger's murder.

"Sure. Whatever lets you sleep at night." His voice lowered to a husky drawl while his lips curled into that wicked grin. "Naked, I'll bet."

I had to laugh. Leave it to Grodie Brodie to make a sexual comment in the midst of insulting me. It was almost impressive. "Sadly, *you*, Brodie Gett, will never find out."

"That *is* a shame," he said, his voice so whiskey-soaked it could melt ice cubes.

I cleared my throat before it could betray me with a moan. "Well, have a nice day." I turned to leave, but he grabbed my arm. The pressure of his hand didn't hurt, but I flinched just the same.

He dropped my arm as if I had the pox. "One day, Charms, you're going to push me too far."

What was that supposed to mean? Was that a threat? This guy's hot and cold act had gotten old about two decades ago.

He blew out a long breath. "How's Jack?"

"Home," I said. "Somehow he made bail."

Ignoring the last part of my statement, he nodded. "Glad to hear it. Grandma Rue had quite a row with Danny the other night about his locking Jack up."

"Really?"

"Like I said, Danny was just doing his job."

"His job sucks then."

Brodie nodded in agreement. "Want to grab a coffee and we can talk some?"

Had Brodie just asked me out? I fought back a shiver of revulsion, or so I told myself about the rush along my nerve endings.

"About your investigation," he added, tone filled with distaste. "Nothing more."

I couldn't blame Brodie for his disgust. My eyes still had a vivid shade of purple circling each of them, along with the cut on my forehead. I wasn't worthy of captain of the football team golden boy Brodie. On the other hand, coffee would both taste wonderful and be a chance to ask Brodie a question that had been bothering me since June had shoved me out of her flower shop. Namely, was Roger cheating on Mary?

"Sure. Why not?" I said.

Staring into my eyes, he straightened, all semblance of warmth gone in a blink. The coldness in his gaze had me rethinking my ready agreement. "That's the spirit, Charms. Way to take one for the team."

CHAPTER

38

"DANNY SAID YOU FOUND a tape of Roger right before he died." Brodie drank deeply from a chipped mug Cindy Mae had set down in front of him a few minutes earlier.

When Brodie suggested coffee, I'd figured he'd meant at the nearby Harker coffee shop. Not so. He had followed me all the way back into town, right into the Gett Diner's dirt parking lot, as if he worried I wouldn't make it on my own. More likely, he'd followed me to make sure I didn't backtrack to June's flower shop and find out what she planned on revealing before he had rudely interrupted us.

With my mouth full of the bourbon-soaked fruit from the Drunken Apple Pie Cindy Mae declared a must-have, I nodded rather than fully form an answer. After all, Jack had instilled some manners in me. But perhaps not sense, considering Brodie was obviously pumping me for information, and I was letting him.

A girl will do many things for a handsome guy bearing pie, even if he is sort of the devil.

"Said you couldn't make out the driver though." He stopped, tilting his head. "Any luck there?"

I chewed, swallowing my last bite and sat back with a smile. "Possibly."

"What's that mean?"

"On a scale of absolutely to impossibly, it falls somewhere in the middle." I laughed at my own joke. "Didn't they teach you anything at the University of Miami?"

"Keep making jokes and I'll make you pay for your own pie."

I winced, remembering the lone two dollars in my wallet. The last thing I wanted Brodie to know was my current financial straits.

Or more to the point, Lucky Whiskey's.

Rue would surely swoop in then.

"Hey," he said, his eyes on mine. "I was kidding. Don't look so sad."

"Sad?" I gave a phony laugh. The same one I used on stage a time or two. The key was, don't overplay it, think of something fun but not necessarily funny. "You're kidding, right? I am this close"—I held my fingers together for emphasis—"to catching the real killer. And I suckered you into buying me pie when you only offered coffee. I'd say I'm ahead of the game."

"Who are your suspects? Maybe I can help." He leaned in, his voice soft, full of warmth and yearning. As fake as my laugh had been. I knew this nicey-nice routine, and it always ended badly for me. Brodie was interrogating me, buttering me up. But for what reason? Was he worried I knew too much? Or was he merely doing his brother, the sheriff, a favor?

"I don't think so," I said quietly.

His eyebrow rose. "Still don't trust me, huh?"

For once, I went with total honesty. "I wish I could. It would be so much easier." Brodie had been surprisingly kind to me the last week or so. Whether or not that was because he'd killed Lucky Whiskey's only distiller and at the very least help shove Roger's corpse into a cask was yet to be determined.

"You can," he said with conviction. "Trust me, that is."

I laughed. For real this time. Right in his gorgeous face.

He jerked back like I'd slapped him. "Hey," he said. "I was being sincere."

My own eyebrow lifted. "Are you sure you know what *sincere* means? I'll let you borrow a dictionary if not." Not that I owned one. Jack had refused to buy one, even when my homework required it. He said I could learn all the words I wanted from his collection of pulp novels. Any of the other words could be learned at the Harker library. After my second fifteen-mile bike ride, one way, to the library I'd re-evaluated Jack's collection.

And today I was thankful I had.

While I wouldn't suggest giving pulp novels to many children, they'd offered me an escape from the sadness and loss of my parents' deaths. In those pages my love for drama and, some would say, melo-drama grew.

"You always were a smart-ass," Brodie said, as if that quality was less than endearing. I knew better. Everyone loved sarcasm. Really.

"And you always pushed my buttons on purpose," I said quickly, "trying to make me lose my good sense. Like the incident at the water tower. Last thing I remember was you daring me to do it, paint bucket in *your* hands." I set my fork down and crossed my arms over my chest. "It's not going to work this time."

"Charms," he drawled softly though his face creased with guilt, "we all know you were born under a bad sign, but sweetheart, I didn't think you were also born without a lick of sense. I am trying to *help* you!"

His words hung in the air, greeted by my silence.

He shifted but his hard gaze never left mine.

After a while, I licked my lips, saying one simple word: "Why?"

He dropped his empty coffee cup on the table, the bang of it ricocheting around the diner. Cindy Mae gave us a worried glance, as did a few other patrons. Brodie lowered his voice as not to be overheard by prying ears. "Why do I bother?" he hissed. "You're so damn oblivious." He threw up his arms. "Fine, have it your way. But don't come running to me when it blows up in your face."

With that, he scooted out of the booth, shot me one last glare, and left the diner.

Without paying the damn bill!

Tears burned the back of my eyelids. Had I made yet another mistake? Had Brodie truly wanted only to help me?

I doubted it. Getts lived and died for Getts. Not Luckys.

We stood alone. Always would.

I was so tired of being alone.

Cindy Mae came over, patting my shoulder. She leaned down to take the check, her big belly brushing my arm. "On me, hon." She frowned after Brodie's retreating backside. "I know better than anyone what it feels like to be dumped by a Gett boy." Before I could argue about my relationship status with Brodie, she added wistfully, "It'll stick with ya for years to come."

CHAPTER

39

I HONESTLY DIDN'T KNOW what was worse. The fact Cindy Mae had picked up the check because I didn't have enough to cover the bill or that the whole town now believed Brodie Gett had dumped me. And I played right into it.

Anger blinded me as I drove Jack's pickup back to Lucky Whiskey.

Damn Brodie. He'd known just how his abrupt departure from the diner would look to the good citizens of Gett.

A bit of Gett revenge.

Just like the night of the water tower incident.

Well, I wasn't about to do something stupid like that again. Instead I pulled Jack's truck into the spot closest to the Lucky family home and went inside.

I opened the front door, surprised to see Rue Gett sitting on the couch next to Jack. The two of them jumped apart like teenagers caught kissing. Not that Jack or Rue would kiss. But something was going on between them. Neither met my gaze.

"Jack?" I asked, fear tickling the back of my throat. "What's going on?"

"Mind your manners, girl," he barked.

I cleared my throat. "Hello, Mrs. Gett. You're looking well," I said, when what I wanted to do was scream. Everywhere I turned there was another Gett. They were like the Florida house lizards, also known as adorable geckos, which were only adorable until you couldn't get rid of them. Then they were simply called pests.

"Good to see you, Charlotte," Rue said, her voice dragging me from my unflattering comparison. "I hear Brodie is helping you with a little problem." She folded her hands in her lap like a proper southern lady. "I hope my boy is behaving himself."

"The *problem* isn't so *little*, but yes, your *boy* Brodie has been a constant *inspiration*."

Jack motioned to the kitchen. "I made some canned beef and potatoes if you're hungry."

I knew he was trying to distract me from the reason for Rue's visit. I decided, after looking at the two of them again, that I'd let him. Jack was a grown man. Lucky Whiskey was his to do with whatever he wanted. As much as selling to Rue Gett would destroy me, he had a right not to see his distillery mismanaged by his granddaughter to the point of bankruptcy. If Jack wanted to sell, so be it.

A tear slipped from my eye, rolling down my cheek. I turned away before either of them noticed. "Thanks," I said. "But I think I'll turn in. You'll be all right?"

"It's only seven o'clock," he said, his voice full of concern. "Are you feeling all right, girl?"

"Yes," I said. "Tomorrow's just going to be a long day." And then I turned around to see Rue's pinched, wrinkled face. To see how she'd react to my next words. "I want to be sharp. Never know who might be gunning for us." With those words, I headed up the stairs and into my childhood room. Faint whispers from below continued for hours.

I drifted off, listening to the almost musical sound of the destruction of Lucky Whiskey.

"Morning, Char," Jack said from his spot at the kitchen table. The warm, welcoming scent of freshly brewed coffee filled my senses, lifting some of the fog from my brain. "Chicory," he said, warning of the extra bold brew he'd drunk since I was a kid. Only in the south did you find the rich flavor of true chicory. Like the best whiskey, it came from the minerals in the water that fed the plant.

"Thanks," I said, filling a cup. The heavenly taste washed away the final tendrils of haze from my mind. "How are you feeling this morning?" I asked, when what I wanted to know was the impact on our lives after Rue's visit.

But Jack would tell me in his own time.

I needed to trust in that, in his love for me and Lucky Whiskey.

"Good." He took a long sip of coffee, eyeing me over the rim of his cup. "Nice to sleep in my own bed."

I understood completely. I, too, missed my queen-sized bed, which still sat in my studio apartment in L.A. "Will you be attending Roger's service today?" I asked, taking another sip of coffee.

"Best I don't."

I raised an eyebrow.

"Half the town thinks I killed him." He shook his head, both sad and proud that people thought a man his age could accomplish the feat.

More than half. I'd bet a bottle of our finest that Rue had made sure of it. "I'm sure—" I began.

"It's okay, girl. Sweet Jayme is coming over to keep me company." He shook his head. "She never did like Roger all that much. Especially the last six months. Something happened between them, but Jayme never would tell me what."

I exhaled a long breath as my suspect list grew yet again, by two—Sweet Jayme and Billy James.

However, I strongly doubted Sweet Jayme would harm a hair on Roger's head. Hell, she wouldn't kill the huge flying cockroaches that infested Gett like tourists at Disney World. But what of Jayme's boyfriend, Billy James? Had Roger done something so terrible to Sweet Jayme that Billy took his life?

My stomach clenched at the thought. Billy *did* have a temper. And he loved Jayme more than anything. The farther I went down the rabbit hole into Roger's murder, the darker it seemed to get. I now suspected people I called friend of murder. It was almost too much.

Especially for the early morning hour.

"Better get a move on, Char," Jack said, dragging me from my dire thoughts. "The service starts at ten. You don't want to be late."

Numbly, I nodded. I surely didn't. For every cop show I'd ever seen promised one thing: the killer always went to the victim's funeral. I couldn't think of a better time or place to see all my suspects in one place. "Call if you need anything," I said, leaning down to kiss his weathered forehead. His skin felt warm, but thin. Easily broken. "I love you, Granddad."

"Right back at you," he said, his voice gruff. "Whatever happens, girl. You remember that."

His words rang ominously in my ears as I headed back upstairs to dress for my final goodbye to a man whose death had done what he'd sought out to do in life: ruin Lucky Whiskey and my family, for good.

CHAPTER

40

I'D OPTED FOR FAIRLY comfortable two-inch black boots and my go-to basic little-black-dress for today's memorial service. Good thing too, since the church was packed with mourners when I arrived and I'd have to stand the entire service.

I took my place in the back, my hands clinched together in front of me, which seemed like proper mourner etiquette. I wasn't sure, since the last time I'd attended a memorial was when my parents died almost twenty years before.

I could hardly remember their faces anymore. That alone broke my heart.

But I did remember my mother's voice, her gently rocking us in the rocking chair my dad had built out of old casks. According to Jack, my dad had been the finest cooper in the land. He could build anything, including whiskey barrels, in a few hours.

Tears rose in my eyes as I thought of the old rocking chair tucked away in Jack's attic. I'd begged him to let me keep it in my room, but he'd smiled sadly. "Sometimes out of sight is the only way to survive, girl, and I want you to thrive," he'd said.

Today I was thankful he had.

Mary, who was being helped down the aisle to her seat in the front row, drew my attention. Not because of her grief, which looked unbearable, but more so for the man holding her upright. Brodie clasped her arms, his face a rigid mask.

Again the suspicion reared its head.

Were those two having an affair despite Brodie's claims to the opposite? The way he held her, softly as if she might break, spoke of intimacy. So much so I turned away—but not before Mary's eye caught mine.

She looked beyond devastated, tears silently falling as they had the day I visited her at her house on Gator Alley.

But with more than sadness this time.

Instead her gaze also boiled with equal parts grief and rage. She stared daggers in my direction. I took a calming breath. I was being paranoid. Nothing more. Mary didn't wish me harm. Why would she? Unless she believed the worst of Jack.

I wanted to scream his innocence but bit my tongue instead.

Seeing her intense rage, I was glad to be close to Danny Gett, who was likely armed. He stood a few feet away, his arm around Nancy Jeanne, the much too young and pregnant woman from the Curl & Dye. The one who ran out crying at the insinuation that Danny was involved with other women. A blush rose on my cheeks. Poor Nancy Jeanne. I could think of ten men much better suited for fatherhood than Danny Gett. Odd, but Brodie's name came first to mind.

The service started with Pastor Ryan welcoming the mourners, and then he launched into story after story about the upstanding, albeit fallen, member of the community—Roger Kerrick.

An occasional sniffle filled the church, but nothing more.

I found that saddest of all.

Halfway through the service, Nancy Jeanne grabbed her stomach. "I think I'm going to be sick." She launched herself away from Danny and ran for the door. Heads swiveled our way.

Instinctively, I smiled at the mourners now openly glaring at me as I too headed from the room. I wanted to make sure Danny's girlfriend was okay, for she had looked anything but.

It had been a while since I'd been inside the church, or any church for that matter, so it took me a few minutes to find the restroom off a tiny hallway by the confessional. Here in Gett, there was one church that all denominations utilized, from the two members of the Jewish faith, to the fifty or so Catholics, and one or two followers of Islam.

Gett, oddly enough, had a long history of religious tolerance. Probably had something to do with it also being the greatest producer of whiskey in all fifty states.

I started to open the door, but Rue Gett's voice stopped me dead in my tracks. "I'll give you money, Nancy Jeanne. But you need to leave. Soon. Before you start to show," she said. My eyes widened with shock. Rue Gett wanted Nancy Jeanne and her future grandchild to leave town? Had I not heard it with my own ears, I wouldn't have believed it.

"Mrs. Gett," the girl cried, "please, I—"

"Hush," Rue cut her off. "You know you can't stay here. I won't—"

The door hinge decided to out me by letting out a loud moan. I winced, debating if I should enter or run back to the service. The mirror hanging over the sink made up my mind for me, for Rue's eyes caught mine in it. I ducked my head. "Excuse me, ladies, I just ..." I motioned to the door hiding the toilet.

"Yes, of course," Rue said, using her cane to stagger from the restroom. Before she left, she turned back, her eyes on mine. "You're still planning on dining with me this evening?" I nodded, wondering if I should try to convince Rue to leave Nancy Jeanne alone to make her own decision regarding her future. "Good. We have much to discuss," she said, and then left.

I looked at Nancy Jeanne, and she at me. She took a ragged breath, slumping against the sink. I rushed to her side. "Are you all right?" Anger made my voice tight. How dare Rue upset her in her delicate condition. And why the hell had Danny let his grandma be his mouthpiece? Yet another reason to dislike the older Gett brother.

"Yes," she said, looking anything but. "Thank you."

"This isn't any of my business," I said, sounding like anyone about to butt into your business, "but I can't stand to see Rue bully you into leaving town." I took a paper towel from the dispenser, wet it, and handed it to her.

The girl choked back a sob. "Rue isn't bullying me. She's done nothing but try and help me." She rubbed her belly. "But I messed up, and ... I don't know what to do ..."

"You didn't mess up alone," I said, anger radiating in my voice. "Danny damn well has a more than equal share in this."

Her brow wrinkled. "Danny? Danny Gett? What does he have to do with this?"

My own brow furrowed as well. "Isn't he the father?"

Through her distress she managed a loud laugh. "Danny? Just gross."

"Oh, I thought ... never mind."

Her gaze turned wistful. "The Getts, most of them at least, have been wonderful since ..." She patted her stomach again. "At first, I was so excited, but now ..."

I swallowed. As much as I wanted to give her advice, I didn't have any experience with pregnancy, let alone experience in being run out of town—which was surprising, considering the water tower incident. "It will be okay," I lied for her sanity's sake. "If you need anything…"

"I know what people are saying about your grandpa." Fat tears rolled down her cheeks. "I don't believe it. Jack's a good man."

"You know him well?"

She shrugged. "I worked at Lucky before Rue hired me to be her office manager. Now," she hesitated, her face twisting, "with the baby, I'm not sure I'll still…"

"You can come back to Lucky anytime," I said. Jack might disagree, but so what? Nancy Jeanne needed a job. Baby or not. I wouldn't allow the Getts to destroy this girl. "I'll make sure of it."

She smiled through her pain. "Thank you. I heard many things about you from…" Heat stained her reddened cheeks. "I'm glad they aren't true."

I grimaced. But before I could ask what she meant, Danny Gett burst into the bathroom. He glanced at Nancy Jeanne and then to me. "You okay?" he asked her.

She nodded.

"Service just ended." He took her hand in his, anger in his eyes when he looked at me. "We should go, before…"

Her head moved up and down again wordlessly. She let Danny lead her away, only once looking back over her shoulder. She gave me a halfhearted smile and then disappeared into the throng of mourners ready to put Roger in the dirt.

CHAPTER

41

FOLLOWING ROGER'S BURIAL IN the Collier County cemetery, the funeral precession drove the fifty miles back to Gett, stopping occasionally for an alligator crossing the roadway. Brodie's Jeep took the lead, Mary in the front seat.

The Gett Diner had graciously offered to feed the mourners. So less than an hour later, a hundred or so cars pulled into the parking lot of the diner as well as the street and intermittently the front yard of nearby houses.

I parked a half-mile up Main Street, needing the fresh air to rid myself of the feeling of loss and sadness today's service had emphasized deep inside me. I doubted I'd ever find complete peace for the parents I'd lost. My memories of them, sparse as they might be, would live on until I took my final breath.

Stop being so melodramatic, I ordered myself.

The sun was shining. Birds circled overhead. Life, even as fragile as it seemed, was to be lived.

I opened the door to the diner, surprised the fire marshal hadn't shut the place down. People were packed in, some of them with feet barely touching the floor as they moved through the buffet line. The smell of overcooked meat and still-frozen veggies lingered in the air, ruining what little appetite I'd had.

I spotted the fire marshal, a plate full of food in his hands, waiting in line for some of Cindy Mae's Drunken Apple Pie.

That explained that.

I decided to offer Mary a quick condolence and then head back home to spend the afternoon with Jack. For who knew how many days of freedom he had left? Carefully I picked my way through the crowd. I spotted Cindy Mae, still as pregnant as ever, taking drink orders.

She gave me a wave, shaking her head. "Haven't seen this many Gettians in their Sunday best since old man Merritt died. Course then, everybody thought he had money. Turns out, he had a whole 'nother family in Tampa. Left all his dough to them. Town surely was disappointed, but not so much as the second Mrs. Merritt."

I let out a giggle. "Is Mary somewhere in this crush?"

Cindy Mae nodded toward the biggest booth at the back of the diner. The one surrounded by mourners waiting to lie about the dead, if only to give the living a small measure of comfort. This was one of the reasons I did love Gett. They came together when one of the community needed support. Helping with Lucky Whiskey was just one example.

This sort of caring wasn't found in L.A. It took a special bond. The kind forged in hurricanes. In poverty. In the struggle to put one foot in front of the other in humidity so thick one could eat it for dinner and have enough left over for breakfast the next morning.

Avoiding the bodies of those fellow men and women, I managed to get less than five feet from Mary. She looked pale, but her tears had stopped. Lester and Brodie stood outside the booth next to her, as if protecting her from further harm. I swallowed back a wave of absurd jealousy.

Where had that come from?

I didn't even like Brodie. Mary needed him, I certainly didn't. Brodie caught my eye and then looked over me, as if making just that point. But his eyes burned hot, angry. Guess he hadn't forgiven me yet. My own anger ignited. Who did he think he was?

"You!" Mary shouted, waving a finger in my direction.

I jumped back, almost staggering into the people behind me.

Mrs. Crest grabbed Mary's shoulders, pulling her back. But Mary was far from finished. "How dare she—" she yelled.

"It's okay, sweetheart," Lester said to her, patting her shoulder awkwardly.

Before I could say a word, Brodie stepped forward, grabbing my arm in a painful grip. "I think you should go."

I flinched, trying to pull away before he added to my collection of bruises. "But … I …" What could I say? Apparently, as the days passed, Mary had come to believe the worst of Jack, of my family. My chest burned, but I refused to cower. I would walk out of here, my head held high. I straightened. "Let me go. Now!" I hissed.

He did, like an afterthought. His attention was on the front door, where Boone Daniels stood. Boone sported a black eye and a violent sneer. I wondered how he'd come by the black eye.

But I didn't wonder for long. Instead Brodie grabbed my full attention. His body stood rigid, practically vibrating. Was he that angry with me? Or was he reacting to Mary's misplaced rage at my family?

Before I could question him, he up and left, disappearing into the crowd in front of me. I stood, my mouth wide. In that moment,

I'd never felt more alone. Rather than seek internal solace, I went with equal parts rage and outrage.

All directed at Brodie Gett.

This was exactly how I'd felt in high school. One minute everything would be cool between us, and then Brodie would flip a switch and either torment me into doing something outrageously stupid or completely ignore my existence. Well, I wasn't going to stand for it. Not now. Not when I was a mature adult. "Bastard," I whispered.

Mrs. Branson gave me the evil eye—that or she was using her one good eye to see who'd spoke. "Is that any way to talk about yourself?" she said in a low voice. "Your mama and daddy did marry after all."

I smiled politely, using years upon years of acting skill to keep my voice even. "Yes, they did. Thank you for the kind reminder."

She nodded. Heck, I deserved an Academy Award for that. Or maybe not. If I had one handy, I'd likely smack her and then Brodie in the head with it. I smiled as a satisfying fantasy grew in my head. My daydreaming ended when a wave of whispers filled the room.

"What's going on?" I asked Cindy Mae, who stood by the window, her face pinched as if in pain. My heart slammed in my chest. Was she about to have her baby right here, right now? "Are you in labor?"

"What?!" She let out a hoot. "I hope not. I have a feeling this one will slip right out. No warning."

I grinned. She did have a point. "Then what's wrong?" I asked.

Instead of answering, she waved outside to the parking lot, where Brodie and Boone squared off, preparing to fight.

I gasped. What was Brodie doing?

Boone would fight dirty, using anything he could to one-up Brodie. I moved to the door as quickly as I could through the crush, throwing it open in time to hear Boone's mocking tone. "Whatcha gonna do about it, pretty boy?" He stopped, his voice cruel. "That bitch needs to know her place. On her knees," he joked. "And I'm the man to show her."

My fists clenched. I didn't know who Boone was talking about, but I felt sorry for *her* nonetheless. My mind flashed to the night he'd attempted to rape me. The feel of his hands on my skin. His foul breath in my face. I gagged. Brodie glanced up, as if we'd relived the same memory.

Boone took advantage of Brodie's distraction, sending his fist flying toward Brodie's face. The punch landed with force, knocking Brodie a few steps back. He wiped a smear of blood welling from his lip, and smiled at Boone. A cold, terrifying smile.

I swallowed. This Brodie could and would kill.

Before Boone knew what hit him, Brodie hurled his body at the smaller man, taking them both to the dirt. Dust flew up around them as did the occasional fist. The sound of fist meeting flesh and bone and sporadic grunts filled the air. A crowd had now gathered in a circle around the fighters. They yelled and jeered. Not one of them tried to stop the beating.

My fingernails dug into my palms. I had to do something.

Brodie managed to gain the upper hand, methodically slamming his fist into Boone's body. Boone howled with rage. Grabbing dirt, he threw it into Brodie's eyes. Brodie reared back, apparently blinded. He swiped at his eyes, leaving his body open.

Boone landed a few hard hits to Brodie's handsome face. Brodie took a few wild swings until his vision cleared and then Boone was in for it. Brodie grabbed Boone's head, forcing it to the dirt. He leaned down, whispering.

The crowd leaned in to hear.

Too late to overhear whatever Brodie had said.

Much to their dismay.

Boone tried to buck Brodie off of him. But Brodie held tight. A flash of steel glinted in the sun. "Look out!" I yelled starting forward as Boone pulled a knife from his boot.

Before I reached the combatants, Danny pushed through the on-lookers. "Drop it!" he yelled, kicking at the knife. It clattered to the dirt. Brodie took full advantage, clocking Boone in the jaw. His head snapped back with a sickening thud.

"Stop," Danny said to his brother.

Blood running from his busted lip, Brodie held up his hands as he staggered to his feet. His once white shirt was stained with dirt and blood. A rip ran down the collar.

Boone laid on the ground, gasping. "I want to press charges." He wobbled to his knees, his own face nearly unrecognizable from the blood soaking it. "Do you hear me, Sherriff? I want your kin arrested for assault."

Danny smirked, much like he did whenever my name was mentioned, as if humored by his disgust. "Keep quiet or else I'll toss your ass in the slammer for illegally carrying that knife." He leaned down, voice so quiet the crowd hushed to hear him. "Got me?"

Boone said nothing, doing the wise thing, for once. He staggered to his feet, pushing through the crowd. Unfortunately, I was between him and his truck. His eyes blazed with such hate that I stepped back, my heart slamming in my chest.

"You better hope I don't find you alone one of these nights," he growled.

"Move along, Daniels," Danny ordered in his cop tone. Just this once, the sound didn't grate on my last nerve. In fact, it warmed the chill currently prickling my flesh. Boone gave me one last heated glare and then stormed off. He leapt into his oversized truck, pulling out of the parking lot, wheels and dirt spinning.

I glanced back to Brodie, who leaned against the wall of the diner. He'd removed his torn shirt, holding it up to his bloody mouth. It was then that I noticed the angry, red scar on his chest. A round, jagged scar. The sort left by a bullet.

Brodie caught my eye.

He spat a glob of blood into the dirt and turned away.

CHAPTER

42

FEELING LIKE I NEEDED a shower after the day's events, I drove home, my mind wandering to the last few hours. I winced thinking of how close Brodie must've come to death. Not today—he had the upper hand during the fight—but while combating terror a world away. The bullet scar wasn't that old. It was still angry and red, standing out on his chest. Why hadn't he told me? Had the wound ended his military career? Was that why he sat, day after day, on a barstool?

Was he in physical or emotional pain?

I blew out a long breath. I didn't need to start feeling sorry for Grodie Brodie. He'd made my life hell growing up, and still tried to do so. Whatever partnership we'd shared over the last week was all a lie. He'd spied on me, on my investigation, in order to protect his grandmother. Noble, if it wasn't also a felony to aid and abet a killer.

I pulled into our driveway, taking a moment to soak in the beauty of the quiet distillery as the sun shone down on it. I would miss it. Miss making something real. Something tangible.

But this wasn't where I belonged. I had a life in another world. Jack would find his way after he sold to Rue. We'd see each other at holidays.

It would all be all right.

I swiped angrily at the tears running down my cheeks.

Blowing my nose on a wad of napkins I found on the truck's floor, I checked my makeup in the mirror. Jack's eyesight wasn't what it used to be, lucky for me. He wouldn't notice I'd cried. And if he did, I'd blame it on Roger's funeral. Though Jack was far from stupid. He wouldn't buy it.

Better to avoid him until the redness left my face.

I sat in the truck, enjoying the sound of water running along the creek. Half an hour later, with one last glance in the rearview mirror, I opened the door and jumped from the truck. My boots left heel marks in the wet, humid dirt as I walked to the house.

Luck was on my side as Jack snored loudly in his chair. Sweet Jayme used a duster on the table next to him. I gave her a wave.

"He's taking his afternoon nap." She grinned down at him. "As you know, it would take a hurricane to wake him. Want some coffee?" Her hand motioned to the kitchen.

What I wanted was a fifth of whiskey, but I settled for a coffee. We moved to the sparkling clean kitchen. A rush of gratefulness filled me. Jack and I were lucky to have Jayme on our side. She was far more than just a nurse, but one of the family. Who also saved Jack from my lackluster cleaning abilities and much too often his preference for canned foods. Jayme's family had always worked for the Luckys in some capacity. Her parents had actually met at the Lucky annual picnic, when there still was a picnic. The last one happened the very day my parents died. As a favor, they'd stopped off to buy ice for the party. Five miles later, they were dead.

Jayme poured each of us a cup of coffee, dragging me from my dark thoughts. She added two sugars to hers, and some cream. I opted for black. "How was the funeral?" she asked, taking a sip of her drink and then adding another sugar packet.

I shrugged, filling her in on the basics, including Mary's reaction to my presence and Brodie's fisticuffs with Boone. Once I finished she shook her head. "Wonder what set Brodie off?" she asked. "He's usually so even tempered."

I would've laughed at her assessment of the youngest Gett, but I didn't want to hurt her feelings. "Boone threatened Mary, I guess," I said, replaying Boone's disrespectful statements prior to the fight. Considering Brodie's protectiveness of Roger's former girlfriend, it made sense. Brodie was an alpha male all the way. He would kill or be killed—I winced, picturing his scar again—for someone he cared about, or maybe even loved.

The thought of Brodie in love with Mary left me cold.

Best not to examine why too closely.

"What was all that with Mary about?" Jayme frowned into her cup. She swirled it back and forth. A drop of coffee leapt over the side, landing on the table. Jayme wiped it up with her sleeve. "She knows better than to think Jack would kill anyone, let alone that weasel."

A frown as unsure as hers grew on my lips. "If you don't mind me asking ..." I hesitated. "What happened between you and Roger?"

Abruptly she rose, heading for the sink and the few dishes in it. She started to run the water. I didn't think she'd answer my question, but she finally turned the water off, focusing her attention on me. "I really shouldn't ..." she began.

"Nothing you say goes any farther," I said. "Please, for Jack's sake."

"I don't want to talk ill of the dead or nothing." She let out a long sigh. "Thing is, I caught Roger one night, let's just say, with his pants down."

I pulled back, shocked. "Roger cheated on Mary?"

"No, no. Not that." A blush stained her cheeks. "I was taking care of Jack one night. He wouldn't stop pestering me for a bottle of last year's small batch. I gave in and headed for the rackhouse for Jack's special stash. But I found something far more hard to swallow."

I chuckled. Jayme didn't drink anything stronger than white wine. She never understood the complexity and beauty of a single blend. "What was Roger doing?" I asked.

"I can't say."

"Why not?" I stood too. "What if I swear on a stack of Bibles that I wouldn't tell anyone?"

She laughed. "I can't say, because I only saw Roger inside Jack's office. I don't know what he was doing, but I knew it wasn't good."

"Oh," I said, disappointed. I'd hoped for some obscure motive for his death, all tied up in a nice ribbon. Nothing had gone my way since I'd found Roger's corpse. It was almost enough to make me wish I'd picked a different cask and we were all just busy speculating where the heck Roger had run off to.

"When I opened the door, Roger popped his head up from the desk, like he'd been searching for something inside." Her forehead wrinkled. "He yelled a foul word and told at me to leave, and I did. The next day, he acted like nothing had happened. But I knew better."

"But you didn't tell Jack."

"It wasn't my place."

If she had, would Jack have caught on to Roger's theft? Another question came to me, one completely unrelated, but forefront in my head. "After Brodie fought with Boone, he took off his shirt."

"Lucky you," Jayme said with a quick grin. "That boy is fine."

I tried not to nod, but my baser self refused to listen. "I noticed a scar on his chest." I pointed to where it had been on my own torso. As I touched my body, I flinched, unable to imagine the pain such a wound would cause. "Do you know what happened to him?"

"Rumor has it, two days before the end of his deployment, a sniper shot a whole bunch of soldiers. Brodie happened to be one of them." She fingered the cup in her hands. "But the boy didn't let a bullet stop him. He pulled two of his platoon to safety."

"How terrible."

Her hand clutched the cup tighter. "Rue got a call in the middle of the night. The doctors weren't sure he'd live."

"How awful."

"He's home now. He can heal." She hesitated for the barest of seconds. "Like you."

"What? I'm fine."

She patted my hand. "You surely will be, Charlotte. Surely will be."

CHAPTER

43

I SPENT A GOOD portion of the rest of the afternoon playing cards with Jack. Oddly enough, we played Gin, while sipping whiskey, in the quiet of the day. Jack asked me about the funeral. I gave him the basic rundown, leaving out Mary's screeching and Brodie's fight with Boone.

As far as Jack needed to know, all was quiet and good in Gett.

"Char," Jack said after he won four hands in a row. "Do me a favor."

"Anything."

"Don't quit acting in favor of playing cards for a living." Tears rose in my eyes, and Jack backpedaled. "Oh, girl, I was teasing. I didn't mean..."

I held up my hand. "Please don't sell Lucky. Not yet." As soon as the words left my mouth, I tried to shovel them back in. "I didn't mean that. I'm sorry. You have every right to do whatever you want with your distillery."

"Our," he said.

"Excuse me?"

"It's *our* distillery, girl." His hand brushed mine. It felt warm and safe. "Where'd you get a fool idea like that?"

Fool idea? Did that mean Jack wasn't going to sell? I asked him as much.

"Hell no," he said. "Rue Gett isn't getting my distillery. Not ever."

"Oh."

"If I'm convicted of this ridiculousness, then you'll take over full-time." He ignored my protest. "I had the Killer draw up the papers. If you want—"

I suddenly stood. "That's not happening, Jack."

"Girl—"

"No," I said. "I won't let you spend the rest of your days in prison."

He grinned. "Planning to bake me a cake with a saw inside? Though, if you're baking it, it might be too tough for the saw to cut through. Best have Jayme bake it."

"Funny."

"I thought so." He staggered to his feet, holding his arms wide. I stepped into them, comforting as nothing else was. "You have to promise me, girl."

"What?"

"You won't do anything stupid."

"Me?"

He snorted. "No climbing water towers for me, Char. I mean it."

"Yes, sir," I lied. Not that I planned to paint the town red, or any other color for that matter. My idea was simpler. Tonight I'd gather enough evidence to prove the Getts' guilt, and Danny would have no choice but to let Jack remain free. Even if it killed me.

Which it might if Brodie caught me hanging around his dear grandma, asking questions about Roger's murder.

I remembered the hard glint in his eyes when he'd dragged me from the diner.

Brodie Gett could and would kill.

I just hoped it didn't come to that.

This time.

———

For investigating/dinner, I selected a black blouse and leggings. I finished the outfit off with my lace-up boots and a string of pearls, easily tucked into a pocket if need be. Friends back in L.A. called this outfit cat burglar wear. Good, considering it might take a few of those nine lives to survive dinner at the Gett estate. I doubted Rue would outright poison me, though. Too easy to trace back to her.

On the other hand, I knew firsthand how she could and would manipulate people into doing her bidding. I'd have to keep one eye on her and my other on my back. Which sounded hard enough, then add in her grandson and I didn't have enough eyes.

My only hope was Brodie would forgo dinner tonight. Maybe he would spend his evening consoling Mary. A pale Mary in his strong arms flashed through my mind. I blinked the image away.

After I finished dressing I curled my hair and put on a fresh layer of lipstick and eyeliner. Not for Brodie's benefit, if he wasn't otherwise occupied, I assured myself.

Butterflies danced in my stomach. Rue wanted something from me. Why else would she invite me to dinner? We had only one thing in common—whiskey. Was she going to make me an offer I couldn't refuse? I smiled, picturing Rue as the Godfather, her thin cheeks puffed out with cotton.

What would I say if she made an offer on Lucky?

I'd like to think I'd laugh in her face. But I had to think of Jack. Of his twilight years. Would he be better off with or without Lucky? I didn't know the answer, though I knew for sure he'd do whatever he could to save it. Even at the cost of his life.

Or freedom.

Taking one last look in the mirror, I turned off the light and headed down the steps toward the front door. Jack had fallen asleep in his chair right after I fed him a fine dinner of skinless chicken breast and a salad, topped off with half a glass of Lucky's finest. I slipped out the door without a sound. Last thing I needed was Jack asking twenty questions.

My motto: *What Granddad didn't know, wouldn't hurt me.*

Since the Gett estate sat less than three miles from the Lucky property, I decided to walk. For one thing, Jack wouldn't bother to open my room door to check on me if the truck was still there. For another, Jack's pickup growled much like its owner had earlier when I served him his healthy dinner. It would surely draw notice, and I wanted to do some snooping. If I was lucky, Brodie's Jeep would be on the property and I could finally read the RFID chip on the decal. I had the reader in my bag.

Thirty seconds in the dark, and I'd have a killer.

I swallowed hard as the night sounds filled the air. The road I walked along was dark, the only light that of the moon above. Thankfully, it was full and hung low in the sky. I could see maybe ten feet in front of me. Just enough to stop before stepping on a copperhead or worse. It felt good to stretch my sore muscles out and I settled into a satisfyingly brisk pace.

The sound of something exiting the brackish waters next to the road gave me pause. It was something very large. With very sharp teeth, I imagined. I swatted at a mosquito buzzing my head and again longed for the bright lights of Hollywood as I resumed my walk.

I arrived at the Gett estate a little before eight. Just enough time to check for Brodie's Jeep.

As a kid I remembered Brodie's daddy working on a car while Brodie and Danny stood fascinated. I wasn't as excited, probably because Rue had forced Brodie to invite me to his tenth birthday party, and I was the only girl there. Brodie had called me a boy, waving to my blue jeans and t-shirt. I'd cried and kicked him in the shin, but he hadn't cared. He stuck out his tongue and then vanished into a group of older boys. Like most of my memories of childhood, Brodie's teasing and occasional cruelty stood forefront in my mind.

But tonight's memory also served a purpose.

I knew just where to find Brodie's Jeep.

Behind the house, at the back of the property, sat a wooden structure long enough to house an army. Carefully I made my way to the garage. The side door was open. I slipped inside, cautious not to make any noise. Inside sat a row of five cars lined up perfectly.

Sadly, Brodie's Jeep wasn't one of them. I let out a sigh. It turned into a gasp when I noticed the other vehicles. Parked side by side was a work truck, a smaller compact car, Rue's 1968 Camaro (bright blue in color), and, best of all, a plain-looking Ford Taurus.

My excitement peaked. Was this the proof I needed? I ran to the Taurus. On the driver's side windshield, a small RFID chipped decal stood out, just like on the video. No need for the RFID reader now. I'd found the killer's car.

In Rue's very garage!

But what to do with this information?

I glanced through the high garage door windows at the Gett home, blazing with lights. Should I confront Rue? As stupid as it sounded, a part of me wanted to let her know her plan didn't and wouldn't work. My excitement gave way to something darker. I pictured Rue in prison garb, her wrinkles deeper, her hair mussed. Then I imagined the same for her accomplice, Brodie. From hero to felon.

Justice would be served.

For Roger.

For Jack.

Before I left the garage, I snapped a few photos of the vehicle in question on my iPhone. Just in case it disappeared. Danny must've recognized it from the video and tried to hide it in the garage. Not a bad plan. I would've dumped it somewhere in the Glades, where no one in their right mind would look. Maybe that was his plan. Let the heat die down, and then get rid of all evidence.

Did that include me?

Was that why someone—likely Brodie, given the damage to his Jeep's fender—had pushed me off the road? Was I yet another loose end?

Anger tingled in my chest. How dare they not only murder Roger, but arrange for Jack to take the fall? I vowed to ask Rue that very question. I stormed out of the garage, around the house, and to the front door, pressing the doorbell with force.

A man in his fifties answered. "Good evening, Miss Lucky," he said.

I flipped through my mental rolodex for his name, though I wanted to call him Jeeves. "Mr. Marshall, good to see you," I said after a moment. For as long as I could remember, he'd worked for the Getts. During one of Lucky's more prosperous times, Jack had tried to snatch Marshall from Rue's clutches. Marshall had politely but firmly declined. He was definitely team Gett.

I'd be smart to remember that.

"Ms. Gett is in the library if you'd like to join her for a whiskey before your meal."

Only the whiskey sounded good. Though it surely would be a Gett brand. "Sure." I moved passed him and into the grand house. And I do mean grand. The double staircases were straight out of *Gone with the Wind*. The place always made me feel small in size if not bank account. Rue had lived here since she married into the Gett clan over sixty years ago.

From all accounts, her marriage had been a happy one, until the eldest Gett had up and died thirty years ago. Now Rue lived alone, in a mostly empty house overlooking Gett Whiskey. Had she not been a murderous villain right out of *101 Dalmatians*, I might've felt sorry for her.

But she'd messed with Jack for the last time.

CHAPTER

44

I FOLLOWED **MARSHALL** **DOWN** the long dark hallway to the library. He opened the door, motioning for me to enter. I did, stunned by the sheer number of books stacked everywhere. Most who owned a room called a library kept expensive first editions of fancy literary works. Not Rue. She had books from every disciple, from every genre, tucked all over the room.

The place even smelled of books. Earthy with a hint of dust and ink.

Rue had so many books I used to fear being buried in an avalanche of words. I couldn't remember why Jack and I had spent time here. Just that Brodie, Danny, and I would be forced to sit quietly, reading, while Jack and Rue went somewhere to talk whiskey business.

I hated those trips to the Gett estate. Jack had as well, but I didn't realize that until I was older. He kept his opinion to himself. And I followed suit. Mostly.

Jack would force me into my Sunday best dress and comb my unruly hair. Brodie would be Brodie, and tease me for something or another. Danny, though, would sit quietly and do as told. Without fail.

I frowned.

Had I gotten it wrong? Was it Danny, not Brodie, who was helping Rue get away with murder?

"Welcome, dear," Rue called from a settee near the window. "So glad you could make it."

"Thank you for the invite," I bit out. I wanted to scream at her, but my anger would be appeased later. For now, I'd wait until she made the first move.

She motioned to a stocked bar. Stocked with Gett whiskey. "Would you like a drink?" she asked, pleasantly. Without answering, I moved to the bar. I poured a highball glass of whiskey. A polite two fingers. What I wanted was an entire fist, but I'd make do, for now. I needed to keep sharp. I took a sip, trying not to grimace, as was my custom whenever forced to drink a rival brand. If, gun to my head, I had to tell the truth—Gett whiskey wasn't bad.

It just wasn't Lucky.

"Please, have a seat." She waved to a high-backed chair to her side. It looked dainty and uncomfortable, much like Rue. "I wanted to talk a bit before dinner," she said. "Is that all right with you?"

"Why wouldn't it be?" I sat, carefully, waiting.

She cleared her throat, lowering her voice so as not to be overheard, even though we were alone in the room. "It has come to my attention that you believe I murdered Roger Kerrick."

I drew back. Shocked. Not because she knew I was on to her, but that she, a lady of the South, would bring the matter up. It just wasn't done. Well-bred ladies spoke in hushed tones of non-confrontational matters, not murder. "I … ah …" I mumbled.

"I'd like to ask why."

I looked down at my whiskey glass, draining it in one swallow. "Mrs. Gett," I began.

"Rue, please, dear."

"Rue," I said. "Can I be honest?"

She gave a chuckle, smooth as the best whiskey. "It would be a refreshing change."

"The thing is," I said in no uncertain terms, "I found the car. In your garage."

Her brow wrinkled, hard to see under her natural wrinkles. "What car, dear?"

My gaze narrowed. Was she lying? Feigning innocence for my benefit? "The car on the video of Roger at a Harker gas station right before he was murdered." I stopped, standing up to get myself another drink. This was harder than I expected. "You can't make out the driver, but the car is definitely yours."

"My Camaro?"

"The Ford Taurus. The one with the RFID chip on the window." I licked my dry lips. "An RFID chip that I'm guessing opens the front gates of Gett Whiskey."

Her laugh sounded like the snap of a gator's jaw in the silence of the night. "And I'm supposed to be the driver of this vehicle?" she asked.

I nodded, less sure than I had been twenty minutes ago.

"It's an employee car, dear." She held her hands wide. "Hundreds of people have access to it at any time. The keys are kept in the visor above the driver's seat."

My conviction of Gett guilt wavered a small bit. Was she telling the truth?

"Don't believe me? Check for yourself."

"I … ah …" I stammered.

She blushed, keeping her voice low as she added, "And as much as I hate to admit it, I can no longer drive at night."

Even if what she said was true, it didn't mean she wasn't behind it, I assured myself. "What about the calls?" I asked. "The ones Roger made to you."

"What are you talking about?" She rose, using her cane. Her tone implied she questioned my mental state.

I couldn't really blame her. Hearing the words acted much like a cold shower on my theory. I grasped at yet another straw. "I found a burner phone, of Roger's." Which wasn't exactly true, but I didn't want to throw Lester, one of the few people in town who liked me, under the bus. "He had outgoing and incoming calls from Gett Whiskey's main line."

"And that proves what, dear?"

I swallowed. What did it prove? "Were you blackmailing Roger into destroying Lucky Whiskey?"

Now she drew back, hurt in her gaze. "I would never…"

But she had, in the past. She'd poached our employees, sent inspectors to the distillery regularly, and even resorted to infesting the rackhouse with rats after Jack won the 2004 Best Whiskey award.

"Roger was embezzling from us," I said. Jack would kill me if he knew I'd told Rue anything about Lucky business, but especially this. "Over the last six months. Right around the time the calls started." I shot her a hard stare. "Can you explain that?"

She said nothing.

"That's what I thought." I set my drink on the table. The jury was still out on her murdering Roger, but one thing was clear. She knew more than she let on. But how much more? Was she protecting someone else? Brodie or Danny?

"Grandma," Brodie said from the doorway. "What's going on here?"

She looked at her grandson and then to me. "I'm sorry you feel that way, Charlotte. I'd hoped, one day, that you and Brodie would heal the Gett divide." She stopped, her face pale. "Brodie, be a dear and eat dinner with Charlotte. I'm not feeling quite up to it at the moment."

Brodie's face turned from suspicion to fear. He rushed forward, giving her his arm. "Are you all right?" he asked, his tone full of gut-wrenching concern.

"I'll be fine." She patted his arm, her wrinkled hands lingering a moment longer. "Now be a good man and take care of our guest."

A shiver ran up my spine at the last part of her sentence. It hit me suddenly that no one knew I was here. I cursed my instinct to protect Granddad. It would be awfully nice to know someone would come looking for me if I failed to make it home.

Brodie looked at her and then to me, his face hard. "For you," he said to her, though his gaze stayed firmly on mine. "I'll do it for you."

CHAPTER

45

MUCH TO MY DISMAY and for reasons unknown, Brodie insisted on feeding me. Not in the literal sense, mind you. But he refused to let me leave until I cleared my plate. Maybe he didn't want to murder me on an empty stomach. I grinned as the thought flickered through my head.

Brodie wasn't about to kill me. At least not at the Gett family dinner table.

I was 90 percent sure.

Besides, he'd have to take Marshall out too, since the man in question currently served an array of delicious foods, none canned, to Brodie and me.

"More whiskey, miss?" Marshall held out a bottle of Gett. Its label clearly printed, white lettering upon black. Straightforward, like the whiskey itself. Not an ounce of creativity went into packaging or the brew. Unlike Lucky. We opted for bold flavors. Packaging and liquor with flair.

I debated the wisdom of another drink, and then decided if I were going to die, I would have at least two more. "Yes, please." I hoisted my glass, smiling as he poured a perfect two fingers. He motioned the bottle to Brodie. "Master Brodie?"

"I'm good," he answered. "No matter how much I beg, Marshall refuses to call me anything but Master Brodie. He knows it drives me insane."

"Rightly so, Master Brodie," Marshall responded, deadpan.

I giggled, eased by the friendly banter. You didn't joke around with someone you planned to kill, right? Another laugh escaped my lips. This one filled with nervous energy.

Marshall disappeared to parts unknown, leaving Brodie and I alone in a dining room large enough to hold fifty. Thankfully Brodie had rearranged the place settings so we were seated across from each other rather than at opposite ends of the long table.

"What were you and Grandma discussing before I came into the library?" he asked after a long silence.

Instead of answering, I asked a question of my own. "What were you and Roger discussing before he was murdered?"

Brodie gave a small shake of his head. "You won't give up, will you?"

Now it was my turn to shake my head. "I can't."

"I know." He blew out a brash breath.

We consumed the rest of the fabulous meal in an uneasy peace. The only sound was the clicking of forks against china that cost more than my apartment. When I finished the last bite of a fabulous tiramisu, I set my fork down and looked up—right into Brodie's steady gaze.

I wiped my face with the linen napkin in my lap. "What?" I asked when he didn't look away.

"Are you ready to go?"

Rather than answer, I pushed from the table. My legs felt rubbery from the whiskey and good food. Not to mention the slight fear I felt being so close to Brodie Gett. He led me from the house to his Jeep. Holding out his hand, he helped me up, his hand lingering a little too long.

"Charms," he said into the darkness, "you have a hell of an ass. Anyone told you that?"

I snorted. "I'm not that drunk. And you're definitely not that smooth. So whatever you're planning, forget it. I'm not sufficiently intoxicated enough to climb any water towers tonight."

Jumping in the driver's side of the Jeep, he started the engine. He started down the driveway. "About that..." he trailed off.

"What?" Was he about to offer an apology? A Gett asking for a Lucky's clemency? Be still my whiskey-laced heart.

Rather than beg my forgiveness, he jerked the Jeep to a stop. "Some idiot left the garage door open again. Stay here. I'll be right back." He leapt from the vehicle.

I winced, knowing just who said idiot was.

In my rush to get to Rue, I'd forgotten to shut the side door. Would he discover my trespass?

Instead of worrying about it, I opted to take advantage of his leaving. I ran my hand along the dashboard, then I looked to the left, and then the right before I popped the glovebox open. When we'd gone to visit Boone, I'd noticed a gun hidden inside. I should've taken a closer look then, but in my defense, Boone had been trying to fill us with buckshot.

There indeed was a weapon inside the glovebox. A snubnose .38.

Was it the same gun used to kill Roger?

My fear, half wrapped in the warmth of whiskey, surged forth. *Calm down, Charlotte.* Brodie wasn't about to kill me on the drive home. Though he had flatly refused when I said I preferred to walk. "Too many hidden dangers," he warned. "I'll take you."

With my gaze resting on a beautiful homemade dessert, it hadn't seemed like a big deal.

But now, faced with a .38, I felt very real fear.

"Hey," Brodie said. I jumped a foot in the air, dropping the gun on the floorboard. It landed with a loud bang, but thankfully didn't fire. Not sure how I might've explained killing Brodie with a ricochet from the same gun used in Roger's murder. Danny would probably give Jack and me a two-for-one deal on prison garb.

Brodie gazed down at the weapon, and then back at me. I swallowed hard as his eyes turned from down-home country boy to cold-blooded solider. "Did you want to ask me something, Charms?"

The hairs on my arms rose to attention. I stared him dead in the eye, and lied, "Nope."

"You sure?"

"Nothing comes to mind."

"Good." He lifted himself back into the driver's seat. Slowly, ever so slowly, he leaned down, between my legs, and picked up the gun. I froze as the whiskers on his cheek grazed the thin fabric of my leggings. I fought the urge to draw my knees together.

After what seemed like hours, he straightened, checked the safety, and then slipped the gun back inside the glovebox. He put the Jeep into gear and started down the dark path toward the Lucky homestead.

CHAPTER

46

As **Brodie navigated the** dark road, I focused on the last couple of hours. What had I learned? For one thing, the car in the Gett garage was less damning than I'd hoped. Rue had laid out an explanation for the car like the best criminal defense attorney. She poked holes in my theory without blinking. My narrowing suspect list was again wide open.

Oddly, Rue hadn't seemed to mind being my number one person of interest.

And she surely didn't deny it.

In fact, the only time I saw any real emotion on her face was when I mentioned the calls and how they coincided with Roger's embezzlement. She looked both horrified and shocked. But, more so than anyone, I could spot a good actress a mile away. Rue was good. She faked shock as well as she faked her sudden illness, leaving Brodie to spend an uncomfortable meal with me.

For a second I wondered if she'd planned that all along. Brodie mentioned that she'd been trying to set him up with women around town.

Did I seem that desperate for male attention? I was being paranoid. Rue had to know Brodie didn't even like me, let alone want to work together to heal a family feud that had been going on for generations.

"I heard you and Nancy Jeanne had quite a chat today at the service," Brodie said as he pulled into the driveway of my family home. The lights, normally blazing inside, were dark. Jack must've gone to bed. I would be quiet so as not to wake him. "Charms," Brodie snapped. "Are you listening to me?"

I blinked. Perhaps I had a little too much whiskey. "Sorry. What?"

He smiled, a grin so wicked and sexy my toes curled. "I asked if you wanted me to come tuck you in ..."

I rolled my eyes. "Yes, I did have a conversation with Nancy Jeanne. What of it?"

He licked his lips and my treacherous body tightened. "Just wondering what she told you," he said in a whiskey whisper.

"Why?" The heat in my lower regions turned to ice as his question penetrated. "Are you worried she told me the paternity of her baby?"

He shrugged.

"Seriously, Brodie," I said with disgust and a fair amount of righteous anger. "She's barely twenty-one years old. You're a pig."

For a second, he sat in stunned silence, and then his face grew hard. "Gee thanks."

I straightened. How could he? "Don't act all hurt. How could you let your grandmother deal with your mistake? I walked in on her offering to buy Nancy Jeanne off."

His shoulders lifted again.

"I thought you were better than this," I said through clenched teeth.

"I guess I'm not." He shoved the Jeep into gear before my feet hit the ground. "Do me a favor," he said. "Keep this to yourself." His eyes grew hard, almost as much as when he punched Boone. "Promise me."

I frowned at the request. Everyone in town knew Nancy Jeanne was pregnant. They only had the wrong Gett brother as the culprit.

"Charms, swear it!"

I nodded numbly.

"Good," he said. He revved the Jeep and drove off. My eyes stayed fixed on his taillights until they faded into the darkness. What was that about? What did it matter if I told the world? Soon enough Brodie would have to deal with his illegitimate child. Unless Rue had her way and Nancy Jeanne and her baby left town no one the wiser.

The Brodie I knew, the alpha who relished being in control, wouldn't let his grandmother pressure his lover like that. Something else was going on. Something I was missing.

I headed for the front door, lost in thought. As my fingers touched the cold knob, a crack of thunder exploded close overhead. It wasn't until wood chips rained down on me that I understood.

Someone had just taken a shot at me.

I dropped to a crouch, yanking the door open with one hand. I prayed Jack wouldn't wake and come to investigate. He'd be in the direct line of fire. This was bad. Very bad. Slipping through the door, I continued to stay low while I searched my pockets for my cell phone. Finally, I found it, and punched in 9-1-1.

"9-1-1," the operator answered. "What's your emergency?"

"Someone is shooting at me," I said in what I thought sounded like a controlled voice.

"Ma'am, please calm down." She paused. "Did you say someone shot at you?"

"Yes." I took a deep breath. "Please hurry. I think they're still outside."

The front window exploded, showering me in glass. It ripped into my skin, but I barely felt it, adrenaline acting as the best pain killer. I threw my hand over my mouth to stifle a scream. I didn't want to give my location away.

"Ma'am, are you still there?"

"Yes, please hurry," I sobbed. This was it. I was going to die, on the floor, in my family home. I just hoped Jack wouldn't be the one to find my body. He didn't deserve that.

Tires screeched in the distance, followed by bright headlights through what used to be our window. I crawled behind a recliner and risked standing up to look. Close together headlights, like those that ran me off the road. The light blinded me. I held my hand up, hoping to see the make and model of the vehicle. Not that the knowledge would do me much good against a bullet. But it just might convict my killer. I stifled a half-crazed laugh.

Glass crunched outside as footsteps approached and I hit the floor again.

"Oh, God," I whispered into the phone. "It's too late."

CHAPTER

47

"CHARLOTTE," BRODIE YELLED FROM somewhere outside. "Answer me, Charms." His tone was filled with desperation and fear. Much the same feeling that kept me silent and practically curled into a ball on the floor. "Damn it, Charms," he yelled. "What did you do now ..."

That got me. "Seriously?" I shouted back. "You're going to blame me for this?"

He chuckled. "Figured if you weren't dead, you'd pipe up at that." His boots moved through the busted glass and wood shavings by the door. With each crunch, I gave an internal cringe. "You okay?" he asked.

"Just peachy," I said, still tucked into a ball. "You might want to get down in case the shooter is still there." I stopped, realizing a very scary truth. What if Brodie was the shooter? The gunshots had carried the same healthy crack as a .38. The same kind of gun as he had shoved in his glovebox. What if, after he supposedly left, he backtracked to shoot me. The words *"Take care of our guest"* filled my head.

The door opened slightly.

I kicked it closed.

"Hey," he yelped. "I'm trying to help."

"Great. Help from outside."

"Charms," his voice lowered. "Do you really, in your heart of hearts, think I'd hurt you?"

Did I? I thought about it. The Brodie Gett who I'd known in high school, yes, but this one? The one who stood protectively by Mary? The one who went with me to Boone's? The one who sure as hell wouldn't knock up a woman and walk away?

How stupid could I be?

I shook the glass out of my hair and slowly rose to open the door. There, I stood, face to face with Brodie Gett.

He gave me a small smile.

But my gaze was focused on the gun so naturally held in his hand.

———

A little less than an hour later, Lester stood over me, his hands filled with bandages and antiseptic. He tried to dab at the cut on my shoulder, but I jerked away as soon as his cotton ball touched the wound. "Stay still," he ordered. "You sure are lucky, Charlotte. None of the cuts are too deep."

"No stitches then?"

"No," he said. "But I would like you to go to the hospital."

"For the last time, no," I said. "I am not leaving Jack alone for a few cuts."

"I understand." He waved to Brodie, who stood talking with his older brother. Behind them, in the backseat of Danny's cop car, sat an unhappy Willow Jones. Every once in a while Danny would shoot her a glare, and then turn back to his brother. For a second, I wondered what Willow had done, but the sight of Jack barreling out of the house ended my curiosity. "Lucky Brodie scared away whoever was taking shots at you," Lester finished.

"Yeah, I feel so lucky," I said, deadpan.

Jack gripped a shotgun in his arms, heading straight toward the sheriff. Not good when a main condition of his bail was avoidance of all firearms. If I didn't intervene, Jack would surely end up back in jail. "Can this get worse?" I mumbled under my breath.

Apparently it could, for Danny snatched the shotgun from Jack in one fluid motion. Jack started to sputter until Brodie but his hand on Jack's arm. I hoped he was reminding Jack about his blood pressure, but from the way the two squared off, I had my doubts.

I jumped from Lester's ambulance without permission. Jack's face had turned red and I worried it would all be too much for his damaged heart. But by the time I arrived by his side, Brodie had calmed him. "I won't let you down, Jack," Brodie was saying.

"Let him down?" I asked.

"Get inside, girl," Jack yelled, pushing me behind his back.

"Granddad," I said with a grin. "I'm fine. No one is about to start shooting with all of Collier County's finest standing around."

Danny straightened. "Are you being insulting?"

"Of course not," I lied. "Response time of fifty-two minutes. I, for one, am glad we pay taxes."

"That's it." He moved forward, Jack's shotgun still in his hand. Before he reached me, Brodie held out his arm, stopping his brother.

"She's been through a lot tonight," Brodie said.

Danny looked to me and then at his brother. "Don't come crying to me when she gets you killed," he said, his tone conveying his loathing.

"How can—" I began, but Brodie cut me off with a glare.

"Did you find any casings?" he asked his older brother.

Danny glowered at me but answered Brodie. "Yep. Like you suspected, a .38."

Brodie's face grew icy. "We need to find him and quick."

I held up my hand. "Wait a minute. What? You know who did this?"

Brodie reached for my hand, then pulled back before making contact. "I thought he'd go after me. I'm sorry, Charms."

"Sorry? For what?" My voice rose to a screech. Even Jack, who was half deaf, winced. "What the hell is going on? Do you know who shot at me?"

"Easy, girl." Jack patted my hand. "No one knows nothing for sure. But Brodie thinks Boone Daniels set the fire at the rackhouse—"

"You know that wasn't an accident?"

Jack rolled his eyes. "Course I do, girl. I ain't stupid. But we don't have time to get into your keeping things secret. Brodie also thinks Boone just tried to kill you."

"For the second time," Brodie snarled.

CHAPTER

48

WAS IT POSSIBLE? HAD Boone tried to run me off the road? And when that didn't kill me, had he decided to use me for target practice? But why? Was he afraid I'd find out he had something to do with Roger's murder? And why set the rackhouse on fire? What had it all accomplished?

I said as much to Brodie, who was currently sprawled out on our couch after he'd refused to leave when his brother and the rest of Collier County's finest had.

"Leave it alone, Charms," he said.

Before I could argue, Lester waved goodbye, taking a long look at Brodie. "Looks like you're in good hands. Go see a doctor if any of those cuts turn infected."

"Was that your version of take two aspirins and call me in the morning?" I asked.

"Something like that," he said. He left me and crawled back into his ambulance, heading into the darkness. I watched as his headlights faded before I unleashed my displeasure on Brodie. "Why didn't you tell me you suspected Boone had run me off the road?"

He opened one eye. "Because I knew you'd make a big deal out of it."

"Excuse me?"

He sighed. "Can we talk about this in the morning?"

"You are not staying here."

"Yes, yes I am, Charms," he said, his tone implying it was useless to argue. Not that, in my current state of agitation, I'd take his advice to heart. "You can say whatever you want," he said, "but I'm not about to leave you and Jack alone with no front window and bullet holes in your door."

He did make a valid point. I wondered briefly if alligators could climb through windows. A shiver rose along my skin, and suddenly my teeth began to chatter. I couldn't stop them, no matter how hard I tried. I held my hand to my mouth.

"Take it easy." Brodie leapt up in one fluid motion, wrapping his arm around my shoulders. He pulled me onto the couch. Our bodies sank down as he held me close. "It's gonna be okay." His weight was reassuring as were his words. If I could believe them. "I won't let anything happen to you," he said.

My shaking eased a bit.

Brodie took a bottle of Lucky from the coffee table, pouring us each a full glass. He handed me one and then drained the other in one gulp. He grimaced as Lucky hit his throat. "What do you make this crap with? Wood polish?"

Anger flooded my body, warming the coldness. The chills stopped. "How dare you—"

Brodie silenced me with a kiss.

A friendly peck that should've ended right there.

But I'd practically died tonight.

Needing his warmth, needing to feel alive, I grabbed the back of his neck, pulling him into a deeper kiss. He obliged, shifting his mouth from soft to hard and demanding. His lips grew hotter, persistent for more and more. His hand gripped my waist, slowly inching downward. I moaned, low and deep. Another, sweeter sort of heat filled my body.

Uncaring of the consequences, I crawled on top of him, keeping our mouths locked in the torturous kiss. I wanted him. A surprising revelation, but one I relished, at least in the moment. My hand twisted in his shirt.

"Whoa," he said when my other hand caressed the hard length of him through the fabric of his jeans. He drew back, holding me at arm's length. "Bad idea, Charms."

His words acted like a cold shower.

The sweet heat vanished, replaced with embarrassment. My face flushed. I glanced down at my hand, pulling away. Not the smoothest of moves. I leapt up and hurried to the stairs. Shame and embarrassment following in my wake. "I'm going to bed. Feel free to let yourself out."

"Charms, wait—"

The rest of his words were swallowed by the slam of my bedroom door.

———

I laid in bed, every nerve in my body tense. I replayed the last few hours in my mind. What was wrong with me? I'd practically jumped Brodie. Was I that desperate? It hadn't been that long since I'd been kissed. Though not like Brodie had.

I forced my brain to stop thinking of how wonderful his lips had felt against mine, and to focus on Boone Daniels, and why exactly he wanted me dead. I remembered his threat, spoken with haste at the diner after his fight with Brodie— *"Don't let me catch you alone."*

I'd been very alone in those few seconds as he shot at me.

I nearly died tonight. The realization shook me. Brodie had very likely saved my life by scaring Boone away. I wondered how long the madman had sat outside in the dark waiting for my return. Thank God he hadn't tried to hurt Jack. Better yet, thank God he wasn't that good of a shot. The shaking from earlier came back full force.

I shoved another blanket on top of the four already spread out on top me.

A floorboard creaked outside my bedroom.

I froze, listening hard. Footsteps hesitated, then slowly retreated. The sound of Brodie's vigil reassured me so much, I was able to fall into a fitful sleep.

CHAPTER

49

THE NEXT MORNING I slowly stepped out of bed. From my window I spotted a glass repair truck in the yard. The closest repair shop was in Immokalee. Not only that, but I hadn't called them, or anyone, yet. But I bet Brodie had. Damn him. Why did he have to control everything?

I showered and dressed, adding a swipe of lip gloss to my tingling lips. Not that I was primping for Brodie. Or any man. My lips were dry. That was all. I checked my hair in the mirror, knowing it was a lost cause. Curls sprung at odd angles no matter how much product I used. Nanette had cleaned up my split ends and brightened my color, but she'd done nothing to create an actual style.

I pulled it back with a clip. This would have to do.

With a sigh I headed down the stairs. When I reached the bottom I was shocked to see—or rather, not see—Brodie Gett. Granddad sat in his recliner, his shotgun resting at his side while two men in Immokalee Glass Repair shirts measured the opening where our window used to be. I hoped the repair shop had a payment plan, for my last check of Lucky funds suggested we wouldn't be able to afford a new window along with tomorrow's mash delivery.

Hopeless mixed with anger, turning my voice shrill. "Where's Brodie?"

Jack jumped in his chair. "You scared me, girl." He held a hand to his heart. "You know you're not supposed to sneak up on a man with a heart condition."

"You're hilarious," I said, kissing the top of his head. "Did you eat breakfast?"

He waved to the next room. "Sweet Jayme's in the kitchen. She made oatmeal thick enough to use as plaster."

"I heard that," Jayme said, poking her head from the kitchen. Her dark hair was pulled on top of her head and covered with a brilliant red scarf. "Do you want some coffee?" she asked me.

Jack answered. "Hell yes."

"Decaf for you," she said. "Extra caffeinated for Charlotte."

I smiled my thanks. "Did Brodie leave?" I asked as casually as the blush on my cheeks would allow. Thankfully Jack failed to notice.

"Yeah." He grunted. "That boy … He just won't listen to reason. Takes after his pigheaded grandmother. I told him to leave the repair shop to me, but would he listen?"

Something shiny under the couch caught my eye.

"Are you paying me any attention, girl?"

"Yeah, I heard you." I picked the object up, surprised. "Brodie left his cell."

"Better call up to Gett, tell him it's here," Jack said, and then promptly focused on the television.

Discussion over, I guessed.

I headed for the kitchen and the promise of coffee, Brodie's phone in my hand. Jayme had just finished pouring me a cup. Steam rose off the top. I blew on it and drank deeply. My body warmed as the caffeine hit my bloodstream.

"So what happened last night, Charlotte?" Jayme asked.

My cheeks burned. "Nothing. Why, did someone say different?"

Her eyebrow rose and she laughed. "I meant with someone shooting at you, but I guess that's not the most intriguing part."

My blush burned so hot I thought my cheeks might set fire. "Leave it alone, Jayme. I've had a rough enough night."

"I bet you did."

"Everyone's a comedian today." I set the cup down on the table. My tone grew serious. "Brodie thinks Boone tried to kill me."

The humor vanished from her face, replaced with concern. "Oh, honey. I'm so glad you're all right. When I think..."

I swallowed passed the lump in my throat. "I know. What I can't understand is why."

"Why Brodie thinks so?"

"No, I get that. Boone and I have history. Add in Evan owing him a stack of money, and my refusal to pay his debt ..." I ran my finger over the lip of the cup. "But why would Boone want to kill me in the first place? I can see trying to run me off the road, that's a crime of opportunity, but waiting in the dark to shoot me? That isn't like him."

"Isn't it?" She frowned. "That man is a menace. A coward too."

I couldn't argue that. But he also didn't strike me as real patient.

"Drink your coffee and I'll fry you up an egg."

"Jack said you made oatmeal."

She laughed. "I wouldn't force you to eat it. The doctor suggested I use skim milk and steel cut oats, cuz it's heart healthy. Can't see how that's healthy though. The stuff is actually stuck to the pot."

"Yummy," I said with a chuckle. "Poor Jack. I'm not sure how much more healthy he can take."

It was her turn to giggle. "What he doesn't know, won't hurt us."

I held up the coffee cup in salute. "My favorite saying."

Jayme moved to the stove, dropping a couple of eggs into a butter-soaked skillet. The sizzle made my stomach growl. I glanced at the clock over the door. It was just after eight. Surely Gett Whiskey's staff would be at their desks. I used Jack's house phone to dial the number I'd memorized after Lester had told me about Roger's calls to Gett.

"Gett Whiskey, how can I direct your call?" a young woman's voice answered.

"Nancy Jeanne?" I asked, recognizing her soft tone. "Is that you?"

"Who's this?" she asked.

"Charlotte Lucky."

"Oh."

"Do you always answer the phone?" I asked.

Silence. Then a tentative, "Yes."

No, it couldn't be. My stomach rolled. In a flash, the pieces began to fall into place.

"Are you there, Charlotte?" she asked, her voice trembling ever so slightly.

"Yes." I held the phone out, debating. "I think we need to talk."

More silence.

Then came a small whisper. "Not now."

"When?"

"After work. At my house." And then she hung up the phone.

I stared at the receiver in my hand for a long moment. Was it possible? Had Roger knocked up Nancy Jeanne? And when he refused to leave Mary, had Nancy Jeanne killed him? It couldn't be. Then again, it made a certain sense. Brodie's questions about my conversation with Nancy Jeanne flickered through my head.

The Getts were protecting her.

But why? What did she have on them?

An old rumor buzzed in my memory. Brodie's father caught in an affair with a Gett employee. Talk of an illegitimate baby. And a large lawsuit settled out of court.

I'd been six or seven at the time. But I clearly remembered my teacher's repulsion as she gossiped with the moms of my classmates.

Was it possible? Was Nanny Jeanne a bastard begot by a Gett? She was about the right age. And she had certain Gett features. Though not their annoying personalities. Nature versus nurture, I supposed. It made more and more sense.

Nancy Jeanne had to be a Gett.

What other reason would the Getts have to protect a calculating killer?

CHAPTER

50

LATER, AFTER OUR FRONT window was fixed and the technicians left, Jack fell asleep in his chair. I considered waking him to ask about the old rumor, but then thought better of it. I'd find out soon enough. Not that I was stupid enough to confront Nancy Jeanne without backup.

I called the one man in the county I knew would help. After all, he owed me for cheating off my exams in high school. "Lester," I said when he answered. "I need a favor."

"Anything."

I smiled at his immediate agreement. "Do you know where Nancy Jeanne lives?"

"Sure. She lives off Route 12. In the one with the white Christmas-looking lights on the porch."

I knew the house he was talking about. I'd passed by it on my walk from Jose's garage when I fixed my windshield. I frowned at the thought of my poor Prius. I really needed to call the insurance company again. But first ...

"Can you meet me there at five? I'm not sure I'll need it, but it would be nice to have backup just in case."

"I'll keep to myself until you say the word."

"Thank you." Not that I was afraid of a pregnant near teenager. I wonder if Roger thought the same thing, right before he took one to the chest.

A shiver raced up my spine, but I chose to ignore it.

For the rest of the day I worked on Lucky business. Sales were up, which was good, but if the small batch failed under my watchful eye, we were officially sunk. Without casks of product aging in our rack-house, the bank was likely to suspend our line of credit—which we'd need in order to buy supplies and pay employees—and call in our current notes—which we didn't have the cash for. Whiskey was a long-term business with frequent short-term deficits, and Luckys hadn't been as successful as Getts at stashing away profits in good times. We tended to reward our employees rather than buy fancy cars.

In the past, a bottle of Lucky Small went for two hundred dollars. The hipsters loved it. Drank it like water. And you certainly didn't hear any Lucky employee complain.

Though that had been while Jack was at the helm.

Fear of failure, the driving force in my life, had always made me reckless. I took risks I wouldn't normally take. Roles I hadn't fully considered, i.e., the STD commercial. Would the small batch follow suit? My mind scrolled through the recipe. I'd stayed with Jack's basic recipe, except for one tiny change. I added corn to sweeten the flavor.

Was it a mistake? Had I just ruined Lucky for good?

Nothing to do now but wait, I thought. We'd casked the small batch twenty minutes ago.

Remy shot a toothless grin in my direction. "You done good, girl."

I smiled back. Hoping he was right. Hoping the Lucky luck, like a new penny, would shine through one last time.

———

At five till five, I dialed Lester's cell number from the driveway of Nancy Jeanne's small cottage on the outskirts of town. The house, built sometime a century earlier, looked inviting and cheerful. White hanging lights decorated the porch where an old swing rocked in the breeze.

"Charms," Lester answered. "I'm on my way. About five minutes away."

"Okay," I said. "I'm going in."

"Why don't you wait until I get there," he said, no hint of question in his tone.

I glanced to the girly decorations on the porch, the soft yellow paint. "I'll be fine." With that, I hung up, carefully making my way up the wooden stairs to the front door. Wind chimes tinkled from one of the houses nearby. I knocked on the door, surprised when it opened under the slight pressure. "Nancy Jeanne?" I called, taking a casual step inside. "Hello? Are you here?"

And that's when I saw her.

Nancy Jeanne was in the kitchen, eyes wild, crazed even.

Seconds later, the sound of a round being chambered into a .38 filled the house.

CHAPTER

51

"**PUNCTUALITY. SO RARE THESE** days," a familiar voice snickered behind me. The scent of cheap whiskey, the same variety used to set the rackhouse on fire, filled the air around me. The same variety I'd smelled at Roger and Mary's house ...

I spun toward the sound, my eyes narrowing. "You?"

"Me," Mary laughed.

"I don't ... why would you set the rackhouse on fire?"

Rather than answer my accusation, she motioned with the shiny .38 in her hand. Light reflected off the barrel. "Why couldn't you leave it alone, Charlotte? You're as bad as the rest of them, protecting this slut." She gestured to Nancy Jeanne, who stood to my right. "At the church and later, at the diner."

I winced. How stupid could I be? Mary hadn't threatened me at the diner. She was talking to Nancy Jeanne, who stood in Danny's protective arms, behind me. "People know I'm here. I have backup," I said, thinking of Lester. Not the best choice for a savior, but he'd do in a pinch. If only I could keep her talking until he arrived.

"Oh, honey," she said with a shake of her head, "sorry to say, Lester's a little tied up at the moment."

As she spoke my cell phone rang. She motioned for me to answer it. I did with a tentative, "Hello?"

"Charlotte," Lester's voice crackled through thick static. "Sorry, but I'm not going to make it. Someone called in a bomb threat at the sheriff's station. It's all hands on deck." He hesitated. "Stay away from Nancy Jeanne. According to Mary, she's dangerous."

I had to laugh at that, but without a bit of humor. "I think you have it reversed."

"What'd you say?" he asked.

But Mary had snatched the cell from my hand before I could answer. She threw it on the floor and smashed it under the heel of her boot. I winced, imagining the cost to replace it.

Why didn't I get the insurance?

"Move," she said, motioning me to stand next to Nancy Jeanne. I hadn't looked at the younger woman since I'd first entered the room, but now I got a closer look. The girl was terrified, and rightly so. Mary was obviously crazy, with more than a little anger mixed in. Crazy anger once directed at her lover, and we knew how that had ended.

"It's okay," I said to Nancy Jeanne, but we both knew it wasn't. Nor would it be. Mary had killed one man; a man she supposedly loved. I didn't see her dead lover's baby mama faring any better. I needed to do something to save us. But what? I stuck my hands into the pockets of my sweater, devising a plan.

"I'm sorry," Nancy Jeanne whispered. "She said she'd shoot me in the stomach if I called out to warn you." Tears rolled down her puffy cheeks. "I couldn't let her hurt my baby …"

"Your baby?" Mary's laugh could've turned the finest of whiskey to swill. "That baby should be mine. Mine! Do you hear me?"

I moved in front of Nancy Jeanne before Mary could cause the younger woman harm. "I understand killing Roger. He hurt you. Cheated on you." I stopped, giving her a small smile. "But that's not Nancy Jeanne's fault. You can still end this, let us go. I promise, I'll do everything I can to make this right for you."

She gave an ugly snort. "I could care less who Roger stuck it to."

"Then why ...?"

She waved the gun at Nancy Jeanne. "I'd be damned if he'd leave. He owed me."

"Owed you what?" I ventured.

"A family. A home. We had plans." She rubbed the gun with her free hand. "But then he knocked *her* up. Six weeks later he planned to slip away in the middle of the night with his side piece and *your* Lucky money."

"You knew Roger was stealing from us?" Anger rippled through my voice, making it tremble.

She snorted. "That's how I found out he planned to take off with his whore over there." She waved the gun at Nancy Jeanne. "After everything I'd given up for him. I just couldn't let him ..." She swallowed, looking sane for a second. "You understand, don't you?"

I tried to nod, but my head stayed level.

And then her mental clarity vanished. "You act so high and mighty." Her voice grew shrill. "Why did you have to come back? You ruined everything."

"I didn't—" I began.

The gun flew my way.

"What's your plan here, Mary? You can't just kill us. People will get suspicious when they find our bodies." I nodded for emphasis. "And eventually they'll track it all back to you."

"You're not wrong." Her voice wavered.

I took advantage. "Let us go. Please. For your own sake."

She acted like I hadn't spoken. "That is, only *if* they find your bodies."

CHAPTER

52

ONE DAY I'D LEARN to keep my mouth shut.

Not today apparently.

I could barely contain my teeth's chattering under the chill of dusk fallen on Gator Alley. Mary had forced us into her car at gunpoint, driving us to the swamp behind her house. Nancy Jeanne and I stood, shivering, knee-deep in the brackish waters. Mary was also there, but insanity clearly warmed the soul, for she whistled tunelessly as she baited the waters around us with chum. She also wore a thick coat and boots, something both Nancy Jeanne and I lacked.

"Please," I said. "Stop this." The water around my ankles swirled, coming alive with who knew what. This was it. Death by gator. My greatest fear.

An odd numbness set in.

Mary paused in her chumming. "Do you hear that? Sounds like a big one."

Crap. Numbness turned to the desire to run, forcing Mary to shoot me, rather than stand around waiting to be eaten by a gator named Boots. I glanced at Nancy Jeanne, her face equally frozen in horrified shock.

If I could distract Mary enough, maybe Nancy Jeanne could get away. Why should both of us, and her fetus, die?

With one last glance at Mary and her gun, I took off running for the mangrove trees about a hundred feet ahead.

90 feet ...

80 ...

Bullets whizzed by my head. I ran faster, faster than I'd run in my life.

Pain ripped through me. I gasped, clutching my side.

Mary had shot me!

At my outraged shock, a laugh bubbled from my throat. Of course she shot me. That was why she had a gun. Dizziness filled my head. I stumbled.

The safety of the trees never looked so impossibly far away.

I wasn't going to make it.

I had but one option left to stay alive.

And that was to die.

I dropped to the wet ground, playing dead. My breathing came in harsh gasps. I tried to quiet them, but to no avail.

Heavy, pregnant silence filled the marsh.

"Did I get you?" Mary asked, sounding less than twenty feet away. Her booted steps came closer. "Charlotte? You still alive?"

Like I was going to answer. Mary clearly had more than one screw loose.

Water splashed closer.

And then came a shriek. A tortured, tormented one straight out of a horror film.

Before I could do anything foolish like lift my head, a single word, yelled with force, broke the silence following the scream. "Charms!"

Brodie Gett thrashed through the swamp toward me. "Hang on, I'm coming!"

I started to answer, but stopped when two dark eyes appeared feet from my head. The infamous alligator, Boots, his broad back and powerful body inches from mine. I recognized him from the long scar along his snout. The blood pouring from the wound in my side must've called him, and now I'd end up a gator after-dinner mint.

"Charms!" Brodie shouted again.

"Stay back," I said in a calm, even tone. A surprising composure, considering.

"Oh, thank God," he said. "You really are a good actress. I thought you were dead."

"So did I," I said. "Still might be if Boots hasn't had his dinner."

"Damn." Brodie pulled to a stop. "You need to get up, real slow like."

"No way."

"Charms! Do what I say," he ordered in only what I could assume was a drill instructor's voice. "Now!"

I started to rise, but my legs buckled. I fell back to the moist earth.

"In my sights," Danny Gett yelled from behind his brother.

"Don't you dare shoot me, Danny Gett."

Brodie let out a harsh laugh. "Not you, sweetheart."

"Oh." Blood loss had made me stupid.

"Stay still," he said. "I'm coming to get you."

"No," I yelled. "Don't. Both of us don't need to become gator chow."

Rather than listen to my more than sensible advice, Brodie moved forward. When he was a mere foot away, Boots jerked up, disappearing into the mangroves. Relief filled me. Along with sleepiness. I wanted to snuggle up, forget the pain burning in my side, and close my eyes.

"Charms!" Brodie's harsh voice burst through my eardrum. "Wake up this instant."

I blinked, trying to focus. "Is Nancy Jeanne all right?"

"She's fine." Brodie's thick arms wrapped themselves around me as he carried me back to the safety of the road above Gator Alley.

"She's your sister, isn't she?" A rude question, but the only one I could hold onto in the moment.

"Yeah."

"It's why you protected her." When he didn't answer, I said, "I like her."

He grinned down at me. "Me too. Now stay with me."

I looked up into his haunted gaze. "How'd you find us?"

The side of his mouth lifted as he carefully set me down. "You called me. Or rather, you called Danny." Brodie reached into my sweater. He pulled out his cell phone, the one he'd left at my house the night before. "Didn't you know?"

"No." I shook my head, which caused it to swim all the more. "It was in my pocket. I pressed whatever buttons I could after Mary smashed my phone. I hoped someone would hear."

"Lucky for you, Ms. Lucky, Danny's on my speed dial."

I closed my eyes. "Thank you."

"Aw, sweetheart," he said. "Don't thank me yet."

"Why?"

"You'll find out soon enough." As he finished his sentence, pain tore through me. No matter how much I struggled, Grodie Brodie Gett poked and prodded the wound in my side. I let out a loud scream as his finger penetrated the bullet hole.

Much to my delight, a second later, blackness filled my vision and blissful darkness swept me away.

CHAPTER

53

I WOKE IN THE back of Lester's ambulance. Lester stood over me, his face as pale as I suspected mine was. "You okay?" I asked through my chattering teeth. For some reason I couldn't get them to stop, even in the stale, humid air of the ambulance.

"Are you kidding me? I'm fine. Thank God you're all right," Lester said. "I am so, so sorry."

"For what?"

"I didn't know … About Mary?" He grabbed my hand. "I told her about your going to Nancy Jeanne's. I thought … It doesn't matter now."

"I'm sorry," I said and meant it. Lester had loved Mary for a long time. I couldn't imagine how he felt, knowing he'd fallen for a killer.

His face cleared a little. "It's funny."

"What is?" For, at the moment, I genuinely needed a laugh. My side hurt like crazy and my brain felt like it was drowning in sour mash.

"Another Gett saving a Lucky."

"What do you mean?"

Lester's cheeks heated. "I thought you knew."

"Knew what?"

"The night Jack had his heart attack ..." His blush grew until his cheeks looked like twin tomatoes.

"What about it?"

He ducked his head as he shot some clear liquid into the IV attached to my arm. "He wasn't alone."

"What?" I still didn't understand. Jack had company? A Gett?

"Rue was with him."

The implication of Lester's words hit me full force. "Are you saying Jack was ... and he ... Oh God."

"Oh God, what?" Brodie said, climbing into the ambulance.

"Nothing."

"Don't fret, Charms." He grinned down at me. "I'll hold your hand all the way to the hospital."

Lester disappeared up front and the ambulance started off, siren silent. Thankfully. Apparently the bullet hadn't hit anything vital, though it hurt like hell.

"I can't believe she shot me," I said with a frown.

"For the second time."

"What?"

Brodie sighed. "It wasn't Boone who shot at you. Danny matched her gun to the casings we found at your house last night." But he wasn't finished. His face grew grim. "She also ran you off the road. With my Jeep."

"I knew it!"

He raised an eyebrow.

"I mean," I said. "I didn't know it was Mary. But I knew it was your Jeep."

"You were right. Sorry I didn't believe you." He stood, ducking his head to avoid the roof of the vehicle. "She asked to borrow it, to do some funeral stuff. That's what she was doing at my house when you saw us together. The day before your 'accident,' she called to say she hit a deer on the highway. She must have planned it already. I never put two and two together ..."

I nodded, slightly mollified as well as more than a bit doped up from the magical mixture Lester had injected into the IV in my arm. "It's okay," I slurred. "The night Roger died, you argued with him about his sleeping with Nancy Jeanne. That's why you wouldn't tell me. You didn't want Mary to find out about the baby."

He shrugged. "She'd just lost Roger, bastard that he was. I didn't want to pile on. It was a mistake that almost cost your life. I'm sorry, Charms." His face hardened, and then grew soft, mushy even. I raised my hand to poke at it. He grinned, pushing my arm down. "Damn, you're cute when you're too drugged up to annoy me."

"Hey ..."

"What?"

What was it I had I wanted to say? And then it came to me. "Jack didn't kill Roger. Danny has to let him go. Take off that ankle monitor."

"Relax, he's on it. I promise."

"Good."

"Lay back." He gazed down at me, his face a bit fuzzy. "We'll get you fixed up and you'll be back to calling me names in no time."

"Sounds like a plan." My eyes grew heavy. They fluttered, wanting very much to close.

"Hey, Charms," Brodie whispered close to my ear. "There's something I've been wanting to say for a long time now."

I blinked.

"I ..." He inhaled deeply.

Was Brodie about to declare his devotion? The thought didn't repulse me nearly as much as it might've a month ago.

"We've know each other for a long time ..." he mumbled.

"True," I slurred.

"And I ... well ..."

"What?" I asked.

He leaned down until his lips were less than an inch from my ear. "You didn't paint the water tower."

"What?!" I tried to sit up, but he held me down. "Then who did?"

He hesitated, pausing for ultimate drama, like the best of actors. "I did."

The End

Acknowledgments

A special thanks to Terri Bischoff, Nicole Nugent, and the rest of the Midnight Ink team, for without you, my whiskey research would feel much more like a drinking problem.

And a huge thank you to you, dear reader. With so many wonderful fictional worlds to pick from, you choosing mine is not taken lightly. If we meet in person, I owe you a whiskey. As long as you promise not to mix it with Diet Coke.

About the Author

J.A. Kazimer lives in Denver, CO. When she isn't looking for a place to hide the bodies, she devotes her time to playing with a pup named Killer. Other hobbies include murdering house plants. She spent a few years stalking people while working as a private investigator before transitioning to the moniker of Writer and penning more than fifteen titles. Visit her website at jakazimer.com and sign up for her "This Little Piggy Went to Murder" newsletter.